# LETHAL BOUNTY

## A DIRTY SECRET

A SAM TRAVIS ADVENTURE

# GK JURRENS
# TOM KASPRZAK

Copyright © 2024 GK Jurrens
All rights reserved.

GKJurrens.com

eBook ISBN: 978-1-952165-34-4
Print ISBN: 978-1-952165-35-1
Audiobook ISBN: 978-1-952165-xx-x
v.240109
**r.240914_0703**

# 1

Charlestown, Massachusetts
June 17, 1775

Ankle-deep in the blood of their dead and dying compatriots, he and his aide crouched behind one of the earthen redoubts his men had hastily constructed on the ridges during the night. The sun now hung high in the clear early afternoon sky, still visible through the dense clouds of smoke in the stagnant air that stung their eyes and burned their lungs. It was an otherwise brilliant day.

Despite an incessant hail of musket balls, they bobbed their heads up from their impromptu command post down the hill to risk yet another glance at the advancing British troops. They were at least double their own numbers and possessed superior training. Ten yards away, the reckless bastards leapt over piles of their fallen to press their advance with ruthless abandon, with fire in their eyes. *Like they have for the last six-and-a-half hours.* These were battle-hardened professional soldiers of the realm. The young colonel now doubted the wisdom of holding these hills against such a force with his now-dying or already dead farmers and shopkeepers. *This is madness.*

Most of his own troops, a thousand strong at the onset, were raw civilians, but harbored a passion for freedom from the oppressive Crown. That passion pounded in their hearts. Those who still lived, anyway. While *this* battle had only been joined at sunrise this day, they were now thrust into the third bloody month of this brutal siege on their own city. They fought to take back their own neighborhoods, their own homes.

But the new Continental army dared not relent as long as their families and friends remained in the clutches of tyrants. Worse, the Crown's considerable occupying force now *terrorized* all of Boston, Middlesex County, and beyond. He shouted over the din of musket fire, now growing more sporadic, "Lads, they've already paid dearly, *far* more than we. In the future, they'll think twice before—"

"Sir, runners are reporting in. Squad leaders report their surviving men have little or no powder remaining. What are your orders, sir?" His aide stood shoulder-to-shoulder with one of their runners. His face of crimson blinked against the blood dripping from his brow into both eyes, but he did not wipe it away.

Colonel William Prescott was a man of action, and valor, but also of conscience. He said to his aide, "The rest of our militia dies here along with General Warren and the others if we do not now retreat. You did well, boys." He glanced around at his youthful command staff. "They'll not soon forget this battle here atop Breed's and Bunker." Then, to the runner and to his aide, "It is time to muster elsewhere and abandon these wretched mounts to the King's ruffians. Order retreat."

His aide saluted and said, "Yes, sir." At that moment, the left side of his aide's face disappeared in a pink mist.

# 2

Western Massachusetts
December 1775

---

Dark and dangerous times. Most were beyond exhaustion, on the verge of starvation, already victims of exposure. Few men were to be trusted. The same could be said of Mother Nature in her brutal splendor. Early December in Western Massachusetts would not suffer fools. Snow refused to fall. Only a smattering of fickle ice crystals floated earthward. One touched down on Henry's nose, but refused to melt. He saw it land, but felt nothing. Now, he stood stiff on a frozen hill in this... wilderness. He was not alone, but stood apart.

A few short months ago, this quiet twenty-five-year-old bookseller from Boston was thrust into the role of rebel warrior and leader. That meant absorbing a great deal of responsibility almost overnight with very little knowledge or experience. And now, he wondered, *Am I up to this monumental task? Circumstance begs my destiny, and I do possess a damn good nose for this bloody business. At least the General thinks so.* Lucy understood. Henry missed her sorely. On this bitter evening, he found himself on the fringe of nowhere, wondering how he had come to this. But he knew. He'd have it no other way.

He longed to smell the pungent smoke of fires in the encampment, but the men could find no dry wood. Instead, they welcomed the stench of cow cakes from their few oxen and almost two-hundred-fifty horses. They offered precious packets of steamy warmth. Not so long ago, as a civilized city boy, he'd have turned his nose away from such vulgarity—no longer. He gazed down the gentle slope to the nearest stout sled fifty paces distant. It bent under the weight of a six-thousand-pound mortar, recently the property of His Bloody Majesty, strapped to its oaken frame which was joined with iron gussets. No amount of gold could fetch that carriage's worth this night. Nor a king's ransom. Not even with the life's blood of every last man in his care—all one hundred and forty-three souls. *Can I live with such a charge? .... I must.*

Tensions between the Crown and the colonies had been simmering, en route to a full boil for these last five years. It came to a head the previous spring. He was a lieutenant then, an active member of the Massachusetts militia that supported the Patriot provisional government. That was dangerous enough. Under cover of darkness and civilian attire, Henry had snuck around side streets and alleyways in his beloved Boston. He'd hid his colors to fight—with naught but his wit and daring. The oppression the Crown now imposed upon everyone and everything he held dear suffocated him. He especially feared for his Lucy. Dearest Luce *never* felt safe anymore. All because the Crown wished to recoup its enormous financial losses in the North American theater of war. Their fight with the French over conquest of territory in the Americas exploded England's national debt. So, they levied an unending stream of taxes on its colonies. Enforcing these levies grew violent. The colonials fought with ferocity. They resisted paying for the Brits' war in Quebec and elsewhere. If only freedom were free....

Five years earlier, at twenty, Henry had witnessed the senseless massacre of a half-dozen friends and acquaintances in his own Boston neighborhood. These same thugs in their pretentious blood-red waistcoats, the King's regulars, had gone mad. They murdered people he knew right in front of his bookstore, not ten paces from its windows. An unquenchable thirst for power had gone to their heads with the King's blessing, thinking they could do anything they wanted to these unwashed masses, these... *colonials*. Pompous brutes with a bloodlust, Henry had stood strong between a row of long guns and his friends—those who still lived. Barely beyond his teens, he had attempted to play the role of diplomat, talking down one bloodthirsty captain, an arrogant Grenadier who obviously loathed being relegated to menial crowd suppression. Especially this far from the Crown. Since then, the time for diplomacy had dissipated in endless clouds of musket smoke.

During his days, Henry had gathered intelligence he had used to save scarce Colonial military supplies from being confiscated by a squad of British thugs, barely escaping with his life. His compatriots recognized him for his cleverness as a quiet man who stood firm behind the more brazen members of the resistance. Rowdies like Revere and Prescott. Unlike them, Henry avoided the more lively subversions, like that massacre on Breed's Hill—they *should* have fought from atop Bunker's higher elevation. That was even the plan. Reckless ruffians, but Henry was glad they were on their side. With ever-escalating violence across Middlesex County and Massachusetts Bay, Boston had become an urban battle zone. So, he and Lucy fled to regroup with those of like minds as open hostilities, now far more deadly and more frequent than occasional street skirmishes, prevailed across the city. And across their beloved colonies.

. . .

Shaken from his reverie, the bitter December wind inspired an involuntary full-body shiver. Henry's black knee-high Wellingtons were handsome boots, though now scuffed to raw hide, not so long ago fashionably appropriate for traversing Boston's finer cobble-paved neighborhoods. But they now did little to forestall inevitable frostbite in this forsaken wilderness, even with extra cotton stuffed in their toe boxes. Many of his men weren't so lucky. Some marched barefoot. Some left bloody trails in the light snow. Though his command was one of the Colonial Army's few artillery units called *The Train*, few of Henry's men wore any sort of uniform. Most layered much of the clothing they owned against the weather. His and the General's primary charge was to keep this rag-tag group of rebels from quitting. Now, as *The Train* became scattered, Henry worried that some men might just make for their homesteads. He worried without end.

Henry Knox lied to himself that smoking his pipe might warm him against the night, even if just a bit. Though frigid to the bone, he burned with patriotic fervor; however, he continued to worry about his train of sleds. He drew deep into his lungs harsh Maryland tobacco smoke from his *little ladle,* his treasured but oh, so fragile clay pipe. Exhaled as tendrils swirled out of his nostrils and rose into the moonlight. Of course, the rigors of a winter march resulted in more than one chip at the end of the pipe's short stem. But that pipe was one of his most treasured and well-guarded possessions out here in this frigid field. *Nothing in all the world like the scent of a pipe on a forbidding eve.*

Henry's brother, William, whispered as they stood close, shoulder to shoulder. Their vast encampment dared not risk discovery. Henry smiled. *Whispering amid their massive gathering comprising dozens of oxen and one-hundred-twenty-four teams of horses to transport forty-two sleds carrying fifty-eight cannons, howitzers, and mortars from Fort Ticonderoga to Boston?* Silly to whisper, but he resisted disparaging his dear younger brother's conscientious effort at unnecessary discretion. "Henry, if we are found out, we surely shall face a firing squad."

"No, William, we shall not. This is the time to make our stand. If we do not, history will judge us harshly. The very success of General Washington's endeavors on behalf of the Continental Army may very well depend on us completing our task. The General awaits our artillery in desperation. Besides, firing squads are for traitors. We are patriots, stewards of our precious rebellion."

---

They'd been on the road for a month-and-a-half already, bone-tired and lower than ever on supplies. The men were dying of exposure and despair. The weather? Worse than abominable. Still, Henry wished for more of the same. He *needed* snow to grease the skids of his sleds. Most of the men wrapped neckerchiefs over the top of their heads to protect their ears from the biting wind. No fancy tricorns or cocked hats for this bunch. Wool caps were a precious and rare commodity. Those lucky enough to own or commandeer a second kerchief or scarf also bundled their frost-bitten faces. And the temperature would continue to plummet if the evening's sky offered a portent of their near future. It was Henry's responsibility to find shelter, and he had failed.

So, they camped scattered alongside the wooded trail where dense stands of spruce and hemlock offered a wind break, at least. The men slept in their bedrolls close to the beasts of burden and the steaming body heat they radiated. The sleds carried not only machines of war, but feedbags. They, too, now collapsed flat—near empty. Worse, with almost no grass visible through the light snow, grazing prospects remained grim. Henry already had lost half of his few oxen reserved for the heaviest of their forty-two sleds, with but two to spare. And most of the horses had lost weight and muscle. Although his teamsters suffered alongside their hungry beasts, they would not complain.

Even though money was in short supply, Henry found a farmer yesterday willing to accept Continentals. The new Continental currency sufficed in lieu of Colonial money, or British pounds, or Spanish coins. They saved their doubloons and other coinage when nothing else would do. Henry had purchased a half-dozen oxen from that farmer, but then he learned with surprise that their financial larder was significantly depleted. Truth be told, he wasn't much of an accountant. He'd talk with his purser, Sergeant Grossman.

Now, here he was, an artillery colonel in the Continental Army, with the constant threat of confronting the finest soldiers in the world—British regulars. That was a daunting prospect in itself. But he *also* dreaded Hessian auxiliaries—world-class mercenaries. The British were known to employ them in conflicts such as theirs. According to the General, the Crown favored using these experienced soldiers in their conflicts elsewhere. It was only a matter of time.

Worse, with loyalties divided within almost every household, every action questioned, and not knowing who might be a British collaborator or spy, no one was to be trusted. *For the love of God, what is keeping us from lying down and drifting off in peaceful slumber?* But no. The General needed him and his train. As General Washington implored him in a recent correspondence concerning his artillery pieces, "the want of them is so great that no trouble or expence [sic] must be spared to obtain them." And he *was* obtaining them.

William asked, "We *are* doing the right thing, aren't we, Henry? I mean, Colonel?"

Contrary to his own conflicted thoughts, Colonel

Henry Knox's condescending glance at his younger brother left no doubt. "William, it is true General Washington has only been in command of the Continental Army since July. And our beloved rebellion *is* only a few months old." He surveyed the vast field of captured British armament before him, now in his charge. "But if our commander-in-chief doesn't have this artillery for his purposes in the bulwarks around Boston, our entire noble effort might be in vain. Then, my dearest brother, the Crown *will* charge you, me, and every man in this company with treason. And they *will* shoot us *if* we make it as far as a firing squad. There is no more hiding. But that does *not* mean we are traitors, only that we are rebels, no longer willing to kiss King George's ring or bend the knee to his royal arse." He hadn't intended his voice to raise in pitch and volume. Theirs was a righteous cause, and he would not accept any doubt whatsoever. William appeared reassured, but Henry thought, *If only my own confidence matched my words.*

They had left Boston six weeks earlier for a secret meeting with one of General Washington's cohorts. Henry, William, and only a squad of Grenadiers had followed the coast south to New York City. After meeting with Major General Schuyler in New York, they then possessed the funds for their expedition. It wasn't much, but perhaps enough to save the fledgling rebellion. They then headed north along the Hudson for a brief stop in Albany. From there, they continued due north to the captured Fort Ticonderoga, where the rest of his command awaited their arrival.

Colonel Knox and his soldiers spent three precious days collecting all the heavy weapons they could gather on a landing at Lake George. It was called Fort George, but was little more than a collection of cabins perched on the lake's shore, guarded by a handful of sentries. The camp didn't even feature a perimeter fence. Not yet, anyway. Their best security remained their obscure location.

In a brief but bloody skirmish, Ethan Allen and the militia he called his Green Mountain Boys had captured Fort Ticonderoga. They discovered the British had all but abandoned the fort just weeks earlier, including an armory deemed too difficult to move with any rapidity. Now, General Washington intended to use those same weapons to eject the admiralty fleet from Boston. Failing to do so, however, could very well spell their end. Henry reminded himself once more, *The General—my friend—is depending on **me**. And the very survival of our revolution may well hang in the precarious balance.*

---

Abraham and Jacob Jenkins huddled together against the night wind as they watched the young colonel and his even younger brother up on the hill, smoking. Of course, *they* had tobacco. Food, too, they wagered. The stench of cow cakes from a big steaming ox standing over them offered a welcomed though meager source of temporary heat. They did not fear being trampled. The oxen appeared frozen in place after a long day of hauling the heaviest sleds. Abe snarled, "I know where they keep the money, Jake."

"But if we get caught, they'll shoot us, sure." Jake kept his hands stuck down the front of his trousers for the warmth. He huddled with his older brother.

"So we don't get caught, Jake. 'Sides, they won't even miss it."

The next morning, the company pressed on. The brothers Jenkins bided their time. They had grown weary of this fool's errand of suffering and dying for nothing, anyway.

# 3

Twenty hours later, the company trudged to a stop as the command echoed back from the head of the column. Most spread a bedroll behind some sort of windbreak and fell into a deep slumber straightaway. Food was in short supply, anyway, with hunger their constant companion. But two men snuck off, each carrying a box. "We bury what we got, see? You listenin', Jake? The colonel will never miss it. Learned from me cousin who gets meals for hisself, he ain't so sharp with the numbers, mate. And the sergeant, hisself's purser, don't know nothin' 'bout security."

Abe shivered as they arrived at a likely spot. The soles of his shoes were more paper-thin than not. And his damn stockings not only needed knitting at the toes and heels, but were soaked and half-frozen. Like his toes. He stood on one foot at a time, leaning against a rock thrice his five-foot-seven height near the edge of a dark abyss. He had already decided this was the spot, at the based of this cabin-sized boulder.

His little brother kept whining. "But if we get caught—"

---

"Ain't nobody goin' catch us, Jake. Now, let's get ta diggin'." The December ground came up rock hard under a thin layer of snow. Worse, the stony patch had Jake questioning the site that Abe had chosen to hide their trove of Spanish gold and silver. But their single round-point wrought-iron shovel won them a foot-deep hole large enough for the pair of boxes, even if it did curl their precious shovel's tip. Deeper was not possible. As Abe supervised Jake's efforts, he said, "These here coins be heavy, but I don't trust no paper money—not Continentals nor even Pounds, anymore. Give me coin a the realm any day of the week, of *any* realm. And the way this little skirmish be goin', no tellin' what kind a paper we'll be usin' to wipe our arses with. Or what'll be good fer fetchin' victuals, eh, Jake? But gold 'n silver? Nobody goin' question shiny metal."

While Abe pontificated, Jake raised a sweat under his threadbare woolen waistcoat. His sleeves had parted from the rest of the coat atop both shoulders. Laboring on his now-sopping knees with the wooden end of the field shovel's short handle clutched in his fingerless gloves, he glared up at his partner in crime. "Ya goin' talk this here box into the dirt *and rock*, Abe? What say you lend a hand ta the effort, here, brother?"

"Right you are, mate. That's deep enough. Save the spade for trenchin' once we fetch the Heights, eh, Jake?"

Jacob growled at his lazy brother. At least Abe was just as greedy. They set the wooden boxes, side-by-side, in the bottom of their shallow hole, placed small stones over it, and covered it with earth before tamping it down. Stacked a trio of large rocks atop their treasure. That would make the spot easier to locate again in two or three weeks. They'd return after the upcoming battle for Boston, still at least a five-day trudge east and south to the battlements at Dorchester Heights above the British Fleet in Boston Harbor. Not that they were feeling too patriotic, they didn't give themselves two spits in the wind for surviving out here by leaving *The Train*.

After what was sure to be a bloody battle they'd be back. Or so they thought.

# 4

May 13, 1989

Walter Bedford, a retired contractor, loved the outdoors. After forty years of hustling customers, contracts, and employees, he craved serenity. Away from noise and away from people. He adored his trusty metal detector. His new rig, this year's model, featured the latest gizmos for locating valuable buried metals, along with plenty of metallic junk. But he so cherished the hunt.

The possibilities consumed him. Its advanced gold detector, a brand new feature in this model, with its easy-to-read display boiled his blood. With headphones and a comfortable grip, he'd work an area for hours without arm fatigue. That didn't mean he lacked sore feet, back pain, and more than a little of the wife's annoyance. Yes, he spent too much time in the mountains with his trusty detector instead of helping around the house.

Walter loved the Southern Berkshire Mountains where he was born and bred. Especially in the Spring. He planned his retirement well, after he and his wife Rose had raised two boys. They grew up smart and successful. Both left the Berkshires in search of jobs not involving farming or contracting. The last few years found Walter obsessed with metal detecting more than ever, at least according to Rose. He thought of himself as a treasure hunter, or more technically, a *detectionist*. Gave him a sense of purpose. And finding an occasional coin, bracelet, or ring? That was far more rewarding than killing a deer or sitting in an uncomfortable aluminum boat for hours betting against long odds he'd catch a fish or two. Besides, seafood didn't float his boat. Nope, detecting gave him his exercise, kept his interest level high, and delivered the sheer enjoyment of finding any type of relic.

Walter lived in a village called Otis, population sixteen-hundred souls. He loved its small-town feel where everyone knew just about everyone else. Hell, he either built, remodeled or restored more than half the homes in town. Some businesses, too. He and his crew earned a lot of respect from the community, and they had more work than they had hours in the day.

Walter grew fascinated by the story of Henry Knox. The colonial colonel passed through this area, and historians called his route the Knox Trail. Traversed early in America's Revolutionary War, this was not a road at all. Rather, this trail wore a mere path from Fort Ticonderoga, New York and ended outside of seventeen-seventy-five Boston's Dorchester Heights. The Heights overlooked Boston Harbor and the occupying British fleet.

Back then, they called it the *Great Road* through the "western frontier" (per the city folk in Boston on the far side of the state). This trail cut through the rugged and undeveloped Berkshire Mountains. Back then, this was the domain of the fierce Mohawk Indians, the Mohicans, and the Nipmucs. Attacks on the white man were worse and more brutal than history remembers, or so Walter's reference books said.

Henry Knox's artillery company trundled cannons and mortars, each weighing thousands of pounds on sleighs for hundreds of miles in the dead of winter. That artillery enabled General George Washington to bombard the British fleet in Boston Harbor and banish them from the city. This was a major turning point in the birth of America's independence from an oppressive British reign.

After devouring this story with relish, Walter became a hard-core Revolutionary War buff. Convinced there had to be historical remnants of that journey, he read book after book on the subject. The literature described the historical role the Berkshire Mountains played during the Revolutionary War. He concentrated his artifact hunting on the Knox Trail rather than scanning random cellar holes and battlefields he *had* been working. Walter learned Knox transported fifty-nine pieces of artillery from the fort to the coast.

During that arduous trek, he only lost one cannon in the Mohawk River not far from where it connected to the Hudson. Walter also discovered it took fifty-six days to reach Dorchester Heights three-hundred rugged miles to the east. During that epic expedition, they loaded the artillery onto barges and made four separate crossings of the Hudson River. Even sunk one barge and re-floated it and its precious cargo.

Walter had acquired a replica of Knox's own diary from a bookshop in Boston that specialized in local history. From that book, he learned they loaded this armament *by hand* onto large oaken sleds. One hundred-twenty-four teams of two horses each pulled forty-two sleds. Yokes of oxen pulled three more, bearing the heaviest loads. Money was tight for paying farmers, teamsters, and supply stations along the way. They seized gunpowder from British sympathizers at no cost. They made do. Walter was enthralled. So, he focused his search on sections of the Great Barrington, Monterey, and Otis townships.

Knox arrived in Dorchester fifty-six days later and met General Washington with fifty-eight big guns. The young colonel's knowledge of moving all this artillery earned him a promotion. Washington placed him in charge of moving these heavy weapons in the dead of night to key positions along The Heights. To the Brit's surprise in the morning, seeing the cannons aimed down at them put them on high alert. But there was no good choice other than a full assault on artillery-defended higher ground. On March fourth, seventeen-seventy-six, a two-day bombardment of the British fleet chased the ships of the fleet that survived from Boston Harbor.

Walter remembered reading one quote. George Washington said of Henry Knox, "There is no man in these now-united states with whom I have been in habits of greater intimacy; no one whom I have loved more sincerely, nor any for whom I have had a greater friendship." *General* Washington then appointed Knox Chief Artillery Officer of the Continental Army, a position of great responsibility. Knox later became Secretary of War under *President* George Washington of the newly formed United States of America and served in that capacity for five years.

If it weren't for this notoriety, there'd be a great deal less historical information for Walter to research. But a major figure like Knox? Even though most folks likely have never heard of him? Yup, plenty of good info for a dedicated treasure hunter like himself. Walter feasted on this information and decided there had to be historical remnants of that arduous odyssey. He studied maps from that period and discovered the trail was now interrupted by modern roads like Routes 7 and 23.

So Walter worked a piece of the trail within the Otis State Forest. The early morning frost of late May exhilarated him. His detector sounded off near a cluster of boulders left by glacial recession in evidence everywhere in the Berkshires. He suppressed his excitement. As he dug, he referred to the detector, and then returned to digging. No longer able to contain his emotion, he whelped in exhilaration at the sight of a... dirty coin? He spit on it and rubbed it on his jeans. It was silver. He trembled. Brought out his magnifying glass and looked at the impressions. Saw a picture of what looked like King Charles III on its face with lions and castles on the other side. He'd reference his research books to determine its denomination—in *reales*. Scanned his surroundings to ensure no one was watching. Then he returned to searching the ground with his detector.

Walter found four more similar coins, but one was larger. He knew *two bits* equaled a quarter and four quarters comprised a reale. But he didn't know whether a reale was gold or silver. Or both? Daylight faded. He hadn't realized he'd spent so much time in this spot. All day, in fact. He rushed home, despite his exhaustion. Ran through the house to his office, ignoring Rose. His perplexed wife had prepared dinner. He interpreted her look of confusion, but ignored her. Headed right for two books: "Numismatic Books and Catalogs" by Daniel Frank Sedwick and "The Practical Book of Cobs," by the same author. Rose hovered over her excited husband. Finally acknowledging her, he said, "Rose, I think I've found something of great historical significance. Maybe even valuable. I need to find it in one of these *bibles*."

"But honey, dinner is ready. Can't this wait?"

He didn't snap at her. Nor was he kind in his urgency. "No, no, indulge me for a few minutes. I gotta do this." Minutes turned into an hour. When Rose heard Walter yelp, she rushed back to his den-slash-office. "I found it! An eight-pence Spanish coin from between seventeen-fifty-nine and seventeen-eighty-eight—because it bears King Charles' face. Worn, but visible."

---

Rose felt excited for Walter, but she worried about a cold dinner. He brought the book to the table and persisted in rambling about the find of a lifetime. He ate a little, but that night, he hardly slept. He awaited daybreak, eager to search the entire area. He'd use plastic yellow construction tape to mark off selected areas. Like he'd seen pictures of archaeologists working a dig. Exactly like a methodical treasure hunter.

Rose worried for both of them. This wasn't... healthy. Maybe not even... safe. If others knew....

# 5

The day broke dark and dreary with occasional wind-driven rain that made even the unseasonably warm mid-May temps in the fifties feel much colder. Walter's outer rain jacket proved useful, but the rain still soaked him. Water dripped down his neck because his perpetual downward gaze left the back of his neck exposed. From there, inside his coat and shirt and t-shirt, water migrated down either side of his spine in a dribble. Regardless, his flannel shirt kept him warm. Besides, he was in perpetual motion. His leather boots now absorbed water rather than repelling it. Walter didn't care a lick. He taped off rectangles in a search grid, *like the archaeologists do*, and worked with feverish intensity throughout the day. With no further results.

Puzzled, he walked farther south while scanning with his detector along the trail. He came upon a rocky ledge where the trail narrowed. A deep gorge fell away to his left—a hundred-fifty feet deep with large and small fallen boulders strewn at the bottom on both sides. Walter spotted official state forest warning signs nearby to stay away from the ledge because of more rocks crumbling away from the wall. Looked like a giant knife had taken a slice out of the mountain. But Walter imagined a thousand years of run-off from a raging river—not the small brook down there now—had sliced this gorge. Reports of deaths along this rugged ridge were common, like the wall had just grown too old to hold together, and careless hikers paid the price by getting too close to the edge. The panoramic view of the valley below appeared serene.

Walter's uncertainty now gnawed at his consciousness. *Should I return to the site where I found the coins? Or should I push on?* He also worried Rose's patience was wearing thin. Deciding to backtrack, he wondered, *Where would they divert to avoid this gorge?* Certainly, Knox's train couldn't have traversed this rugged valley. There had to be another now-grown-over section of the trail they would have taken.

Two-hundred yards back he saw the remnants of an old trail base now obscured by mature trees. But these were newer trees than the two-hundred-year-old stands on either side. Walter knew these men were practical enough to divert away from the valley with their heavy artillery sleds. He started down that overgrown trail, spending a good deal of time asking himself, *What would I have done if I were them?*

Walter wormed his way around the area and focused on a stand of birches nestled up against a cluster of several house-sized boulders. Then his detector sounded off. Scratching through the hardscrabble soil, he discovered nothing but a short nail. *But what kind of nail?* He examined it at some length. A tapered square nail with a point so rusted it curled. *Must have once had a sharp point, judging by the taper.* After more scanning, the rain stopped, and the sky began to clear, but he had eaten up most of his day. He'd head back here in the morning.

The next day dawned. After a hearty breakfast from Rose's magic hands, Walter grabbed some water and venison jerky. They kissed goodbye. "Be careful out there," she called out just as he started his old green seventy-two Ford pickup. Her voice penetrated the crisp morning, but he didn't hear her. After his hike back into his dig site, he looked around and listened. No blue jays, crows, or mockingbirds he was used to hearing. The forest had fallen quiet after yesterday's rain.

So, he re-started his methodical scanning with his detector. He didn't stop for a water and jerky break until midday. Fatigue hit him after an exciting two days. He came to an enormous boulder, leaned his detector against it, and sat down on a smaller rock. Reached into his pocket for a strand of jerky. Walter didn't know it yet, but the next five seconds would change his life.

As he stretched to unclip his canteen from his left hip, his elbow knocked over the detector, which he had forgotten to turn off. It whelped. "What the—?" Stood up and retrieved the toppled detector. Ran it around the rock. It went crazy near a concave section of the enormous boulder behind a cluster of basketball-sized rocks. After pulling away the small rock cluster, he took out his trusty backpack shovel and dug. Then a quick scan. *Yup, something's down there.* He kept digging. *Thunk.*

Said it again. "What the—?"

# 6

Walter carefully scraped the loose dirt away from something that he saw was man made. A very old wooden box. Could be cedar, as it was still in good condition. The box featured almost black metal corners, maybe tarnished brass, held in place with small tapered nails with the same patina, also rusted. A few were missing, like they had worked their way out. And a swing-up latch over a pad-eye secured the lid, but featured no lock. The rather decrepit box was one foot square, and about that deep. Old, some combination of wood and metal (not tin). He coaxed the box from the ground. It box was heavy. His heart pounded. *Slow down*, he kept telling himself. He opened it.

Walter's eyes popped as he lifted the lid. A box full of gold and silver coins, tarnished, but he had no doubt they were gold and silver, in one box-filling heap! He looked around the area again. Nobody around. Not surprising. He'd had to scrounge his way into this overgrown spot next to this clustered stone outcropping. He did not remove any of the coins, but slid the heavy box into his backpack, dirt and all. *Is that it?* But he had taught himself to double check an area after a discovery. BEEP, BEEP, BEEP. More? He dug further down and farther back. Another small rusty nail. Swung more to his left. Did another sweep. BEEEEEP. Set the detector down and grabbed the shovel again. When he got down to the same depth as the first box, a second box appeared not that far from its twin.

Now delirious, he brushed off the second box and without even trying to open it, put *its* substantial weight right into his backpack on top of the first, each a one-foot cube. Walter worried whether his old backpack and he were up to handling the considerable weight. Filled in the boxes' holes, covered them with leaves and pine needles. Replaced the small pile of miniature boulders. Time to head home.

Walter arrived and bounced through the door. Dropped his now-bulky backpack to the floor with a resounding *THUNK* on the ancient oak floor and grabbed Rose by the waist. Spun her around twice in the kitchen with his biggest grin. "What? What did you find now?" she said. Skepticism laced with chagrin sculpted her wrinkled but still beautiful face.

"Come look." He took her hand and lugged the backpack out to the garage. Switched on the workbenches' three overhead fluorescent shop lights with their pull chains. As he drew the two heavy boxes out of his backpack, still filthy from their extraction, he watched Rose's eyes grow round with intrigue. Walter bubbled and gushed like a child on Christmas morning. One by one, they took the coins out of the first box using only their fingertips. That took over an hour. Didn't have any gloves other than heavy construction leather. Not workable. They counted one-hundred-seventy-four coins. Some were gold, others silver. The second box yielded one-hundred-eighty coins. Three hundred-fifty-four coins total. They looked the same as the five individual coins he'd dug up earlier, but different sizes.

Walter howled, "We're rich!"

"Where did you find these, Walter?"

"Behind the gorge to the right of the trail. These must be artifacts from the Henry Knox expedition from Fort Ticonderoga to Boston."

"Why would they bury and leave this?" She waved her hand over the collection of coins now spread on a sheet that covered Walter's workbench.

"Can't rightly figure, dear."

Rose's hand descended to her hips. Her face grew

grim. "That's on state land and there's probably a law that says you have to turn them in."

"*No way, Rose.* I am not turning this in to *anybody.*" Walter realized he had *yelled* in Rose's direction, but his eyes never left the prize, *his bounty*.

"Then how do you suppose you're going to turn this into money?"

Walther then realized his conundrum. *Have to think about this.* They cleaned off the coins with plain water and dried them with a soft towel. Arranged them by size, then by color and similarity. While doing this, Walter's head spun. They were helpless tearing their eyes away from the sight of this treasure. *How **do** I convert these coins into cash?*

Neither of them slept that night. They dismissed ideas and suggestions almost as rapidly as they conceived them. At last, Walter said he'd do some research and find out what he had. The next day he took his *coin bibles* and went through them one by one, page by page. He determined with satisfaction that ninety percent of the coins were in excellent condition, though he remained uncertain of their worth.

Coin dealers were a shady bunch. At least, that was his experience. A grading service like PCGS (Professional Coin Grading Service) or NGC (Numismatic Guaranty Company) would provide him with an approximate value. But they'd turn him in as they'd realize these coins were Revolutionary War relics protected by state and federal law. He looked up the laws using Rose's computer, with her help. Did not know how to operate the damn thing, but they figured it out together.

Walter learned the National Historical Property Act, the National Stolen Property Act, UNESCO, and the US Archeological Resource Protection Act did indeed protect these coins. He also learned Interpol even staffed a dedicated team for protecting artifacts and coins. Plus, he learned of even more state laws with heavy penalties. *Oh, snap!* Violations of these laws had prison terms and fines associated with hoarding or selling his find—ten years for each offense? *But how did Mel Fisher keep the gold from his Atocha discovery in Florida waters?* Maybe some salvage law of the sea? Was there a similar loophole to save his find?

He'd be damned if he'd just turn *his* treasure in!

# 7

Walter grabbed an old phone book, thinking someone in Westfield or Springfield could help him sell his coins to private collectors for a share of the profit. *But how do I find one of those guys who will keep his mouth shut **and** keep me out of prison **and** without cheating me?*

Walter searched for two days. At last, he came up with three places. They were all in New Hampshire. That was the *Live Free or Die* state. He made one call from a pay phone in the larger city of Springfield with a population of one-hundred-fifty-six-thousand people. He hoped for some degree of anonymity. Certainly more than in Otis.

The first coin dealer did not know how to proceed, though he seemed willing—greedy—enough, as

Walter hinted at an *inheritance* comprising *a few dozen Revolutionary War coins.* He hung up on the guy's apparent ineptitude. The next dealer sounded more relaxed with the right words and questions that he wasn't prepared to answer. Walter was still unsure, never having offered his name. He grew nervous again and hung up. He clenched his fists and seethed with anger, berating himself for his lack of preparation. He stumped back from the pay phone to his truck to regain his composure and to write down his questions.

Time to make his third call to a shop in Portsmouth. Heavy with anxiety, Walter tromped back to the pay phone at the edge of a wooded park, dialed, and heard, "Hello, Browning Diamond and Coin. Ethan speaking. How may I help you?"

"Hello, my name is Robert Walsh. I've inherited some old coins that I'd be interested in selling for the right price."

"Well, Mr. Walsh, I will need to see your coins to determine age, weight, fineness, and rarity, among other criteria. What type of coins do you have?"

"Uh, I'm not sure, but from what was in the will and what I can make out, they might be from the Revolutionary War period."

The pregnant pause on the line further elevated Walter's anxiety. But he hadn't made the long drive to Springfield just to keep hanging up on coin dealers. He screwed up his courage and did not hang up. The man asked, "Are they gold or silver? And what types of insignias are on them?"

Walter forged onward. "I have both gold and silver. Looks like dates from seventeen-seventy-one to seventeen-seventy-five. A face appears on their front. Pillars on the back."

"Hmm, those coins are indeed rare, and if they're in good condition, they possess considerable value. Where are you located, Mr. Walsh, and how many of these coins do you have?"

"Uh, I'm in Worcester, Massachusetts" said Walter.

"Mr. Walsh, you're calling from Springfield, not Worcester, according to caller ID."

"Caller what? You can do that? Uh, sorry Mr. Browning. I'm being careful with my inheritance."

"Understandable, Mr. Walsh, if that's your real name. Let's do this. Bring up a small sample of the coins you have and we'll see what we're able to do for you, alright?"

"Okay, um, yeah. That sounds fair. When is a good time?" They set up the meet for Thursday—day after tomorrow—at one PM. Walter brought a dozen each of silver and gold coins. He grew nervous and excited at the same time.

# 8

Thursday came. May nineteenth. Walter drove Rose's car, not his truck. Her car was smaller and more reliable. Besides, the old truck was a standout. The town itself was a typical New Hampshire burg with a commons—a town square—sprinkled with old-growth maple trees, benches, and public trash cans. A high-steepled white church looked down from a small rise toward retail stores and a pharmacy. Nothing appeared out of the ordinary. He parked on the diagonal at the curb to his right, three blocks from the church at the top of the hill.

Walter carried his two dozen assorted coins in a flannel-lined cardboard coin holder tucked under his right arm inside an old top-loading briefcase. Its shoulder strap was long gone. He had secured the coins in the holder's molded spaces. Fifty feet later, he stood in front of Browning Diamond and Coin, a non-assuming store with a small display area visible through its dirty storefront windows.

Walter opened the door, heard a bell tinkle overhead. A musty odor assaulted him. Illuminated glass cases displayed dozens of rings, bracelets, and necklaces adorned with diamonds or birthstones. A single large case toward the back contained an impressive array of a few hundred old coins in a variety of shapes and sizes. He wasn't familiar with most, but recognized a few. A man came out from the back room. A magnifying glass with an integrated high-intensity light still burning rode high on his forehead, as if he'd slung it up and out of the way a moment earlier. Looked like a third eye. Walter squinted as the man's light flashed across his field of vision.

The man mumbled, "Sorry," as he reached up to switch off his third eye. His rumpled clothes, including one of his shirt tails that had come untucked, advertised the intensity of his focused personality. He appeared a little absent-minded. This was a man serious about his craft. He sported at least a day's growth of beard, maybe two. While he appeared disheveled, he wore decent clothes and shoes. Carried his average height and weight like an aging athlete, but with a slight limp and more than a few decades of hard miles.

Ethan Browning introduced himself, offering his hand with a congenial expression to back it up. Walter responded in kind and gave the man his real name during the handshake. Browning said, "Mr. Bedford, please come into my office, where we can talk freely." Walter followed the man. So far, he seemed okay with this stranger.

Now at ease, Walter settled into the inviting guest chair. He looked around at a dozen wall hangings. They included plaques from grammar and high school sports teams to which the man contributed, a Better Business Bureau award, and family pictures. Walter relaxed. This guy appeared to be a valuable member of his community. "From what you told me on the phone, your inheritance includes Revolutionary War coins. Is that correct?"

"Yes, Mr. Browning. I've brought some samples for you to examine, as you requested." He pulled his coin holder out of the old briefcase he still clutched to his chest and laid it on the desk. Kept the briefcase on his lap.

Browning counted the pieces with care, jotted down the number 24 on an appraisal form, and examined them with white-gloved hands. He remarked, "There's a lot of oil and contaminants on fingers and hands, so I do my best to limit exposure." It had occurred to Walter he should have taken the same precautions. Browning examined each piece with meticulous attention using his magnified headband light. He did not make any comments during the inspection. When finished, he asked Walter, "You say you got these as an inheritance?"

"Yes. That's correct."

"Well, these are indeed authentic Spanish coins from the Revolutionary War period. Their condition is remarkable except for what appears to be dirt in the edges and indentations of the raised figures on the coins. The patina looks genuine. These coins weren't properly stored wherever they came from." Walter said nothing. Browning continued. "Further, the intrinsic value of the gold pieces will be worth more than the silver. You're looking at perhaps twenty thousand—my price to you—for these twenty-four coins. They're naturally more valuable at retail. How many of these coins do you have, Mr. Bedford?"

Moment of truth. Walter was still enthralled with digesting the twenty-thousand number. *Do I tell this guy the truth?* He felt perspiration dripping down his back inside his shirt. "I have three-hundred-fifty-four coins, Mr. Browning. Two-hundred-twenty-five are gold. The rest are silver." He did not include the five individual coins he'd found. Those would stay in his own collection.

The coin dealer whistled, looked at Walter with

suspicion and said, "That's quite an inheritance, Mr. Bedford; however, I must be honest with you. My twenty-five years in this business tell me these coins smell, look, and feel like coins recently recovered from parts unknown. Am I correct in that assumption?"

Walter was so nervous that beads of sweat popped up not only on his forehead, but on his upper lip and now ran in a river down his spine. "It's possible, Mr. Browning."

"Then, depending on where you found these coins, I must warn you, that they're likely subject to federal and state laws regarding their recovery. If that is true, they need to be turned over to the authorities." After delivering that warning, Browning stared at Walter.

Now Walter wasn't sure he'd done the right thing. His bouncing knees, wrinkled brow, with right thumb and forefinger rubbing a rough pattern on his chin broadcast his apprehension. Browning spoke. "Mr. Bedford, there are methods to dispose of these coins through a private market with complete discretion. I will handle such a transfer for you, along with your access to a tidy sum of untraceable money, minus my commission, of course."

Walter now had no choice. He must trust this total stranger. "Well, I'd be interested in hearing the actual numbers first. May I call you Ethan?"

"Of course, Walter. You found these coins, am I correct?"

"Yes."

"You realize at about one- to two-thousand per coin you're in the neighborhood of half- to three-quarter million dollars, less my commission, which is thirty-five percent."

"That's a little high, Ethan."

"Not when you consider I convert your coins to cash while skirting legal entanglements. Few businesses are able or willing do that reliably *and* with complete discretion."

Walter knew he had no choice. "I suppose not. So, how do we go about completing this transaction?"

"First, you turn your entire collection over to me. I inspect and rate each one for quality, clarity, and fineness. I then factor that into the price of each coin."

"Understood."

"Tell me something, Walter. Do you think you got them all? My experience with these situations is that there's often more to be found in the same area." Walter quizzed himself with new doubt. *Is it possible? I did stop looking once I found the second box.*

"Worth one more look, Walter."

"Not sure. I'll go back tomorrow and check once more."

Browning held a palm up toward Walter. "That's good. Then, I'd like you to bring up the rest of your find on Saturday. I'll photograph each coin for your records before you turn them over to me. I will then give you a receipt for your entire collection.

"You'll be open on Saturday?"

"I have a collector in mind, and he's more likely to be available to take my call over the weekend. But before I make that call, I need to examine your entire find so we know what to ask for your... collection. Fair enough?"

"Oh, yes, of course."

"Excellent. Walter, if this goes well, within a week you won't ever again have to worry about money. Now, if you'll complete this short contact form which stays in-house...."

"Okay. You hold on to the coins I brought today after you give me a receipt. I'll bring the rest of my find to you late Saturday morning after I give the site another once-over tomorrow." They completed their business and Walter left Browning Diamond and Coin treading on air. Got into his wife's car sedan and sat there. *Wait until Rose finds out! We'll pay off the mortgage, travel, buy a new pickup, and remodel the old place.* His mind raced.

Walter drove home, slower than usual. He focused on the road with some difficulty. Every few seconds, he glanced down at the receipt on the passenger's seat. He was dying to tell Rose. In his excitement, however, he failed to read the receipt earlier. It did not have any business identification, just "twenty-four gold and silver coins from Walter Bedford, 117 Ridge Road, Otis, MA" with a date and an illegible signature. Walter grew concerned, but remained distracted by the day's events.

Ethan Browning picked up his land line and dialed a number. A man answered. Ethan said, "Got a job for you." A pause. He continued. "Good. Stop over. I'll fill you in."

# 9

On Friday morning Walter kissed Rose good-bye. He had shared his news with her the previous night the moment he'd arrived home. Her face had lit up, but inside she remained more analytical than Walter. She knew he was prone to flights of fancy without sufficient forethought.

Walter drove away. A minute or two later, Rose heard a knock on the door. She thought Walter had forgotten something, as he did so often. But he wouldn't knock. Upon opening the door with a smirk on her face, her eyes widened as she gazed up at a large, masked man standing there. He held a... a gun?... with some kind of tube on the end of the barrel. *This must be some sort of mistake*, she thought, which turned out to be her last one. "You must—" She heard two quick *PFFT* sounds as she tumbled backwards. Rose never even heard or felt the third shot.

---

The man with the gun, clad in a black t-shirt and boots with black and gray camouflaged pants, tucked his rather large weapon in small of his back. Felt the spent energy that warmed its barrel and silencer in his butt crack. He smiled as he picked up his spent shell casings. Stepped over the old woman's body and hurried back to Bedford's home office. The assassin found coin books and notes about coins scrawled in a spiral-bound notebook. He found Walter's stash of coins in a ratty-looking fake-leather case beside his desk. Took them and their now-empty boxes. Stormed out of the house with his booty, roared down Route 8 in his SUV to catch up with his second target on the only road leaving the old couple's cabin.

---

Walter arrived at the logging road. He parked with the nose of his truck down in the trees alongside what was more of a trail than a road. *Are there more coins out here?* Stuffed a packet of jerky and his canteen into his backpack and snatched his trusty metal detector from its case in the bed of his truck. Locked the doors and embarked on the forty-five-minute hike.

---

Concealed a few hundred yards up the road, the man in the SUV watched Walter as he trudged up the trail with his gear. Though he'd had plenty of experience taking lives, he really wasn't an assassin, just a soldier on a mission.

---

Thirty-five minutes into his hike Walter thought he heard a twig snap a short distance behind him. He stopped and listened for a good thirty seconds. Nothing. Now wary, he arrived at the trail that led to the gorge—not to the boulder—*away* from his last find. Just in case. He needed to be certain no one followed him.

Upon nearing the summit overlooking the gorge, he spotted the small stream far below. That's when he heard someone running towards him through the low brush. He turned toward the noise. The last thing he saw before being shoved off into the abyss was the blur of a black face and gloved hands at the end of tattooed arms. As he fell, he only felt... surprised and confused.

The man removed his now-unnecessary mask. Stared down at the mangled body far below on the rocks. He confirmed Walter was dead, took and developed a picture with his collapsible Polaroid Land Camera, and hiked out. Never occurred to him to wait for that little old man to complete his search for treasure. Didn't care. Not the mission. He had completed his assignment.

# 10

EPO Sam Travis slumped at his desk in his home office at 11:00 AM. That low time long after his morning coffee, but before refueling at lunch. The phone rang. Bob Newsome, the Otis State Forest supervisor, informed Sam that a hiker discovered a body at the bottom of *the gorge*.

"Sam, we need your expertise in recovering the body."

"Yeah, I'm familiar with that place. Helluva drop. Bob, please block the trail at both ends and let no one through. I'll meet you at the trailhead in about a half hour."

"You're thinking foul play?"

"Dunno till I see it. Better to err on the side of caution. We'll pull together a plan for this recovery."

"You got it. I'll station a ranger at both ends of the gorge trail."

Sam met the forest supervisor at the trailhead. They walked side-by-side until they met the ranger at the south end of the trail. Newsome said, "Any traffic?"

The part-time ranger said, "Nope. A quiet day."

"Same request. Nobody passes if they ain't wearing a uniform."

"You got it."

Newsome raised a portable radio that was clipped to his hip. Called *his* boss. "Sir, on scene with EPO Travis—," but in mid-sentence, Sam threw up his right arm to stop Newsome as they approached the precipice. The forest supervisor dropped the arm clutching the radio. "What's up?"

"A favor, Bob. Stay here." The two men made eye contact. Sam answered Bob's wordless expression of befuddlement. "Until we know differently, we assume this is a crime scene. It's possible that someone overestimated his hiking skills. There are other possibilities, but I wanna look at tracks and anything else of interest. The less traffic up there, the better." This was new to the forest supervisor, but that's why he had called Sam Travis, expert tracker and body recovery specialist. "Another set of footprints is an unnecessary risk. Stay here, okay Bob?"

"Sure thing. Standing by. I'll be on the portable if

you need me." He raised and waggled the handheld radio to emphasize his point.

Sam nodded and proceeded up the trail, treading with deliberation, eyeballing each step. He spotted a near-invisible boot mark in a muddy spot. Peered at it and identified it as a Vibram pattern, a popular and much-imitated design for boot soles. Near that impression, a few bent leaves low on a bush verified the recent passage of someone with an eleven- or eleven-and-a-half boot size. Whipped out a folding ruler from the backpack slung over one shoulder. He figured on a narrow trail like this, a twenty-two or even a twenty-inch stride was far more likely than the full thirty-inch average. When he lost continuity of the track because of flat rocks, he continued measuring in twenty-two-inch increments.

Picked up the trail again and spotted two broken twigs, their interior still fresh, to his left on two different bushes. Their trajectory approached the precipice at an angle on an intercept course with the Vibram sole. He found no distinct boot or shoe imprint, but didn't need one to know there was a second person here. Not a popular trail. *Huh, **this** guy coming in at an angle wears moccasins or special military boots designed to leave no tracks, just impressions?*

Now standing at the edge of the gorge, Sam saw the body at the bottom. He retraced his steps and re-evaluated the evidence before him. *Another man comes from this direction at a thirty or thirty-five degree angle from behind, and from concealment with longer strides. He or she rushes up to Vibram. The scuff mark from the Vibram looks like a step out of place. An expensive metal detector does not follow the hiker down. Why wasn't it still attached to his forearm? Was he pushed?*

Sam now backtracked at a snail's pace after taking some Polaroids to document his speculation. He called Bob Newsome on his portable.

"Bob, this trail and the area near the edge of the gorge up here where the hiker went over is closed until further notice."

"What did you find, Sam?"

"Not sure yet, but enough to be suspicious. We need to get the State Police and their crime scene techs involved to confirm my theory."

"Oh, jeez."

# 11

Massachusetts State Police troopers and techs arrived ninety minutes later. Sam briefed MSP Sergeant Dolan. He also briefed the techs and turned over his Polaroids of the broken twigs, tracks, and his conjecture about the approach of a second person. They said they'd take casts, measure strides, boot or footprints, any torn clothing, gun wrappers, partially smoked cigarettes, and anything that might help the case. This assured Sam they'd confirm his observations.

Sam turned his attention back to Sergeant Dolan, who also waved one of his techs over to listen. "Sergeant, we'll need to approach the victim from the bottom of the gorge and extract him with a tech taking pictures from down there to up here. At the risk of stating the obvious, the measured distance he landed from the wall will also indicate the possibility of a push, not a fall. I suggest that when you call the ME and an ambulance, ensure we request a crew with experience in removing a body from a rocky, wet, boulder-strewn remote area."

Sergeant Dolan agreed and added, "Let's see if he has some ID on him. Judging from this distance, the look of his head, extremities, and deformation from the fall might be tough without it." Sam nodded in agreement. Five techs swarmed over the scene, performing various meticulous tasks; a sixth tech accompanied the ambulance crew to the bottom of the gorge and took various measurements and more photos before the EMTs removed the body. It had landed at the edge of a burbling brook. The old ME met them at the hearse before transporting the body to the morgue for a full autopsy.

The MSP sergeant had rummaged through the victim's pockets and found an ID: Walter Bedford of 117 Ridge Road, Otis, MA. "Sam, seems we have concurrent jurisdiction here. How you wanna handle this?"

"I'd suggest you folks take lead and I will add my thoughts during the investigation. That work for you, Sergeant Dolan?"

"Sure does. I'll give you what I have when I get it. Will you handle the notification?"

"Yeah, let's ask Trooper Day to accompany me to have another woman present with Mrs. Bedford."

"Can do. Where do you want to meet her?"

"Otis Town Commons—say an hour. It'll take us at least thirty-five minutes to hike out of here."

"Roger that. Thanks, Sam."

Travis nodded. Notifications tore at him... at his emotions. Surprise, denial, disbelief, shock, tears, then an instant of clarity. That's usually followed by a grudging acceptance, anger, but always shocking grief. *'Yes, ma'am, we'll do everything we're able to catch who's responsible.' Dolan owes me for doing this.*

## 12

EPO Travis met Trooper Janice Day at The Commons in the heart of Otis and exchanged greetings. "We meet again, EPO Travis. Notifications, not my favorite thing. Okay if I call you Sam?"

"Of course, Janice. I asked for you because you showed a great sense of empathy on the Josie Currant case. We're gonna need that for this."

"Thanks, Sam. So, let's do this. One cruiser or two?"

He nodded down to his still-open notebook clutched in his right hand, a pencil in the other. "Let's do two because I'd like to make a diagram of this gorge crime scene stuff while it's still fresh in my mind once we notify the wife. And it won't tie you up after."

"Okay, let's roll."

They arrived at the Bedford residence, hood to rear bumper. Sam knocked. No reply. Trooper Day shrugged, her thumbs hooked on her gear belt. Another knock. "Mrs. Bedford, Police. We'd like to talk with you, please." Nothing. Sam spotted a car parked in the driveway. Had to be hers. Mr. Bedford's truck was still at the trailhead awaiting a tow into the Otis PD's impound lot where the MSP techies would go through it with great care taking samples and labeling everything.

"What do you think, Janice? Is it time for a well-being check?"

"Yes, I believe that is called for under the circumstances."

Sam opened the unlocked front door, barely enough to enter. Blocked. He pushed further against the resistance. They observed a pair of feet and a prone body they presumed was Rose Bedford. Once they shoved the door open enough to slide in, they spotted the bullet hole in the center of her forehead. They drew their weapons and cleared the house, room by room, picking each step with care in what was now yet another crime scene.

They then snapped on gloves every cop carried and examined the body. Trooper Day said, "Looks like a double-tap, two forty-fives to the heart? Too big an entrance wound for a forty or a nine mil. Followed by an insurance shot to the head. A pro hit?"

Sam kneeled, glanced up at her. "Yeah, I agree with your assessment. No casings either. Why don't you make the call? I'll poke around here, see what there is to find." She agreed with a grim nod. Upon entering Mr. Bedford's office, Sam spotted a coin collector's reference book, and another, and a receipt for two dozen coins, twelve gold, twelve silver, with an unreadable signature; however, a date was legible. Yesterday. No business name or address on the receipt. *Yeah, that'd be too easy. Let's hope phone records give us something more.* He picked up the receipt with his gloved hand and placed it in a plastic evidence bag. Filled out the required chain-of-custody info on the bag's exterior and resumed his search. He came up with nothing more of interest. Maybe the techies would find some DNA, or hair, or other useful trace evidence.


Sam also made a courtesy call from the Bedford's kitchen to the part-time Otis police chief informing him of the deaths of two citizens in his jurisdiction. This long and arduous day had already presented him with one definite homicide and another possible. He searched the rest of the Bedfords' house and found more books about *detectionists* and their finds. *You had it bad, Walter. What did you find? Something that got you and your wife killed?*

Walter told somebody about his find. *Coins? From state land where we found hubby? I'm betting he was looking for an appraisal and to move them to a private collector.* If so, that violated at least a half-dozen state *and federal statutes* based on where they likely were found. That meant neither he nor the Massachusetts State Police commanded sufficient authority, especially if Walter crossed over into New Hampshire, not far north. *Yup, gotta call the feds. Better let MSP know first. Protocol. Avoid bruised feelings.* Sam made a quick call to his friend Sgt. Dolan—he agreed and said, "Well, you did some work with the FBI on that Appalachian Trail case. Anyone you know you over there you trust?"

"Yeah, I do, but she's a profiler, not a field agent. So I'm not sure they'll let her in on this."

"See what you mean. Give it a go. Make shit up if you have to." Dolan smirked so hard Sam could hear it over the phone. Or maybe it was Dolan's mini-snort that gave away his smart-ass attitude.

Sam chuckled back. "I never make up shit." *Yeah, right.* The techs arrived, the ME arrived, the whole crime scene drill all over again. A long day already. Sam handled the receipt for the coins with his gloved hands in case there were prints and/or DNA. He'd do nothing to impede handwriting analysis, either.

Handed it over. Watched the techs re-bag, label, seal it, and signed for assuming possession of it from Sam.

Now, who'd kill an old retired couple, and why? An armed robbery gone bad? But why kill them in two different locations? No, this was not only pre-meditated, but meticulously orchestrated by one or more killers. This was no amateur snatch 'n grab.

# 13

Sam arrived home. He punished both his fiancée, Kate and his thirteen-year-old son, Brian with extra-intense hugs. Then he took his time to kiss Kate. "You're late, cowboy. Busy day?"

He sniggered. "You didn't hear anything from all your ears to the ground, Ms. Investigative Journalist?"

"Day off."

Brian looked up at his dad, but spoke to Kate. "I've seen that look on Dad's face before. I think the poop hit the fan."

Sam turned and kneeled. Gazed into Brian's hazel eyes and scooped him in close for another hug. "You're so damn smart. You've got me figured out. Love you, son."

Kate now got a sense of how tough Sam's day must

have been. Reluctant to press him for more information, especially in front of Brian, she chirped, "Hey, let's eat some chow and chill."

Sam hoisted a tired grin at her obvious cheerleading. "I'm starving. No lunch again." They sat down to eat. Talked about school, the paper, anything but Sam's day. Later, Kate and Sam plopped onto the sofa in front of the stone fireplace, their favorite *together* spot. Brian dropped to the floor as only kids can do. He flipped the channel to Nat Geo, a show about predators on the Serengeti.

"Homework done, sport?"

Brian looked over his shoulder. "Yeah, Dad. Pretty much."

"Does 'pretty much' mean all, most, or part?"

"Uh, most, I guess."

"Why don't you run upstairs and finish it like the good student you are?"

"Aww, geez Dad. I hate math."

"Me too. But at least give it a try and you'll have an excuse if you screw it up, but I hope that doesn't happen."

"Okay, I'll give it a shot."

"There ya go. I'll be up with Kate later, okay?"

Brian turned off the TV and trudged upstairs. Kate's anxiety had not abated. "Whenever you're ready, hon," she said.

Sam turned to her on the sofa and shared everything he'd discovered about the Bedford case. She asked a few questions, demonstrating her expertise as a sharp reporter, but observed that Sam was drained. Her one pressing question: "How will you get Letty involved?"

"How do you—?"

"You know her, you like her, you worked with her before on the AT case. It's logical you'd seek a federal agent you trust. Hell, you almost died together on that last one."

"You *don't* have to worry about me and Letty. That's a non-existent bridge to cross. I have no romantic interest in anyone but you."

"Hey, big guy, if I were worried, it would mean that I don't trust you. And if our relationship is to keep growing, there is no room for dishonesty or distrust."

Sam edged closer to her on the couch. "Between you and Brian, I can't hide anything, can I?"

"Nope, so don't bother even trying." She tossed him a playful grin.

"Let's say g'night to Brian and I'll coax you into giving me a back rub. Sure could use it. And after that, we fix a big ole cocktail and head back up?"

"Deal."

The phone jangled Sam awake the next morning. He rolled out of bed with body language that broadcast his displeasure. He hadn't set his alarm and nine AM had come and gone. Kate still slept. As he slid into his slippers, he walked around the bed to peck her on the cheek. She murmured but did not wake up.

Sergeant Dolan said, "Sam, we got a hit on three coin dealers in and around Portsmouth. Want the names and addresses?"

"Yeah, sure. Let me get a pen." Sam scribbled down the information. "Okaaaay. I'll call in the feds this morning now that we're crossing state lines, Sergeant. You already ran all three places, right?"

"Ya got me. Of course, we ran them. One of them sticks out a bit. The other two appear to be legit."

"Which one?"

"Browning Diamond and Coin. There's a sealed record with the ATF and IRS. What do ya think of that?"

Sam speculated. "Not sure, but it's a flag. I know those boys don't like to open a sealed file, so someone's gotta know someone to get that done. And pretty far up the chain, I'd think."

"Yeah, I agree. But this shit happens all the time. A court order could open it, but we have no probable cause to get one. Maybe make up some shit, or does your profiler have some yank to get an 'unofficial' peek at it? For probative purposes only, of course. Worth a shot."

"Agreed. I'll do my best to make up some shit. You're pretty creative yourself."

Dolan laughed. "Later," he said and hung up.

After stumbling downstairs to start the coffee, Sam

sauntered into his office, jerked open his top right desk drawer, and rifled through his law enforcement business card collection. Kept them under control with a heavy rubber band. The stack had grown to almost two inches thick and got thicker by the week. A good thing. The more contacts, the better for an investigator. He found Letty's card and dialed. Left an urgent message.

Sam showered, dressed, and bumped into Kate. They both ran late, but grinned ear to ear. Kate grabbed and squeezed Sam's right bun and chirped, "Bri's already off to school. See you tonight, lover boy."

"Roger that." They both flew down the front porch steps to their respective vehicles and off they sped. Kate, now at the Berkshire Tribune as an investigative reporter, held a coveted head start on a double homicide, thanks to Sam Travis, EPO, a.k.a. lover boy.

# 14

Sam piloted his old green Bronco toward the FBI office in Springfield on a hunch that Letty was there. He'd heard she had transferred from DC to Boston, but landed in Springfield... on temp assignment? Sam enjoyed the drive on this beautiful summer day, with lush greenery on both sides of the highway set against the bluest sky ever. He rocketed east on the Mass Pike and cruised into the flats region off Blandford Mountain. Spotted a DMV—a Disabled Motor Vehicle—on the side of the road. On any other day, he'd call the MSP barracks and let troopers handle it. But since no specific appointment drove him, he pulled the Bronco in behind the DMV with his wheels pointed toward the ditch. So some inattentive driver plowing into his Bronco would more likely to push it farther off the road instead of into traffic or the into disabled vehicle ahead.

Travis exited the Bronco with his rear blue lights activated. As he approached the car, a man got out of his SUV... with a... gun! Sam quickly evaluated the situation. He spotted an adult woman's head in the front seat and a smaller head in the back. "Whoa there, fella. No need for any pistol play."

The man looked right through Sam with the gun hanging at his side. *Good sign,* Travis thought. Keyed his collar mike and radioed, "Dispatch, get MSP to my location on the Mass Pike, eastbound lane, mile marker eight-three. Fast. Man with a firearm. Over."

"Received unit twenty-three."

Travis advanced at a snail's pace until about twenty feet away. The man wore a button-down collared shirt and tie with nice shoes, a decent haircut... not a shit-bag. But still dangerous, and in obvious crisis mode. "Talk to me, sir. Tell me what's going on. You don't need that gun." Sam down-nodded toward the weapon, its business end still aimed at the ground. But the man's right index finger was inside the trigger guard. "Let's calm down and figure this out together." The man said nothing. But Travis observed he was under extreme pressure.

"Your wife ever leave you for another man?" The man's eyes pleaded but did not yet make contact with Sam's.

"No, sir, I lost mine to cancer. Let me ask you this,

how many friends, family and acquaintances have gotten divorces? Lots, right? They didn't do what you're thinking about. They moved on with their lives. You can too."

The man paused before muttering. "Well, Susan told me she's leaving me and taking my son with her. That isn't gonna happen." His head jittered back and forth with only the slightest movement. More like an involuntary tick, or spasm.

Sam took it all in. His voice remained low and smooth. "Sure not easy, but if you use that piece, your life will be over."

"It's *already* over, now that she's done with me."

An MSP Trooper arrived. He parked behind Sam's cruiser. Sam heard him speak into his shoulder mike. Muttered a few abrupt but unintelligible words. Travis nodded to him and held his hand up to stall him. The trooper nodded, but his hand rested on his sidearm, not snapped in. Sam: "I want to help you get through this. I appreciate it all seems too much to take, but the alternative is much worse. What's your name, sir?"

The man shook his head in a bigger sideways arc, but said nothing. While mulling over his options, Sam half-whispered to the man who now shivered and was sweating profusely. "See that trooper behind me? In about five minutes, there will be six more. And they will not let me continue this conversation with you. They'll be in charge. Who do you want to talk to? Me or them?" The man wiped his brow on the sleeve of his gun hand, looked up, and up-nodded as if to say, *You.*

"Okay, let's start by putting the gun on the ground."

"*No.* She's gotta pay for what she's doing."

Then, louder, Sam said, "This isn't the way to do it. There'll be court and a judge where you can argue your case. You look upper-middle-class and well-educated. Probably have a pretty good job. All points in your favor. Use your head, man. You kill your wife and son and maybe me and then what?"

"I don't care," the man said.

"Sure you do. What if you get custody? You'll be able to raise your son. Watch him grow into a man. You want that, right? Or do you want someone else to be his father *instead of you?*"

The man hesitated, then nodded side-to-side again. Another sliver of certainty.

"OK, then." Travis baby-stepped toward the man, his hands staying clear of his own weapon. "You'll get through this. She doesn't deserve you, anyway. Why die for someone like that?" The tension eased a little. Sam now stood less than ten feet from him. "C'mon, let's figure this out. Don't do anything you'll regret for the rest of your life. If these troopers don't shoot you dead, that is. Maybe catch your son in the cross-fire" Two additional MSP cruisers pulled in behind the first and a Staff Sergeant advanced toward the two men. Travis couldn't tell him to stay back, but he turned his head and pleaded with his eyes. The Sergeant held his ground four feet from Travis, next to the other trooper.

"You see where this is going, right?" Sam's voice took on a pleading tone. The man looked up. He exuded a sense of hopelessness. Sam's experience told him this might still go bad in an instant. Since the man didn't tell Travis to stop advancing, he continued his slow approach. Still talking in a soft and calm voice, he observed the man now silently sobbing. "C'mon, let's resolve this without anyone getting hurt and making your chances of getting your son impossible." That seemed to hit a nerve. Now within arm's reach, the man could still lift the semi-auto up and put a hole in Travis. Before he could reach his own weapon or before the troopers could draw down on him. No traffic on the Mass Pike in either direction now. They'd closed the highway.

Travis said, "You know I'm right. Be smart. Use your head. Hand me the gun. You don't need it. What you *need* is a good lawyer to fight this the right way." The man looked Travis right in the eye and then lifted his gun hand up. Still not clear whether he'd surrender or fire. Then, the guy fell to his knees as if gravity were just too strong. The gun clattered the remaining few inches to the road's asphalt surface. Travis slowly reached down with both hands, one onto the now-sobbing man's shoulder and the other to retrieve the pistol. "Thank you for being smart. The troopers will take over from here. I do wish you the best, sir."

Travis turned to hand the firearm to the sergeant, who said in a quiet voice, "Nice work, Officer. You were lucky, and I don't know if I'd be able to do that." Travis looked back over his shoulder at the man, still sobbing, still on his knees with his now-upturned palms in his lap. The troopers stood him up, handcuffed him, and checked on the passengers. They scurried around while Travis made his escape and checked in. "Unit twenty-three to base. All's well that ends well."

"Nice work, twenty-three. Your supervisor is calling you. Please contact him as soon as possible."

"Received. Will do."

# 15

Travis slumped behind the wheel of his cruiser. He thought, *That's how Dad would have done it. Always cool on the job, that trooper. Not so much at home, though. An angry man.* Sam punched the wheel. *Gotta learn from Dad's job performance <u>and</u> his mistakes.* Almost no visible tremor in his hands, now. Because he clenched the steering wheel to control it. Dropped his head onto the backs of his white knuckles. A few beats later, a light tap on the window startled him. Jerked his head up and to his left. Travis rolled down his window. A concerned trooper with a slantwise look of concern asked, "You good?"

A deep breath and a brief pause later, Sam said through a big exhale, "Yeah, I'm good. Thanks."

"Excellent work, Officer Travis." Sam nodded as he started the Bronco and eased into the rightmost traffic lane. Didn't even check his mirror. He now focused on meeting with the FBI. Windows down, fresh air surging around him, he filled and emptied his lungs. Several times. In quick succession.

Travis arrived in Springfield at 1441 Main Street Parks in Springfield. Presented his credentials to the security guard in the modern lobby who asked him to sign in. The guard did not ask him to surrender his firearm. Sam asked for Agent Letty Mather. After checking his log, he learned she was due in at noon. "Might anyone else assist you, Officer?"

"Who's the SAC these days?"

"The Special Agent in Charge is Jack Malone."

"Is he available?"

The guard called upstairs and asks, "What is your business?"

"Tell him two murders occurred yesterday in Otis and our investigation now crosses state lines. We need the Bureau involved."

The guard picked up the phone, punched in four numbers, and relayed the message. He said, "Fifth floor, room 501."

Sam took the stairs. Approached and entered 501. A sharp secretary behind her tidy desk screamed efficiency. This outer office was spacious and smartly decorated. No art work, but a gaggle of plaques, photos of dignitaries, diplomas, certifications, and commendations. Sam said to himself, *Subtle chest pounding*. He introduced himself as he flashed his badge and ID. She asked him to take a seat.

"Thanks. Your name, ma'am?" He beamed his most fetching smile.

"Jennifer Weaver. Call me Jen."

"Thanks, Jen. Nice to meet you." The door to Malone's office opened. An enormous man appeared in a blue suit, crisp white shirt, and a designer red tie with yellow stripes. Sam stood.

"Hello, I'm Special Agent Jack Malone. How can the Bureau be of service?" Malone was six-four and at least two-twenty. Former linebacker, for sure. He *owned* the look. At six even and a solid one-ninety, Sam felt small. "Please, come in. Let's talk." Moments later, "Have a seat EPO Travis. Coffee, tea, water?"

"No, thanks Agent Malone. Thanks for seeing me."

"Tell me, EPO Travis—"

"It's just Sam."

"Okay, Sam, what brings you here? Alone?"

Might as well have posted up a frown, but the big man didn't. Jack said, "You're wondering why my supervisor or some higher-ranking person other than myself isn't here. It's because my lieutenant is already at a staff meeting in Boston with our senior staff. Someone murdered my sergeant and we haven't found a replacement yet. So it's just me. Is that a problem for you?"

"Well, I'd like to be certain that your management

allowed you to represent your department in this serious matter."

Travis grew agitated. *Damn feebs.* But he understood what was happening. "Well, since I'm the lead investigator and working with the State Police on multiple murders, I'd agree this is a serious matter."

"This," his index finger pointed down toward the ground carved out a circular patter, "is unusual."

Sam figured better to get it out before disclosing what he learned about the case. Once he let them see what he had, they'd relegate him to the role of observer while they did the work and grabbed the credit. Sam had been down this road before. So, he looked Malone straight in the eye and said, "Are you interested in who is giving you the information or what the information is?"

Malone said, "I don't understand."

"Let me be plain, Agent Malone. I am a lowly field officer speaking to a supervisory FBI Agent. A disparity, to be sure. But the information I have is no less relevant than if I had bars, oak leaves or stars on my epaulets. Did you serve, Special Agent Malone?"

"No, I did not, regrettably."

"Well, I am a former Marine Corps staff sergeant and I dealt plenty with men and women who possessed a higher pay grade than me. I knew more about what was going on than they did. I'm used to it. I think you should get used to it too. If not, I'd be happy to take my leave of this office. I'm positive the

New Hampshire State Police would be more than interested in what this Massachusetts state officer has to say, and I'd still be free of jurisdictional constraints."

SAC Malone stared at Sam as if reappraising his opinion of this officer. He paused, then said, "Well, Sam, no one has dressed me down like that in several years. Okay, you have my attention. Let's get to it."

They both relaxed. Malone walked around his desk and sat across from Sam in a second guest chair. Sam described the coins and the now-established state forest murder, thanks to his freezing the crime scene and applying his tracking skills. He told Malone about Rose Bedford's murder in her home. And that the assassin stole what they assumed was the bulk of Walter Bedford's find, sure to be more gold and silver coins. "Professional hits, both. Our people estimate the worth of Bedford's entire find to be worth at least a half-million, could be twice that much. Let's say our suspect is an outstanding member of his community. But let's also say it's a cover for fencing, or maybe something worse."

"Worse? What are you saying, Sam?"

"This has earmarks of organized crime or something even more... nefarious. Don't know."

"Lots of speculation here with no evidence to back it up."

"True, but not an improbable scenario. I need to do some more digging. You can help by talking to your gang people, your organized crime people, see if there's been any unusual chatter."

"Pretty wide net you're casting."

"What? You want me to throw a small one? I suggest we both get to work on this, and if it's nothing, you can call this swamp cop an alarmist and never entertain speaking with another field officer again. *Only* speak to folks with bars, oak leaves, and stars who will profess to know everything but get their information from people like me. That about right, Special Agent in Charge Malone? And I need another thing from you."

Letty's FBI boss smiled in amusement. "Why am I not surprised?"

"I'd like to work with Special Agent Mather on this since we've worked together before. I need a psychological edge with this *respectable* coin dealer, Ethan Browning, during an interview I plan to conduct in New Hampshire."

"You don't ask for much, do you, Officer Travis? I know that you and Agent Mather recently worked well together on that AT case."

"I am reaching out to be thorough, as I know you will be, Agent Malone."

The head of the FBI Springfield field office drummed his fingers on his desk while he mulled over his next words. Sam remained silent, holding this high-level suit's gaze. Malone finally spoke. "Okay, Sam. I'll talk to my people about this and see if there's any fire to your smoke. Plus, I'll grant your request for Agent Mather. I am impressed by how you handle yourself and make your case. I do, however, require a call from one of your superiors confirming this is indeed a sanctioned operation. I must cover my bases, too."

"Done." They both arose and exchanged business cards with their confidential numbers.

"Stay in touch, Officer Travis, and good luck," Malone offered his big mitt.

Travis countered with his best firm handshake. "Thank you, sir, for your assistance and cooperation."

Sam left the FBI office rather than wait for Agent Mather. He had a ton of things to do in his office at home. But he'd call her that afternoon. Headed home to write a report that his boss awaited. *Paperwork.* Didn't mind an uneventful trip home on the Mass Pike. He also remembered to ask O'Neill to call SAC Malone to sanction the EPO side of their dual-agency operation.

---

While sitting at his desk in his home office filing his report, Sam called Letty to brief her. And to find out when she'd be available to visit their primary suspect, Ethan Browning. Dialed the number, punched in the extension, and waited.

# 16

"Special Agent Mather here. How may I help you?"

"Uh, I need a hand setting up a tent in a remote location for some frog hunting. I was wondering if you're available to assist."

"That's the best you got, Officer Travis?" They both chuckled. "How are you, Sam?"

"I'm fine. Great to hear your voice, Letty." He felt boyish and excited to speak with her again.

"What kind of mischief are you up to now, and how does it involve me?"

"Boy, so much for small talk. Froggin' doesn't excite you?"

"Hmm, not so much, but a midnight boat ride is never a bad idea."

"Hey, I'm working a double murder with MSP. I visited your office today and spoke to your SAC."

"Yeah, he's already spoken to me. You made one hell of an impression on him. I don't have a clue how you even got in to see Malone, much less got him to act so quickly. This is the FBI. Frozen molasses moves faster than we do. So, you've got a double homicide and a coin dealer you suspect is not quite legit. You suspect either gang or mob ties, and you want my help to catch something in him you might miss." Not a question in the bunch.

"Yep."

"Well, what's your schedule look like? I have one meeting at ten that'll last an hour. Want to hook up for lunch and then go to *our* interview?"

"Sounds like a plan. I'll brief you more thoroughly at lunch before we hit Mr. Browning. I'll call him now and make the arrangements. *Or* how about we just pop on in and take the chance he's there to gain the element of surprise?"

"I like the idea of dropping in unannounced."

"Where do we meet? How about eleven-thirty at the last rest area about five miles before the interchange to Portsmouth?"

Letty paused a beat before she responded with an obvious smirk in her voice. "Sounds fine. How do you want me dressed since last time you asked for casual?"

"Oh, stop. Your usual work clothes. I'll be in civvies since I'll be out of state. See you in a couple hours."

The late spring day was turning a dull, gun-metal gray with a light drizzle, soon to be a steady rain according to the weather lady on channel six. *Yeah, I'd trust TV meteorologists with my life,* muttered Sam to himself. The interchange outside of Portsmouth was full of cars parked at the liquor store. Such stores in New Hampshire were always packed. Unlike Massachusetts, they levied no sales tax on booze. Sam spotted Letty's black Crown Vic, standard FBI issue, regular plates and unmarked except for a small one-foot antenna sticking up from the middle of the roof.

They greeted each other with a firm but friendly handshake. Sam suggested they get vending machine coffee, a donut, and return to her sedan to avoid what he called "nosy ears." Letty said, "Same old Sam, paranoid to the Nth." She passed on the snack. There was a reason she maintained a sinewy hundred-fifteen pounds. Rain now poured down in earnest.

He ignored the comment and dropped into her passenger side, sopping wet after scoring a cup for himself. "Here's what I got. Let me know after I'm done what you think." He described the double murder, showed her eight-by-ten black-and-whites of both scenes. The tracks, the gorge with Walter in it, the measured distance from the base of the cliff, and more photos of Rose, and Walter's desk with the coin books. Whipped out the receipt in a sealed evidence bag labeled with chain-of-custody information and handed it to her.

Letty took her time digesting Sam's briefing. Then, she summarized, "A double homicide by one or more unknown killers. Motive: theft of an unknown number of rare coins, value unknown, but likely substantial because of the murders. What about comms?"

"Not much. Walter Bedford's phone records revealed nothing. That suggests pay phones."

"That's not a problem. There's so few in these semi-rural areas that we'd be able to track the two or three dozen in a fifty-mile radius in both New Hampshire and Mass with a federal warrant delivered to NYNEX. They have lots of problems with striking unions. These days, phone companies need friends in the federal government. They'll cooperate. We'd be looking for calls made from Mass to New Hampshire, I'm guessing during the day, to coin, jewelry, or hock shops. That'll narrow down our search."

Sam's jaw dropped and stayed there until he spoke. "Wow, you can do that?"

"Yes, and the SAC will approve it with a priority."

"Okay, let's get on that. In the meantime, let's find out what Mr. Browning has to say."

# 17

They arrived in Portsmouth minutes later. The late May rain and heavy traffic had slowed them down. Sam glanced over at Letty, who furrowed her brow in contemplation. He said, "So, how do we want to do this? You take lead?"

"No, Sam, I want to study his reactions to your questions. If I'm talking and formulating follow-ups, I won't be devoting my full attention to his body language and verbal cues. If he's hesitant, pauses too long before answering, is evasive, demonstrates involuntary nervous twitches, eye movement, hand positions, I want my full attention on spotting those tells. I'm sure you'll be throwing every flavor of crap at him and this approach is our best shot to catch him in a mistake or to reveal his tells."

Sam smiled. He liked this plan. "Okay, let's rattle his cage and watch what tumbles out."

A tiny bell above the door announced their presence in Browning Diamond and Coin. Mr. Browning emerged from his back room a few moments later with his illuminated third eye. He appeared to be surprised, as if his gut was telling him, *This handsome couple isn't interested in coins. Maybe jewelry, maybe not customers at all.*

Letty led off to nip in the bud any jurisdictional beefs later. "Good afternoon, Mr. Browning. My name is FBI Special Agent Letty Mather, and this is Officer Sam Travis from the Massachusetts Environmental Police." They both produced their IDs, complete with pictures and badges... and visible sidearms. His eyes darted between their probing eyes, digesting what was happening and why. He recovered. "Nice to meet you. How can I help you? Uh, and why is the *Mass Environmental Police* in my humble shop?"

Sam started shaking the cage. "Someone committed a double homicide in my district, *and* on state forest land, also in my jurisdiction. I discovered both bodies."

"How awful. How am I involved in this matter?"

"May we sit down? Somewhere private?" Sam wanted to learn the layout of the store.

Browning said, "Certainly. In my office. Right this way." The small office was perfect for Letty. She read it like a book. Chamber of Commerce citations, Little

League plaques of appreciation, an on-line gemologist certificate, and more. Letty could observe Browning up close in the small space. She also perused his bookshelves without being too obvious about it.

Sam said, "You've been in business here quite a while, haven't you, Mr. Browning?"

"Yes, almost twenty years now. I am proud of my devoted clientele."

Sam wasted no time. The goal was to apply pressure. He pulled out a sealed plastic sheet marked with big letters—EVIDENCE. It contained the receipt he found in Walter Bedford's office. "Do you recognized this receipt?"

Browning hesitated for a micro-beat before recovering just as fast. Sam caught Letty's eyes flash. "Uh, yes I do. I gave this to a man, a couple of days ago. A Walter Bidford, Bedford... his name was something like that."

***Was?*** *Interesting use of past tense. He already knows one of our homicides is Bedford. How does he know that?* "Please tell us the details of that meeting."

Browning started in on his story, which sounded truthful and synced with what they knew. But was he stalling? "Uh, I received a call from a nervous man, Walter Bedford, telling me he had valuable coins he wanted me to appraise. We set up a meeting, and he came up from Massachusetts. At least that's what his car's license plate suggested."

*So, now he knows his name was Bedford, not Bidford.* "Why do you say he was nervous?"

"Well, he was hesitant and at first gave me a false name."

"Can you elaborate on who said what?"

Browning broke eye contact and paused. "Well, I asked how he came by these coins and he told me it was an inheritance."

"Did you believe that?"

"I had no reason to doubt him at that point."

"So, at what point did you suspect he lied to you?"

"It seemed like he didn't keep his coins in a secure or clean area. A dirty patina covered the coins. Someone who has valuable coins would take better care of them."

"What coins and how many did he bring to you?"

"A dozen gold and a dozen silver coins from the Revolutionary War period, as written on the receipt. They were in good condition. He said he had more, and it was my professional opinion that they were indeed valuable."

"Did he say how many he had? And how he came by these coins, Mr. Browning?"

"Umm, no, he did not."

Letty twitched.

"Did you ask?"

"Yes, but he was evasive."

"How?"

"He was reluctant to tell me. Look, I'm a well-respected businessman here in Portsmouth and I resent this machine gun type of interrogation, Officer Travis."

"Doing my job, Mr. Browning. And if you're the honest businessman you say you are, you have nothing to fear from us. Did you inform him of the legal implications? That if he found these and didn't surrender them, he might be subject to civil and criminal liabilities? I'm sure you must be aware."

Browning looked down and to the side before answering. "Yes, I may have mentioned it." Letty twitched again. Almost invisible.

"Either you did or you didn't, Mr. Browning. If you don't remember, then say that. If you didn't, say you didn't." During this grilling, the chinks in Browning's armor surfaced. Sam didn't wait for a clarifying response before he continued. "So this meeting was on Thursday the eighteenth, correct?"

"Yes."

"What happened on Friday?"

"Nothing. He said he wanted time to think about his next move."

"Did you tell him what these coins were worth?

"Yes, I gave him an approximate value."

"How much?"

"About twenty-thousand dollars."

"Okaaay... Knowing that, why another appointment with him on Saturday morning at 10:00 am?"

"I'm not aware of another scheduled meeting."

"Well, on Mr. Bedford's desk calendar at his home, he had written your name and time for Saturday the twentieth. Why would he do that?"

"I have no idea."

"Someone murdered him on Friday, the nineteenth. We discovered his body on a trail in a state forest. I've asked myself why Bedford ventured out onto state land. We believe he'd been there before. Was he going back out there to revisit a site where he found the coins? Was he looking for more coins? Maybe not an inheritance at all. May I see your calendar, Mr. Browning, a record of deliveries, appointments and such?" *No surprise to him that Bedford is one of our homicides.*

"No, not without a warrant, Officer Travis." His response was immediate, his voice was soft, cold, and left no doubt.

Travis looked at Letty, raised his eyebrows, and paused before continuing. "Might be a serious hobby, detecting old coins, diamond rings, anything old and buried. Perhaps he found a stash of old Revolutionary War coins and was looking to convert them into cash."

"No idea about that, Officer Travis."

"You met with the victim the day before his murder. You confirmed that. And another meeting with you on his calendar the day after. I'm sure you understand why that perplexes us, Mr. Browning."

"I've told you I had no meeting scheduled with Mr.

Bedford on the twentieth. I'm saddened to hear of his demise. He seemed like a nice old guy."

"From what we've learned, he was. Do you have the coins here with you today?"

"Yes, they're in my safe."

"Get them please."

"Certainly, I'll only be a moment." Browning limped out of the room. Sam was about to ask Letty a question, but she held her vertical index finger to her lips. Pointed to a wire on the desk that led to a file cabinet. Travis nodded and remained silent.

Browning arrived with the coins in a blue velvet box. Twenty-four coins nestled in four neat rows, fitting perfectly into slots that appeared tailor-made for them. "I will need a receipt, Officer Travis." Sam nodded toward Letty. She nodded back.

"Sure, like the one you gave Mr. Browning with no business name, address, only a date and a scribbled signature? That letter to a client on your desk on your business letterhead has your signature on it with almost perfect handwriting. Is this scrawl your signature too?" Sam thought he'd shake this guy into saying something he didn't mean to say. He held up the receipt in the evidence bag containing Browning's own make-shift receipt and shook it a little. Rattled, Browning was unsure how to reply. "It's okay, Mr. Browning, I'm guessing you were rushed, but I don't understand why there's no letterhead on this receipt you gave to Mr. Bedford versus that one on your desk. Do you have two different receipt books?"

Browning now exuded a rainbow of micro-expressions and body language that he failed to conceal. "Uh, yeah, I have one for in-house stuff and another for official business. I guess I grabbed the wrong one."

"Doesn't explain your signature. Why an in-house receipt book?"

Browning stalled. "Why is that relevant?"

So many things smelled sour. Sam and Letty exchanged non-verbals. They'd need to seize the rest of coins before they disappeared. The receipt, evasive answers to almost every question, and two sets of books? Sam continued his barrage. "Did you or anyone you know have any connection with the death of Walter Bedford?" A now-rattled Browning shouted, "*No!* I had nothing to do with his *or* his wife's death, okay?"

*He knows about Rose Bedford, too!* "Okay for now, Mr. Browning."

"What the hell does that mean, 'for now'?"

"It means as of right this moment, we will take you at your word unless future evidence dictates otherwise." Browning fought to maintain his composure. Letty looked at Browning without expression. No, that wasn't right. Her eyes were not only neutral, they were... cold. The man now perched on the forward edge of his chair, not sitting back like earlier. Yet another tell.

Letty interjected herself into the interrogation. "Mr. Browning, do you have any employees working for you either part-time or full-time?"

"I have one full-time and one part-time who does pickups and deliveries."

"What are the full-timer's responsibilities?"

"Well, Josh is my right-hand man and is learning the business. He does some appraisals, orders gemstones and bracelets, takes inventory, and fills in when I attend civic functions."

"Did Josh meet Mr. Bedford?"

"No, he was out of the office."

"How about your part-time guy? Did he see Mr. Bedford?"

"No, he didn't work on Thursday."

"What are your employees' full names?"

"Why is it necessary for you to know that?"

"Details matter, Mr. Browning."

"Am I a suspect in this case, Agent Mather?"

"Not at this time, sir. Their full names, please."

"Josh Bingham lives here in town. The part-timer is Andrew Lofton. He lives in Derry. Do you need addresses too?"

"Yes, please." Browning jotted down the information for Letty. She nodded at Travis, who stood up and offered his hand. "Thank you so much for you time and information. If there's anything else that occurs to you, please take my card and contact me at anytime."

Browning accepted cards from both Letty and

Sam. Letty also handed the man a receipt she had scribbled on a piece of notebook paper she'd commandeered from Browning's desk.

"Oh, Mr. Browning, did you offer to purchase the rest of Mr. Bedford's coins? Is that the reason for the Saturday appointment written in his book?"

"No, but I offered to appraise the entire collection."

"Why? If you knew they were the subject of federal and state Recovery and Artifacts laws?"

"Uh, I guess personal interest in seeing so many rare coins from that era."

"I imagine many private collectors are potential buyers."

"I suppose so, depending on how many and what condition they were in."

"Good day, sir, and thanks again for your time. Your insights are helpful." Travis tipped a casual salute in the coin dealer's direction. They both left the office and saw Browning staring at them through his dirty storefront window.

# 18

Once out of Browning's line of sight, Sam eyed the man's company van with the same logo as on the building. Parked in the adjacent alley, Sam retrieved a bulky tracking device Letty had stashed in her trunk. He crammed the half-brick-size device inside of the van's rear bumper with the powerful magnet on the bottom of the device. Back in the car, Sam smiled. "What's the range of that thing?"

Letty had checked the device out of the FBI Springfield office's armory. The *half-brick* was a new generation of tracking device based on the latest Global Positioning System technology originally developed for the military. Federal law enforcement organizations were the first non-military users.

"Range? About fifty miles if you're following the ground-tracker side of this device. The battery is good for about ninety-six hours. Its satellite tracking capabilities both locate and record. But my ass is grass if I don't return this costly little unit. I thought it might come in handy."

"Nice toy, Letty. Good call. Who'd you have to kill to get access to that kind of tech?"

"It is possible I bandied about the phrase 'national security potential.' Who knows? Might even be true." She flashed that devilish smirk Sam had grown so fond of.

He smiled back. He proclaimed a little louder than he intended, "You lied your ass off. Said it before, I'll say it again. You're okay for a feeb."

Letty reached into her small purse and turned off her recorder. Sam looked down at the device and said, "And you're a sneaky feeb!"

Letty smiled and said, "We have to work fast. This guy will cover his tracks. I'll get a warrant for a phone tap on his business. We now have enough probable cause if I shop the right judge. There was so much info he dumped on us. Only some intentional. I need to go over all of it again. He lied or didn't tell the complete truth more often than not. We need a complete background investigation on him and his employees. Something stinks here and we don't have a lot of time. Did you see the predominant 'Live Free or Die" plaque on his office wall? I spotted a few books on his shelves that lead me to believe we may be on to something bigger than a double homicide and robbery. Books like *Refreshing the Tree of Freedom*, *Weathermen* by Bill Ayers and Bernadine Dohrn. Also—"

Sam's perplexed expression drew Letty to explain. She told Sam the *Weathermen* was a domestic terrorism organization that the FBI ranked as a major national security threat during the seventies, estimating a membership of thousands. The Bureau later learned their *Weather Underground* was a small organization that made a lot of noise—by detonating bombs. "Sam, the point is this guy reads a lot of extremist literature. If he's our guy and he off'd the Bedfords to steal their treasure, there will be more than greed at work here. God only knows how many coins Walter discovered. If this was a major find, Browning could fund almost any kind of operation. I guarantee a guy like that has a healthy network of fences to convert those coins into cash. From there—"

Travis piped in; "Holy crap! A lot of speculation, there, Special Agent. But if you're on target, yeah, we gotta move fast. I wanna see where this guy lives. Gotta get to the courthouse and look up land records, where this guy came from. His pals, too. Browning didn't pull this off by himself."

Letty said, "One small word he uttered tripped my wire more than most. When you asked him if he offered to buy *all* of Bedford's coins, he knew Walter held a lot more than twenty-four. And the Bedfords are dead less than twenty-four hours after Browning gets a bead on Bedford? Before they moved the coins elsewhere? Plus, the wife gets triple-tapped at home on the same day Walter falls off a cliff out in the middle of s state forest? Yeah, Browning didn't limp up to the edge of nowhere on that prosthetic leg, for sure. Didn't seem all that surprised to hear that Walter had been murdered. And Sam, he knew of Rose's death before we mentioned it."

Sam piled on. "Prosthetic leg? Jeez, I missed that. Just spotted the limp. Maybe Browning offered to fence Walter's find at his going rate. But why take a commission when you got boys who'll snatch the whole enchilada for you?"

Both believed Browning was the man. But what was he planning to do with all the money from the sale of those coins? They didn't know. Yet.

# 19

Ethan Browning had been waiting a long time for a score like this. Now, the time had come. The plan he'd spawned a decade ago with his *Patriot Guardsmen* was about to hatch. *Generations yet unknown will study our efforts to restore the freedoms established by our illustrious founding fathers. They fought the same injustices we now battle.*

Alone again in his office, Browning picked up the phone and dialed. "Josh, you and Andrew need to get over to my office as soon as possible." He hung up without waiting for a response. Walked to the front of the store and locked the door. Flipped his "Open" sign over. Limped back to his office and closed the door.

Opened a substantial wall safe behind his desk hidden by a magnificent painting of General Washington. He retrieved Bedford's two now meticulously cleaned cedar boxes, each a one-foot cube. Lifted the lids of both boxes to examine "his" coins. *Our day of reckoning is coming, and soon.* But then a smile turned into a frown. There should be three-hundred-fifty-four coins less the twenty-four the FBI confiscated. A quick count revealed only three-hundred-six. Twenty-four short.

Josh and Andrew knocked on the store's locked front door. Browning hollered, "One minute, on the phone! Go get a couple of coffees." Needed a beat to ponder the missing coins. This was not a surprise he relished. He knew who took them. Only one person had access, and he was sure of his count. He placed the boxes back in the safe, locked it, and replaced the large framed painting of General George Washington. Portrayed him and his staff crossing the Delaware River on Christmas evening, December 25, 1776— painted by the German-born American history painter, Emanuel Leutze in 1851. A remarkable oil he had admired for decades before acquiring it by illicit means.

*A sneaky son-of-a-bitch, that General Washington. Men, supplies, boats, cannons, all set for a Christmas present for the redcoats, and in a blizzard, no less. Genius.* Ethan admired the old ways of his country, how it was founded, its valiant rebellion against an oppressive regime, and later fought two world wars against multiple enemies. Won both times. Not like Korea, Viet Nam, and the sand wars. *Now, every politician is a millionaire or multi-millionaire within their first few years in office.* He loathed today's government. Pompous, arrogant, entitled, *and they get nothing done!* The country was being torn apart from within: drugs, illegals, Muslims, homeless, once beautiful cities destroyed by anarchists and the staggering greed in Washington. *They need to be reminded of what it's like to be humbled. Now is not the time for timidity. We must grab these fuckers by the balls and hang 'em by 'em. Need to get back to the country's roots.*

His plan was coming together sooner than he thought possible because of good old Walter Bedford. Another knock on the front door. He walked over, opened it, and shook hands with Josh, who hailed from Huxford, Alabama, before they served together. He also shook hands with Andrew Lofton, originally from Ivanhoe, North Carolina. Served with both. Good ole boys from the south like Browning himself from Seminole, Texas. *My Patriot Guardsmen.* They were a good team with a unique combination of skills and knowledge, but most critical? Their combined commitment to their cause. And they trusted each other with everything, including their lives. Again. Or so Browning thought.

"C'mon in and set a spell. Wanna drink?" Both accepted, now setting aside the coffees they just paid for without question. Ethan poured three fingers of

Chestnut Farms Kentucky bourbon in each of three glasses from the bar next to his bookshelves. "Gotta go over some new events with you both. Most of it is good, but some not so good. Nothing we can't handle." Josh and Andrew looked at each other and gave their leader a single nod.

"Boys, we got lucky with this treasure trove that will allow us to speed things along. Josh here brought us a couple of old boxes from *our* Revolutionary War. Their contents are extremely valuable. This will allow us to complete the prep for our mission in weeks instead of years." Andrew was nearing forty, but looked thirty. A solid two-hundred pounds and on the high side of six feet, he spoke first. "Boss, since I've been up at the north camp, I need to get caught up a bit."

"With our recent financial windfall, it's time to send a message. It won't come without a price, though. This is why I asked y'all to come by. This windfall accelerates everything, but we have a concern. Actually, two concerns, and one of them is you, Josh."

"*What?*"

# 20

Josh's astonishment spiraled him into an incoherent response. "What, ah, concern, um, might you, ah, be havin' 'bout me, boss?" In the next fraction of a second, a small dagger appeared in Ethan's hand. He sent that razor-sharp knife on its way. The throw missed Josh's throat by an inch and stuck with a pronounced *twang* in the back of his chair. Andrew froze in astonishment. Josh felt the flat little throwing knife's breeze as it zinged by, and its reverberation in the high-backed chair as it struck its intended mark. With uncanny precision.

Ethan said, "Josh, we've been through thick and thin, boy, and I find out you *stole* from me? Why would you do that?"

"What you mean boss?" In another second,

another identical knife appeared in Ethan's hand, as if by magic. Josh squealed, "Wait!"

"Talk to me, boy, before this one severs your carotid artery." With the fire of fear now in his eyes, Josh glanced at the nasty little flat-black blade cocked in Ethan's right hand, like nothing more than an evil but lethal shadow. "You'll be unconscious in fifteen seconds and dead inside of three minutes."

"I, I, I'm sorry boss. I never crossed you in all these years. I jus' looked to set up my ma and kin for a better life! I shouldn't a oughta done it."

"Where are the twenty-four coins you stole from me, boy? From *our* fuckin' *cause?*"

"In my apartment behind the TV in a small locked box. I can get it for ya."

"There were three-hundred-fifty-four coins. The two dozen I got from Bedford I surrendered to the cops. Then I counted three-oh-six. Should be three-thirty." In a loud voice, Browning yelled, "You'd betray me—the *cause*—for two dozen coins, Josh? Like Judas and his pieces of silver?"

"I, I, am so sorry boss, but it wasn't for me."

Now Ethan wasn't shouting. His voice scraped low, like a chair on a stone floor. "Don't matter who it was for. They don't belong to you—belong to the Patriot Guardsmen, to our cause—and *you* took it. I've taken good care of you all these years and this is what I get back? I oughta kill you *mean*." He shook that little shadow knife to punctuate the depth of his emotion.

"*No,* please boss, give me a chance. I'll make it up to you." Browning settled down. At least he fell silent. Andrew glanced back and forth, not sure what was going to happen next. He feared suggesting anything. One of the boss's knives might end up in his own neck.

---

After considering how much Ethan needed Josh's experience with explosives, he finally spoke. "If I get even a whiff of anything sideways with y'all, I'll cut you a thousand times and feed you your own balls. Got that?"

Josh now whined, not only from fear, but from shame. His two co-conspirators read that in his face. "Yessir, yessir, I'll never do anything like that again; promise to God."

"We'll see. You're on thin ice, Josh. You best be on your toes and do things right, the way I order it. Nothing less, nothing more. Got it?"

"Yessir!"

"Now, back to my second concern. We have some trouble with the FBI and some environmental cop from Massachusetts. They interviewed me here today about Walter Bedford and his wife Rose. Thank you, Josh, for your excellent work."

Josh looked astonished. Ten seconds earlier, he was close to being killed by his boss, and now received a compliment for his wet work? Yes, he looked confused. Good. Ethan also needed Andrew's mechanical and fabrication skills that were nothing short of brilliant.

"Where do we start, boss?" asked Andrew.

"First, we need to shake up this FBI lady that came to visit today. Pretty thing, but didn't say much. I'd say she was observing my reactions to the environmental cop's questions. She's the smart one. That other cop came on strong, and she just watched. Shouldn't take too much to slow her haste to stick her Yankee nose into our business with a bit of unfriendly advice. The other cop seems a harder item to deal with, but we'll take care of him too. Andrew, go with Josh. Get my coins. Bring them back. If he tries any shit, kill him. Slow."

The men left, shaken. They needed strong leadership, especially for the upcoming mission, now possible thanks to their benefactor, Walter Bedford. *The political football called the Viet Nam "conflict" humiliated our great nation, cost me a leg, and the lives of more than a few of my fellow patriots. Soon, we'll send a message that can't be ignored....*

Browning sat in his chair. Rubbed around the edges of his stump and under the straps that held it in place. God, he hated that thing. Thought about how to get to that FBI lady. The enemy. When she had offered him her card, it listed the Springfield, Mass FBI field office. Plus, he'd copied down the plate number from her car. A good start.

After his soldiers returned from Josh's apartment in record time with the pilfered coins, Browning said, "I want both of you to head to Springfield. Put a tail on this Agent Mather. I looked up the address of the FBI office there. Here's the info." He handed them a slip of paper with an address and the Yankee bitch's plate number. "Here's your mission. Find out where she lives. She drives a dark blue Crown Vic. Stake her out. Look for entry and exits to her house or apartment, her neighborhood, neighbor proximity, security alarms, the whole bit. You both understand that? Take my van, but without the magnetic signs on its sides. Don't let her pick up your tail. She's a trained FBI Agent, so use extra caution."

The boys answered in unison, "Yessir."

*Good boys.* "Call me when y'all know where she lives. Here's some cash for fuel, food and anything else necessary for this part of the mission. No credit cards and no toll roads."

"Got it, boss." Josh was now eager to please.

# 21

Letty and Sam met in her office in Springfield. They'd tap into the massive amount of information available within the FBI's computer networks. Letty said, "After the Bureau pressured them, NYNEX informed my SAC the specifics of three calls from Springfield to New Hampshire. They were made from the same pay phone, all within a single thirty-minute period. One call lasted just forty-five seconds, the second lasted seventy-five seconds, and the third almost three-and-a-half minutes to Browning Diamond and Coin in Portsmouth. So, we've confirmed that Walter had the most contact with Browning. We're still waiting for results from our military friends at the NPRC in St. Louis. Sam, you likely are aware the National Archives Records Administration at the National Personnel Records Center should enable us to dig out military records for Browning and his two employees. What's next?"

Sam said, "Let's listen to your tape of our Browning interview to see if we pick up anything we might have missed. I most want to hear your psych perspective on this guy. My gut's serving up a feeling, but I'm gonna wait until we learn more."

"Good idea."


They had started with a fresh pot of coffee. Both recognized from experience this could be a marathon skull session likely to wear down their brains. Letty kicked them off. "First impressions. Browning has had experience being interrogated. That's now obvious to me. I saw that only after you leaned hard on him. He grew defensive, evasive, and less sure of himself based on his choice of words, growing jittery, and offering certain answers after hesitating. But then he pulled together some calculated answers. He dodged a few questions to gather his thoughts based on what he heard we already suspected. He knew more than he was saying. Most troubling for me was his demand for a warrant to see his personal calendar or appointment book. That screamed at me he had something serious to hide. Five'll get you ten Bedford was on his calendar for Saturday the twentieth, the day after he was murdered. And I'm betting that was his Plan B in case his boys failed to end Bedford. Rose was just a loose end."

"I agree," Sam said as he rewarded Letty with an appreciative gaze and a soft punch to her shoulder.

Letty continued. "Also, I'm sure you noticed him looking away to buy himself think time. And an innocent citizen doesn't need to remind law enforcement, more than once, that he's a respectable businessman. Might as well have screamed, 'I'm not a dirtbag,' or 'I'm not lying. Really!' Broadcasts just the opposite."

Letty's phone rang. She held up her left index finger and mouthed exaggeratedly 'NPRC.' Sam nodded and relaxed while he ran over the points in his head they'd reviewed. "Uh huh... yes, Browning, Bingham, and Lofton. That's right, we'd appreciate a fax... Within the hour? Perfect. Thank you, Captain."

Sam's expression revealed what he was thinking. He said it anyway. "That was fast. Nice."

"Okay, let's go over everything again from a different angle. I'm also troubled by several volumes of extremist literature on Browning's bookshelf. And did you see that giant portrait of George Washington on his wall? That looked to be an Emanuel Leutze original oil. One spendy wall hanging for a cluttered and cramped business office. I'm envisioning this guy fancies himself a highly committed patriot, and he thinks he's smarter than everyone else, especially you and me. That kind of extremist commitment and illusions of superiority fit the profile of a militia-minded fanatic. I fear more than ever what this guy plans to do with a buried treasure."

"Are you thinking terrorism, Letty?"

"I think it's decent odds."

"Shit. Okay, that's good enough odds for a working assumption. What else?"

Before she answered, an administrative assistant knocked on Letty's door, entered, and handed her several fax pages. The young man left after receiving an appreciative nod from Letty.

Sam said, "NPRC?"

"Yup." She scanned the first couple of pages and grew excited. "Listen to this revealing after-action report:

**CONFIDENTIAL–EYES ONLY**

*Summary, After-Action, January 30, 1968*
*Tan Son Nhut Air Force Base, Saigon,*
*South Viet Nam*

- Staff Sergeant First Class Ethan (NMI) Browning
- Specialist First Class Joshua L. Bingham
- Corporal Andrew T. Lofton

*3rd Squadron, 4th Calvary Regiment*
*Commanding Officer Colonel Jeffrey*
*Armstrong, US Army*

*PCRS AUTH: 24-62-405*

"The report is lengthy and written in non-military terminology for the most part." Sam leaned over Letty's shoulder and followed along with her narrative. "All served in the Army's First Division during the Viet Nam War and were stationed together for the usual one-year 'tour' until their rotation for reassignment came up. SSgt. Browning was stationed at the air base in Tan Son Nhut. He was in charge of both Lofton and Bingham, as well as an entire squad.

Browning's direct superior officer, a Lt. Steven A. Saucier, had only been in-country for a month. Fresh out of Officer Candidate School and basic training at St. Anselm College in New Hampshire, Saucier was young and eager to make a name for himself. Oh, and this is interesting. Specialist First Class Josh Bingham was an explosives expert who had served ten months in Viet Nam by this time. Corporal Andrew Lofton was in equipment repair and replacement within the same outfit. He, too, had been in-country for ten months.

"They saw cyclical enemy activity. Conducted daily patrols with occasional night sorties. These sporadic enemy actions produced minimal casualties. Bingham's billet included rigging the base perimeter with two rows of anti-personnel mines and claymores targeting anything on or near the ground. This was his specialty and his primary job, along with five other enlisted personnel. He also ensured the perimeter was properly rigged with concertina wire, tank barriers, observation towers, and he supervised regular perimeter inspections."

Letty continued to read. "Corporal Andrew Lofton's primary mission kept M-113s in operable condition. What are M-113s?"

Sam knew all too well. "Armored Personnel Carriers or APCs. These babies transport troops from one point to another. They're equipped with tracks like tanks. Go about anywhere."

"Oh. According to this report, with spare parts in short supply, Lofton's ingenuity created ways to keep them on the battlefield. For that, he gained widespread recognition."

"Yeah, I've known guys like that. Sounds like he was able to cob-job just about anything."

"According to this, he commanded a reputation for manufacturing parts to keep the M-113s combat-ready."

"From my time in the Marines," did Letty now notice a residual quiver in Sam's voice? "I know these APCs were quite the machines and critical to the war effort in Viet Nam. I imagine that made Lofton a pretty handy guy to have around. Of critical operational importance, even. M113 APCs would carry a dozen or more troops and were about the only ground machine that made sense in the rice patties of Viet Nam."

Letty said, "This is interesting. On January 30, 1968, the Tet Offensive began at night. The NVA regulars and... VC?"

"Viet Cong, enemy guerrilla troops that backed up the North Viet Nam Army regulars. Some hardcore suckers. Sneaky bastards, too. A formidable enemy."

"Right. Well, says they struck in strength at several South Vietnam cities and U.S. bases. Almost seventy-thousand enemy troops were involved. As Tan Son Nhut Air Base came under heavy fire, chaos reigned. Command posts, observation platforms and perimeter barriers of barbed wire and fences proved no match for enemy numbers.... Okay, here we go. The Marine command made specific note of Lt. Saucier's lack of combat experience. Also, that he ordered ten men, including Browning, Lofton, and Bingham, into an M-113 to engage the enemy. Ssgt. Browning protested. Said that was a suicide mission and served no purpose. Saucier again ordered them to proceed. Senior officers had already fled, anticipating a complete rout, and took classified materials out of danger. Browning and his men faced an overwhelming force, charging straight at them. Says here enemy sappers had already taken out the concertina wire. What the hell are sappers, Sam?"

"Combat engineers. Responsible for breaching fortifications. Shitty job."

"Well, the report says RPGs had already eliminated the base's observation posts—"

"Rocket-propelled grenades—"

"Yeah, I actually knew that one. This report further says that hordes of NVA were pouring through the gaps. Evidence suggested that, before removing himself from the action, Ssgt. Browning fired upon Lt. Saucier in the back with a three-round burst. The incident was later classified as a 'friendly fire incident.'"

"Not sure you're familiar with the term 'fragging,' Letty. This is it. More common than the Army would ever admit. Was the evidence strong enough to prosecute?"

"Doesn't say in this report. Only 'evidence suggests.' It says that as Browning and his ten-man squad traveled parallel to a runway, an incendiary mortar round struck the rear of their APC. Four men survived the blast, those who were in the vehicle's front. Only parts of the remaining men were scattered around the blast. Browning discovered he was unable to walk. A large red-hot piece of shrapnel had embedded itself in his right leg. As the APC continued to burn, SSgt. Browning sprang into action. Grabbed a rag and used it to pull the piece of hot metal from his mangled right leg. The rag then became a tourniquet. He crawled to drag Bingham, Lofton, and a PFC Hetaera from the burning wreck. Hetaera later died from a hole in his stomach that left his intestines more out than in.

. . .

"Since Browning was unable to walk, when they regained consciousness, Lofton and Bingham in turn carried Browning to a reinforced company building three-hundred yards away. There, they re-joined the rest of the company in full retreat. The medics took SSgt. Browning away for treatment of his wounds. The after-action report includes the trio's heroics. Later, when the body was recovered, the autopsy of Lt. Saucier showed three entry wounds to the back from a 5.56-caliber rifle. Superiors suspected that Lt. Saucier had been... fragged, and that put them in a difficult position. The only three survivors swore they did not fire upon, nor did they see anyone fire at Lt. Saucier. They speculated that an NVA regular, an enemy soldier, had picked up an American M-16 rifle and shot the lieutenant. They had no choice but to award the three men, as there was no contrary corroborated evidence. Browning, Specialist First Class Bingham, and Corporal Lofton each received a Bronze Star for their actions under fire.

"Browning lost his right leg from the knee down. They fitted him with a prosthesis. Later, they also awarded him a purple heart based on testimony from Bingham and Lofton. The Army transferred the three men back stateside where they completed their period of service. Browning received an honorable medical discharge. The Army honorably discharged Specialist First Class Bingham and Corporal Lofton at the end of their enlistment period. And that's the end of the report."

---

Sam mulled over everything Letty had read or paraphrased. "I'm guessing Browning blamed Saucier for losing his leg. I'd also speculate he's fostered a hatred for what the Army and the government did to him. Saucier should never have been in command. *And* they should have all been evacuated after the first perimeter breach. I bet he's been on a slow burn ever since. Or not so slow. I know the feeling. I saw more than my fair share of snot-nosed ROTC graduates placed in charge when they should have still been partying at their frat houses. Assholes like that got more 'n one of my own friends killed. And damn near did the same to me." It surprised Sam how retelling that one memory set him to shaking with anger. He had always kept that buried deep inside.

---

Letty noticed that. She decided not to say anything about it and moved on. "I agree, Sam. Combine that with the literature we spotted in his office, and his general evasiveness, I'm convinced more than ever that he's good for orchestrating the Bedford murders. And that one of both of his two lap dogs were his triggermen. But now, more than ever, I also fear something worse than simple greed as their motive for ripping off the Bedford's Revolutionary War bounty."

"So we have one hero pissed off at the government, an expert fabricator, and one explosives expert in the thick of it here. What does this spell?"

"If I had to make an official judgement call, more than ever, I'd say this definitely spells the potential for a domestic terror attack in the making."

"Okay, what's next, Special Agent?"

## 22

Neither the anger nor ghost pain in Ethan Browning's lost leg abated, even with the passage of time. Both grew worse. *Stupid war. We had no business being there to begin with. And no woman wants a one-legged man.* The government didn't give a shit. Oh, sure, after he got out, the VA gave him a chunk of wood and metal and leather to stump around on, and they kept him supplied with pain meds. *Thanks a lot.* But he had to *do* something.

Browning's epiphany came to him in a blazing flash of brilliance when walking—limping—past a jewelry store not long after his discharge. The display piqued his curiosity as he shopped for a ring. The owner was pleasant. He purchased a simple ring featuring a large blue sapphire in the center, his September birthstone.

The two men engaged in a conversation while standing at the shopkeeper's cash register. Browning learned enough that day to open his own small jewelry store in a different town. Everything about the concept appealed to him: huge mark-ups, no heavy lifting, no shift work, or nights, and closed on Sunday. He grew excited about finding an occupation that interested him *and* offered him a lucrative career. This would be it.

So, Ethan completed his on-line gemologists course, bought equipment with his VA disability settlement, and opened his small shop. Both Andrew Lofton and Josh Bingham had stayed in contact with him. Once settled in, he invited "the boys" to move up to Portsmouth and to for him. Browning Diamond and Coin enjoyed almost overnight success. Ethan knew success wasn't possible by himself. At least, not probable. He needed help. But he was thinking about more than the shop, too. With Andrew and Josh at his side he remained in the store selling. And thinking. And plotting.

The boys made deliveries and ran errands. His clientele grew. He became a businessman who leaked his wartime exploits to the local newspaper for an article which brought in more patriotic customers. Plus, he was not above exploiting his employees' combat experience. His secret hatred for the Army and the United States government kept intensifying. The act of sending young boys into senseless wars to be maimed or killed was worse than senseless. It was criminal that politicians used wars as chess pieces while they sat on the sidelines.

Now this bullshit government talked about normalizing relations with Viet Nam, including with the damn Commies! The first war that the U.S. ever lost. Forty-eight thousand-two-hundred-twenty lives lost. And for what? Political bullshit. When he, Josh, and Andrew got drunk together, which was often, the three men spoke of some type of retaliation, to wake up those who did nothing.

As Ethan Browning's business expanded, and his standing in the community grew, he came upon a few opportunities to "fence" stolen jewelry. He was not above taking advantage of those opportunities. Such merchandise remained untraceable, especially among older pieces, artifacts of estates. He also acquired inheritance pieces for pennies on the dollar that no one wanted. Legitimate shoppers then bought a lot of that stuff. Browning and his business thrived.

The talk of retaliation against the government never waned. No, it was more than that. They believed they'd be able to make a difference in the future of America, which had gone to shit, run by a government that got nothing done. But how? Just a strong statement, not an overthrow. But people would still die.

People died in war, too. About time they learned a lesson.

And so they gave birth to the Patriot Guardsmen's full-on conspiracy. They pulled together their plan. No rush. Plenty of time to do it right. Josh's knowledge of explosives was key, and Browning charged Andrew to devise a delivery system. But what were they going to use to make their *statement*? A building? The John Hancock Tower? The iconic USS Constitution, a.k.a. Old Ironsides? No, symbolic, but not enough punch. That's when Browning scanned the local newspaper and saw a picture of an LNG—a Liquid Natural Gas tanker ship—coming into Boston Harbor on the front page of the Portsmouth Daily Ledger. The gigantic ship, surrounded by more than a dozen police and heavily armed Coast Guard vessels, meant this type of vessel was both important and volatile. The time had arrived to do more than scan articles. He read every word of that piece and then spent hours at the local library devouring everything available about LNG tanker ships and the organizations that protected them. They worried about the implications of such vessels being attacked. Or worse, what if one was sunk in a major entrance to a port vital to American commerce? Like Boston Harbor? Yes, important and volatile with a lasting effect, *if* he engineered their mission for maximum effect.

Ethan learned Environmental Police from Massachusetts formed an outside perimeter whenever such a vessel entered a major port like Boston Harbor. His imagination fired white hot in the forges of his newborn conspiracy. What if he'd provide Josh with a powder keg comprising a third of a million barrels of liquid—fourteen-and-a-half million gallons, equaling 1.2 *billion* cubic feet of explosive gas—going off before an LNG got to its mooring in Everett, Massachusetts? What a Bunker Hill Day celebration *that* would be! Back in June 1775, a small force or rebel patriots made a much larger occupying force pay dearly for their arrogance. *In Boston*. That's it! Symbolic *as well as* imposing an enduring impact—their *monument* to a victory that would remain visible as it rested on the harbor's floor, for all to see. For years. Maybe forever.

And with many private collectors drooling to acquire Bedford's fortune, now his fortune, achieving his vision was now within reach. He called Andrew and Josh. They met at Ethan's house out on Barnes Road. "Boys, we are going to throw a party, one that the Republic will never forget."

From that day forward, they burned through countless hours of serious planning sessions over bourbon and beer and barbecues. They agonized over how to penetrate the security ring around an LNG. What kind and how much explosive materiel would light the ship's fuse? Ethan learned that the liquid itself wasn't explosive, but the vapor was, just like gasoline, only more so. Although Josh explained from memory that while LNG in its gaseous form is exceedingly flammable, its ignition point is high—twelve-hundred degrees. That made it safe to transport. But with the right ignition source, they'd deliver a helluva message. They'd create *their symbolic monument* in Boston Harbor. Ethan looked to Josh for an answer. "So, how do we expose the vapor to the air for combustion?"

"We'd need a serious hull *and* tank breach. I read that these tankers are constructed with an outer hull and an inner 'hull', which is also the tanks' membranes. We'd have to breach both to expose the liquid gas to the air with a high-threshold heat source for ignition."

Lofton scratched his stubbled chin that was drooping into grayish jowls these days. "Hey, what if we used a swarm of small three- to four-foot remotely controlled fiberglass boats each carrying a payload of C-4?"

Both Ethan and Josh perked up at the outrageous suggestion. Ethan turned to his explosives expert, who was already evaluating the idea. "Toy boats loaded with explosives? That work, Josh?"

Before Josh answered, Andrew said, "They're too small to be spotted by radar. Lost in surface clutter like waves. Plus, no way they'd be lookin' for tiny toy boats."

Josh looked intrigued. "Yeah, cause a breach in the first hull, followed right behind with a second boat as insurance. A second C-4 explosion would definitely breach the insulation between the hulls as well as the inner hull, which I'd think would be constructed of a lighter metal like aluminum. Maybe the first impact would do it, but guaranteed a second explosion at the same impact point exposes the vapors and causes ignition. Then *BLAM*. How about half a dozen boats at three impact points, two boats each? We load each with, say, three to five pounds of C-4. Yeah, boss, that could work."

Andrew felt thrilled that his idea appeared to have merit. "Hell, yeah."

Ethan said, "Where do we get boats like that?"

Andrew's confidence as a master fabricator had never been an issue. "Hell, I make 'em, or we buy 'em and I modify 'em."

Ethan grew animated over this idea. "Okay, now where do we source C-4? And how do three of us control, say, six boats?"

Andrew fell silent in thought. Then, "Well, each of us controls two boats with two controllers each and some basic automation. We launch from precise coordinates at precise times, assuming we have exact coordinates for the target, and we walk away. This'll work, boss."

Josh grinned. "And for C-4, we break into an armory a distance away from here. Take what we need."

Ethan frowned, "Except for two problems. First, armories don't carry explosives. Only small arms. I don't even think they carry ammunition. Plus, a shit-ton of red flags go up when explosives go missing."

Josh turned to Andrew. "How much weight will these baby boats carry?"

"Well, I'd have to draw up some specs, but I'd guess at least three or four pounds each, maybe a little more."

"That'd do it, assuming the outer steel hull isn't more than about two inches thick, and they're not hardened steel. Can't imagine any more 'n that. And the inner hull? No problem. Like rice paper to C-4."

Andrew looked at their leader. "So, where do we get the explosives?"

But Josh answered. Scratched his chin. "Got C-4 on most Army and Marine bases, but that'd be like busting into Fort Knox. And forget about getting it on a naval ship. How about the point of manufacture?"

Ethan snapped his fingers. "They have to transport it from the factory to the bases, right?"

Josh thought out loud. "Those trucks are fireproof, bulletproof, built like tanks, and resist tire punctures from a .50 cal. Armed escorts, too. Gotta be an easier and lower profile way. Plus, that'd send up a lot of flags, too."

"Is there a black market for this stuff?" asked Lofton.

Ethan said, "Josh, you still have any contact with the guys in your old unit?"

"I haven't kept in touch, but I know this one shady

guy who never got caught. He was three gallons of crazy in a two-gallon bucket. The MPs were after him every week. Heard rumors he skimmed stuff here and there. Never proved it, but they watched him awful close. Then, they changed inventory procedures. That made it a lot harder to clip product. Carl Devon, Devlin... no, Devors. That's who it was. Hated the military. Traded or bartered everything and anything. He'd steal and sell. Every company had one of these scroungers, but this guy did it all. Devors got involved in small arms, prostitutes, even some drugs. You name it, I'm bettin' he'd get it for us if I can find him and he ain't dead."

Ethan perked up. Pointed an index finger over at Josh with a smile. "Find him. Reach out. I'd bet he'd heard about Saucier's fragging. That's your bona fides, but don't come right out and admit it, of course.

"You wasted Saucier, not me."

"Yeah, well, he doesn't know that. Who's to say or know except us here in this room? Everyone else is dead."

"Huh, yeah, Ethan. Let me go to work on that. He was from Mississippi, if I remember right. We got along good. I saw shit he did and never ratted him out. I'll put an ad in the Military Times. Try that. I'll also hit an old phone book, look for him or his kin. I'm sure they'd tell an old army combat buddy how to get a hold of him. We got enough cash to score a hit if I get lucky?"

Ethan said without hesitating, "Yeah, we got whatever we need. Make it happen, Josh." He didn't tell his boys he'd moved their Revolutionary War bounty to a private collector in Mumbai for a cool half-million. No muss, no fuss. And how ironic the same funds that were destined to fuel a revolution against a tyrannical government two-hundred-fourteen years earlier now will fan the flames of a new revolution. Or, at least, to make a statement he dared fat rich politicians and other patriots to ignore. Just like back then, they had to feel like he and his boys did now—righteous.

"On it, boss."

## 23

Letty and Sam sat in her Springfield office in once more. As a behavioral analyst with DC and Quantico credentials, unlike most field agents who sat out in the "bullpen" here, she warranted a pleasant office, albeit small. Windows, even. They peered at each other across her desk. Sam summarized what they identified from his ex-military perspective. "This crew is decorated Army infantry with combat experience in explosives, fabrication and repair. The after-action report we received from NPRC stated that the investigation showed Lt. Saucier had three 5.56 rounds in his back from close range. Doesn't add up to anything but fragging by this crew. Letty, let me ask you this. If your base came under a coordinated heavy attack and someone ordered you to go on a mission with zero military value and resulted in certain death, would you go?"

"Hmmm... I'd try to reason with the lieutenant to explain the futility of that order."

"In combat, there is no time for discussion. Plus, it's not a democracy. It's authoritarian. What if the lieutenant ordered them into this hopeless firefight with zero military value and meant certain death? The lieutenant had thirty days in-country. Hardly enough time to get his boots muddy. Pretty clear to me the Army suspected three co-conspirators in the murder of their lieutenant. No one left alive to dispute that. But the Army had no evidence to prove it. Further, it appears they had no political choice but to give medals to these turkeys. You're a behavior expert. What's going through these guys' minds with this report as their shared history?"

Letty whistled through her lips. "Rough stuff. Yeah, depends on a lot of other factors in their lives. But I'm thinking of the shared camaraderie of combat. The literature says they're about as committed to each other as any human beings are capable. They'd die for each other. Plus, if they, um, *fragged* their lieutenant, they've committed murder, or at least conspiracy to commit, if only one or two shooters. In their current relationship, with Browning calling the shots, we must assume his two employees are much more than employees. They'll do *anything* for this guy."

"Yeah, that tracks. And if *he's* a fanatic—"

"So are they. That's the classic definition of a terrorist cell. Hey, I'm no field agent, here. What's our next move, Sam?"

He took some time to think about Letty's analysis. Then, "We start humping on the legwork, the research, the intel. In other words, we investigate."

"And we start where?"

His words now banged out on full auto. "I want a full work-up on Browning and his two associates. Everything you can find. I want photos or videos of each one of their residences. I want tax returns, deeds to properties, credit card and phone numbers, vehicle registrations, boat registrations, firearms licenses—"

"Whoa," yelled Letty, "I can't write that fast. Slow down, big fella. You sound like a damn field agent."

"Okay, sorry, but the case is only as good as our evidence. Time to collect it. It's gonna take time, but you've got a dozen agents here, and your SAC likes you." Sam winked. "Crack the friggin' whip and get 'em humping. I'm getting a terrible feeling about this whole thing."

"Okay Sam. Yes, me too."

"What was your opinion of Ethan Browning?"

Letty continued. "He's being evasive, untruthful in fact, judging by his body language and his choice of words. The warrant demand was also telling. I think he didn't want us to see the follow-up meeting with Bedford on his calendar, which is now sure to be ashes. Did you also notice that he didn't even mention his military service, awards, decorations or even have any pictures? He wants that erased. How many combat vets don't keep a picture of the guys and him with or without firearms in fatigues, cigars and a beer in their hands? I bet you even have one, or you'd at least mention your service."

Sam reflected on his Marine days. Yup, he had a picture of himself posing with the men his life depended on, but didn't mention it. She already knew by his silence. The machine in his brain now ran at flank speed. Letty spotted that tell, too. She knew something was missing. Sam muttered as he gathered himself for a hasty departure. "Okay, I'm headed back to the hills to brief my lieutenant. I'll brief Larry, too." His boss's boss, Captain Larry Jamison, liked to be kept in the loop as much or more than his direct supervisor, Lt. Paul O'Neill "Also, one of these days I gotta get my nose into a few books since the sergeant's exam is coming up and I'm going for it. Hoping for a lull as your guys do their thing."

"*Sergeant* Travis? Has a ring, Sam."

"Let's meet again when you have enough information on these turkeys and we'll pull together our plan."

"Roger that, Sergeant Sam!"

"Knock it off or I'll solve this case without you."

"You don't stand a chance solving this case without *mois*. Or at least. my access to resources."

He just grinned. She was right.

# 24

Josh Bingham started the search for his C-4 source. Called information and checked listings the impatient operator gave him for his Army buddy, Carl Devors. But he wasn't getting lucky.

"Yes. Eucutta in southeast Mississippi. Any other Devors? Anywhere in that county?"

He heard it in her voice. The operator had given him too much time, with too many unsuccessful attempts. She gave him a number and disconnected. So, Josh dialed. The voice sounded like pure South. "Yeah, who is this and what'chu want?"

"My name is Josh Bingham. I'm looking for Carl Devors. I'm an old service buddy of his. We're putting together a reunion for our company that served at Tan Son Nhut Viet Nam in sixty-eight."

"Well, he don't live here. I'm his kin brother. You got the wrong number."

"You have his number? I'd like to reach out. We'd love him to attend. He was a damn special part of our crew."

"Ah don't give no numbers to no strangers, sport, even if y'all were buddies. But give me yours. If he's a wantin' to call you back, I reckon he will." Josh gave him his number. The old boy hung up without so much as a *by your leave*. Nothing to do now but wait. He knew if Carl didn't respond, Ethan would send his ass to Mississippi to find him. *Fuck! Mississippi this time of year? It's so damn hot down there, roast a pecan right on the damn tree.*

---

Meanwhile, Ethan Browning sat in his office. Andrew Lofton had fetched coffees for both of them from the pot near Ethan's office door. Andrew sat down in a guest chair. They sipped their coffees before Ethan spoke. His prosthesis perched atop his desk reminded Andrew of his debt. He'd be dead without Ethan. That wood and plastic and steel leg lso reminded him Ethan paid every day for both their lives. Ethan said, "So, Mr. Wizard, I need you to develop a working model of a radio-controlled bomb. It must be capable of surviving a one-foot swell, waterproof, and carry at least four pounds of cargo, batteries excluded."

"Huh. What kind of range you lookin' for, boss?"

"Figure one mile, two tops."

A pause. "That's a lot, Ethan. Those RC boat controllers are only good for four- to five-hundred feet. Some of them boats have an anti-capsize feature, and their batteries are only good for twenty- or twenty-five minutes. We'd need a longer antenna driving a signal booster for sure. Running at forty MPH, which is doable, in twenty minutes they'd travel..." he performed a quick calculation in his head, "more 'n thirteen miles. No way I control a boat that far away. Want lights on 'em or run dark?"

Browning wasn't deterred. "Andrew, I need a three-foot boat, capsize-proof, no lights, but I do need a one- to two-mile range."

"Hmm... let me think on that, boss. It's a tall order. I read about a company that carries higher-end RC boats. I'll look into 'em because it would save us a lot of time to buy 'em instead of makin' 'em. I'll get seven."

"Seven?"

"Yeah. One for testing and six for the mission."

"Andrew, this is something the three of us have talked about, drank over, and schemed for years."

He watched Ethan's crystal gaze and thousand-yard stare. "Huh. We're gonna do some real shit, aren't we?"

"Bet your ass we are, son. These boats don't need to do forty. Twenty-five, thirty'll do to save on battery power, although that doesn't sound like the key issue. I'm going to be looking at the Boston Harbor Islands State Park and see how close we'll be."

"Okay, I'll start working on some prototypes. Is time a factor?"

"I'm thinking we make our statement middle of next month. June seventeenth is Bunker Hill Day. Know what that means, Andrew?"

"Not really. Some Revolutionary War shit, right?"

"Precisely. The British kicked the Colonials' butts under Colonel Prescott's command, but Prescott made the bastards pay. We'll likely get our butts kicked, too, but we'll make them pay, just like our country's original rebels. Andrew, that means you have four weeks to test and ready your boats. Must be one-hundred percent functional, reliable, and simple to operate. Plan on the need to evade obstacles in the harbor."

"What you mean, boss?"

"Pleasure boats, Coast Guard, EPOs, State Police, even Boston PD. Factor in the wind, tides, all that nautical shit. Anticipate and evade any possible interference that might get in the way of contacting the target and detonation. We're gonna launch from points where we have line-of-sight on the target, so land masses won't be an issue."

"Want me to set up shop at your farm?"

Ethan said, "No, I've got something else in mind.

My next-door neighbors have a four-stall garage they rent out when they go south for the winter or on cruises. We'll keep the stuff off my property in case we're being watched. We need good operational security, camouflage, and eyes peeled for the unexpected. Just in case the feds or that fuckin' EPO snoop around the farm. I called the Livingstons in Florida. Wired them rent money for the garage, and they provided me with the alarm code. So, we'll set up a shop with tools, electronics, and materiel. With less than a month from D-day, I need you to make up a list of must-haves for quick acquisition."

Andrew grinned like a kid about to experience the best Christmas morning ever, not that he ever enjoyed that as a kid. "Sounds great, boss. I'll need some cash to pick up the stuff I'm gonna need ASAP."

Browning reached into his bottom desk drawer, the one reserved for important shit, and handed Andrew ten thousand in a banded pack of bills. "That'll get you started. Keep a record so I can track you ain't spending it on booze and whores."

"Boss! I'd never cross you that way"

"Better not. Livin' is better n dyin", son."

# 25

Sam left the spacious FBI field office in Springfield, headed for home. His head spun like a wobbling top. *What did I miss? Where else should I be looking? Who else is involved? What'll Letty dig up using FBI resources?* The forty-five-minute drive was uneventful and uninspiring, but peaceful. Pulling into the driveway, he saw Kate was home early and it was obvious Brian had been home from school for a while They were in the sloped front yard playing catch with a hardball and gloves. Still sitting behind the wheel after he shut off the engine, Sam took a few beats to enjoy the view. As he slid out of his Bronco, he hollered across the yard, "You both have arms like noodles. Let me toss you some real heat!"

Kate turned in mid-throw, grinned, and yelled back. "I've seen turtles get to the plate quicker 'n your fastballs, cowboy!" She completed her throw to Brian, her hair swinging in a soft pony tail.

"Horse feathers!" He smiled, leaned on the Bronc's door frame, taking another couple of seconds to reflect on his good fortune. Helped him forget. Kate wore a tank top and skin-tight leggings. She looked mighty fine. Brian still wore his school clothes - t-shirt, jeans, sneakers. Sam thought he looked awfully skinny. Reminded him of himself as a kid until he had filled out in high school. Had to. Needed to defend himself, not sure how much of that was his own fault. Trouble had always followed Sam around. Part of that was his attitude. A drug addict for a mom, and her sleazy friends hadn't helped. A state cop for a dad who carried around a damn powder keg on his back with a short fuse in the middle of a dumpster fire. Sam wanted better for Brian. Shook his head, an involuntary coping mechanism to rattle away the memories that weren't *all* bad. Smiled again at his good fortune. He *was* breaking that cycle, wasn't he?

While tossing the ball around, they talked a little about the day. But Sam was getting hungry. As the resident chef, he said, "What do you guys want for dinner?"

"Haute cuisine." Kate liked to eat well. That would surprise most people to look at her, especially after seeing her in that damn tank top and throwing a respectable fast ball.

"Shit. Yup, a mistake to ask. Crabs on toast points coming right up."

Brian always hated to admit he liked pretty much whatever Sam would sling. He hollered in his over-dramatic under-developed pre-teen squeak, "Yuck!"

Now feeling pretty good after a dose of normality and anticipating some kitchen time, Sam whipped up one of his specialties: poached cod in a court bouillon, with rice pilaf, grilled asparagus, and hollandaise sauce. Extra lemon with capers, of course. The way Kate liked it. After dinner, Sam and Brian involved themselves in a few private moments in the living room. Brought back memories of his own dad. Never got the chance to spend much time with him. As a state trooper, he was gone most of the time. Sam vowed not to make the same mistake. He still broke that vow more often than he cared to admit, and that made him mad at the only person he could blame—himself. But he was here, now. They lounged on the floor near the fire he and Brian had built while Kate cleaned up after category five Hurricane Sam demolished the kitchen. "So, how's school? You fixin' to play ball this year?"

"School's okay, Dad, but math really su_ uh, it's not my favorite. And yeah, I'm thinkin' about trying out for the team."

"That's great news, Bri. You'll learn a lot of good stuff, like being a part of something beyond yourself. Sportsmanship, discipline, hard work, *and* fun."

"Will you be around to help me with my swing and fielding?"

"I'll do my best to be here for you, son." *What the fuck kind of answer is that? I sound like dear old Dad's weasel excuses.*

"Well, not sure what that means, Dad. You work an awful lot, and we don't do much together anymore."

Yeah, it's getting away from me again. *Shit.* He said, "Son, I'm a work in progress and I give you my word. I'll make more time for you and Kate." They both knew this promise was already on thin and cracking ice the moment he spit out yet another oath. Every case just took so much time and energy. *Shit, shit, shit!*

"Bri, why don't you run up and get some homework done? Then, come down and we'll check out a little TV together, okay?

"Sure, Dad. That sounds great." *Is it my imagination, or is the kid walking away in utter disbelief?*

Sam got up from the floor a little slower than a few years ago and a lot slower than his son, plopped down on the couch in front of the fireplace. His favorite spot in the whole house. Kate dropped next to him to plant a lingering kiss.

"Hi, there." He couldn't shake the feeling that what was most precious to him was slipping away.

"Hi back, handsome. Whatcha got going on? Besides working that double homicide, your suspect up in New Hampshire, and working with Letty, again. That going well?"

"Well, my gut tells me there's a whole lot more than meets the eye here besides a double homicide."

She raised her eyebrows, somewhere between intrigued and perplexed. "What can you share with me, Sam?"

"I have my suspicions and trust my instincts. This guy is a dangerous man, Kate. Maybe even explosive."

"What's driving your gut?"

"Dunno yet, but I'm gonna find out. Lots of work to do before we take any action. The proof isn't there yet, but I smell it. I can taste it. And it ain't sweet."

"I did some checking myself at the paper on Ethan Browning, Sam. Some kind of war hero and wears an artificial leg. His childhood is pretty obscure. An aunt raised him, not his parents. He did okay in school and no police record."

"Yeah, a real upstanding citizen. His store looks normal, too, but we unearthed quite a few inconsistencies and questions that Letty's team in Springfield are digging into. Listen, I think I need to spend more time with you and Brian. I'm losing touch under all this work shit, again, and you've been so patient with me. I appreciate that. Gonna make a genuine effort to make sure we get our quality time."

"I'm glad you recognize that, Sam. But that's only the first step. When is step two coming? When we spend time together as a family, and not just after a bad day."

"Yeah, I deserve that. How about tomorrow we go to that Chinese restaurant you both like?"

Kate's face transformed. "You're on. We go out for a change. Sounds lovely. Get you out of the kitchen. What are you doing tomorrow?"

"I gotta study for that sergeant's exam, straighten out my office, take care of some calls. Yeah, spend an admin day here at home."

"Okay, Officer Travis. Dinner at six, then. But for tonight, what say we catch a little TV, get Brian to bed, mix a couple of monster cocktails, and go to bed early?"

"Are you suggesting...?

"Why don't you try it out, cowboy, and see what happens. Maybe you get bucked off!

*Why do I feel like sweat's gonna pop out on my forehead?* "You're on, cowgirl."

"Math's finished." Brian called down the stairs. He was getting better at not entering a room unannounced. After he flew down the stairs, cowgirl, cowboy, and cow pup watched a sitcom. Sam sank deep into his spot on the couch and dozed. Brian's devilish grin didn't give anybody a warning. He stood behind the couch, blew up a balloon, and hit it with a pin. *WAP!*

Sam flew off the couch, still half asleep, and reached for the service weapon that wasn't there. Eyes wild and scanning the room, he realized no imminent threat loomed a pulse-pounding instant later. He didn't scream, but came close to it. "What the hell? Brian, n*ever* do that again. Loud noises like that sound like gunshots and that kicks in my intense mode. That is *not* something I want in this house, understand?"

Brian transformed from a devilish grin to near tears within the span of a few seconds. Sam just watched, a flushed frown still burned into his face. He muttered, "Sorry, Dad. I was just playing a trick."

"Son, that's not the kind of trick I want you to play on me, okay? Got it? Brian?"

"Got it. Goin' to bed. 'Night." As they watched Brian slump up the stairs with his chin buried into his chest. blood still pounded in Sam's temples. He was breathing heavy. *Should I congratulate myself for not pulling my piece on my own kid had it been there? Yeah, right.*

Still on the couch next to where Sam launched from—Kate hadn't moved—she cracked the awkward silence and said, "Sam, he's still a kid. You know kids don't realize everything they do may cause unintended consequences. You were a little rough on him. He was being playful."

"Yeah, I know I'm jumpy. I'll go up and tuck him in, make it right."

"Good idea. I'll mix us those drinks. He'll be asleep in ten minutes, but *we* won't be."

He recovered from his guilt and snorted at her innuendo, but didn't trust himself to say anything yet. *Let it the fuck go, Sam!*

# 26

The next morning, Kate snuck off to work early, leaving Sam sleeping with a smile still on his face. Brian made his PBJ sandwich, grabbed his books, and hoofed it to the bus stop. The phone's ringing awakened Sam at nine AM. He usually got up hours earlier. Snatched the phone off his bedside table, mad at himself for sleeping so long. Way too cheerfully, Captain Larry Jamison said, "What's shakin', Travis?"

"Uh, just about to grab a mug of coffee before hitting the books for the exam."

"Well, I wanted you to know that Lt. O'Neill brought me up to speed on your double homicide case. What's your infamous gut telling you, Sam?"

He had meant to update Larry himself. He was a

good shit. Always trusted Sam's instincts. "I think these are just the first two bodies to drop, boss."

Silence. Then, "Talk to me."

"Well, a trio of disgruntled ex-Army war dogs look to be planning something, but Letty and I haven't figured out what yet."

"She working out?"

"Yeah, she's fine, Larry. And we're leveraging her resources to the hilt. Once we get some more data on our three suspects, we'll assemble a plan."

"Sounds fine. I want you to include me in your daily narratives, side notes, and gut feelings every step of the way." That was a small rebuke for not already updating him. *Shit.* "Like you, Sam, I'm convinced there's more to this story."

"Okay, Captain, you got it. Thanks for calling."


Travis found studying impossible. A hike in the crisp mountain air always brought him some clarity and inspiration. As he walked along an old logging road west of his house, he patted his trusty three-five-seven holstered high on his right hip. Never went anywhere without it and a small canister of Mace spray. Four- or two-legged predators were always possible threats. Occupational hazard to think like that. About two miles into his hike, he spotted two men kibitzing in a clearing less than twenty yards from the road—more like a trail, now—off to his left. They carried long arms and had not spotted him. Wasn't sure if they toted rifles or shotguns. It was in Sam's DNA to sneak up on suspected lawbreakers. He slowed his pace and chose his steps with care as he moved closer. At about seventy-five paces, he eyeballed them and their weapons more clearly. Overheard the man in a red flannel shirt. "Place it here and we'll locate our stands on either side, *but* not so we're shooting at each other."

It was warm for an early summer day, but not hot. The other man wore black attire from his hat to his boots. *Huh. What the hell's **that** all about?* Sam kept advancing until he was within fifty paces. Remained hidden by a six-foot mountain laurel, but spotted two fifty-pound burlap bags filled with corn. Yup, baiting either bears or deer, both illegal. They also had rigged portable tree stands and a pair of battery-powered recording trail cameras that were motion-activated. They had set them up to cover the clearing. The men spread the corn in a straight line, versus just tossing it. Looked like they were practicing. As the animals would take that bait, their sides'd be exposed to either tree stand. These guys knew what they were doing. Now, what to do about it?

They weren't in their stands. Their firearms rested against a nearby tree. No way to prove they were hunting. He'd have to catch them *in* their stands with loaded guns *and* the bait spread out in a leading pattern. That might not happen for days, and Sam didn't have that kind of time to invest in their little operation. He waited until they took off, maybe for lunch and a beer down in the village. By then, Sam had decided to play spoiler. They left their matching three-hundred-dollar stands with ladders in the trees so they wouldn't have to keep lugging them in and out. They, of course, left the trail cameras to show them what was coming in and when.

After they roared out in their pickup—sounded like a big diesel—Sam climbed the ladder, exercising care to stay clear of the cameras' field of view. Took the stands down one by one. Used one ladder to access one of the cameras from behind. Turned it off, released the strap that held it to a branch, and stuck it in his pocket. He then moved the ladder to the next cam. Swung only his hand around into the lens' field of view and flipped them the bird. He took out his pad and pen to write:

*If you want your shit back, contact Environmental Police Officer Sam Travis to pick up your citations and gear. Call 413-555-0520.*

He put that in front of the camera for a full five seconds so they'd get the picture. They'd only see his hand-to-man gesture and the note. He then turned it off to stop its recording, but left it in place. Hiked home to pick up his Bronco and drove back. He then scattered the grain around and loaded up the stands on the Bronc's animal carrier. Smashed the ladders until they were unusable and drove home, humming all the way. He'd never hear from them, the chickenshits. *Serves you right for setting up your little poaching operation just down the road from a game warden's home.* After a suitable waiting period, he'd donate the expensive tree stands to a sportsmen's club raffle. He kept the camera for use on the job. Yeah, he'd stick it on a tree to monitor his driveway and house—since his cabin also housed his official home office.

Sam felt good now and got serious at his desk to his pile of already-opened service manuals. Studied night lighting requirements on vessels over fifty feet. Then, the required day shapes that boats and ships must fly on their masts, and light configurations after sunset. He moved on to memorizing the charted location of the ColRegs Demarcation Lines in Boston Harbor—the invisible boundaries where inland rules change to international rules of the sea. Later, to change things up, he switched to studying search and seizure. Now *that's* something he threw himself into, but studying about it versus doing it? *What three elements are necessary to make a consent search valid? More interesting than boating laws, at least. But hauling in a feisty poacher who's in deep guilty? Sign me up!*

# 27

Josh Bingham and Andrew Lofton headed toward the FBI field office in Springfield, Mass to stake out the lady FBI agent who had gotten under the boss's skin. But first, they removed the *Browning Diamond & Coin* magnetic signs from the side of Ethan's van. And in thirty seconds, it became a nondescript vehicle. They also were careful not to use toll roads with their ever-present cameras. Once in Springfield, they spotted several black cruisers lined up outside in the field office's outdoor parking lot. With binoculars, they scanned the plates. Found one that matched Ethan's hand-scrawled note. Lucky it wasn't in the parking garage which required ID to enter.

Josh observed, "She must be leaving soon if she

parked outside." An hour later, Agent Mather appeared. The boys got a little nervous when she scanned the area, but figured that was standard agent shit. A paranoid bunch, alright. Not too surprising. She got into her vehicle and headed out. Weaved her way toward East Longmeadow to a small but tidy house at one-eight-one Washington Street. She parked in the short driveway—not in the garage. Entered the house using a key in the front door. They figured they hadn't been spotted.

"That's it, Andrew. Looks like thirty feet between houses, story-and-a-half, a one-car detached garage, two security cameras near the front and side doors. Call the boss and ask him what he wants us to do next."

Andrew walked three blocks to an intersection they'd passed on the way in and used the pay phone on the corner of a broader avenue to call Ethan. "Scare the shit out of her, son. Send a message. Make sure she can't recognize your voice. Only one of you talks. Tell her the next time she'll never see it coming, and nothing more. Got it?"

"Got it, boss. We'll wait 'til dark. A knock on the door and another on her head. That sound okay?"

"Yeah, but be careful, quick and quiet."

"Roger that." Took only three minutes to walk back and hop into the van around the corner from the FBI lady's house. Andrew conveyed Ethan's instructions to Josh who hopped out, looked around, and slapped duct tape over their license plates to ensure that a nosy neighbor didn't pick up their tag numbers. Two hours later, new darkness cloaked their approach. First, they both snapped on a pair of rubber gloves and ski masks before Andrew located the security system's box and cut its power feed. They were hoping for no battery backup. He then neutralized the two cams on the house's exterior. As insurance, Josh slapped a two-inch length of duct tape over the cams' lenses. Josh reached up to unscrew the porch's light bulb (it wasn't on and they wanted it to stay that way). He knocked on the front door while Andrew hid to the left, out of sight. Both wore dark clothes besides their masks. They waited. Knocked again, softly, back still turned toward the door and the peephole.

The door cracked open with the safety chain still secure. With a violent thrust, Andrew threw his two-hundred-pound bulk at the door, shoulder first. He crashed through and into Letty, fracturing the door's jam, lock and all. Knocked her down as the door banged into her. Both charged her now-prone form, flung her onto her face and zip-tied her hands behind her back. Josh ripped off a four-inch length of duct tape. Stashed the roll into a cargo pocket on the side of his left thigh. Slapped the tape over her mouth and crammed a coarse black sack over her head. Dragged her into the kitchen toward the back of the small house by the back of her shirt, and threw her onto one of her kitchen chairs.

In a hoarse half-whisper meant to obscure his voice, Josh's baritone hissed Ethan's warning to the captive FBI agent. "Stop what you're doing. Or you won't hear the shot that kills you." Andrew delivered a solid backhanded right fist to her right cheek that sent her and the chair sprawling. Her head bounced off the floor, rendering her unconscious. Andrew tore off her hood. That bounced her head again, like a chunk of solid wood hitting the linoleum tile floor. He and Josh then hauled their own asses out the way they entered, leaving the woman still unconscious on her kitchen floor in the darkness. Closed the front door behind them against the now badly damaged jamb.

The nondescript white van drove with slow deliberation from the neighborhood. A short distance later they stopped. Josh jumped out to remove the tape from their license plates. No need to get stopped for something as stupid as a concealed plate on the trip back to New Hampshire.

# 28

When Letty regained consciousness, she took stock. *What? Attacked? How long have I been out? Still dark... this can't be happening again.* She remembered the last time she felt this powerless, and had vowed never to let it happen again. Yet, here she was. After her initial rage subsided, she took inventory as her academy training kicked in. *I was unconscious, now a severe headache. Possible concussion. My hands bound behind my back, I'm on my kitchen floor. No sign of my attackers.* Time for the tough stuff. She looked down at her own bare feet. *Pajamas still on, no pain 'down there.'* She breathed a sigh of relief. *Okay, likely no sexual assault.* This time. *No unusual sounds in the house. Assholes must be gone. Two of them. So much for eating a TV dinner in my PJs.* She remembered the whispered warning: *'Stop what you're doing. Or you won't hear the shot that kills you.'* *This is about the Browning case. But no direct reference. What balls!*

Letty had to free herself and make some calls. During her training, instructors taught recruits how to free themselves from zip-ties. After a wave of dizziness passed, she sat up by rolling on her side and inched her way up to a sitting position. Slid her butt on top of her hands. *Oh, my aching wrists!* Struggled through the pain to get her arms in front of her. After five minutes of torquing muscles in ways they weren't meant to be stressed, including her back—*this was a lot easier at the academy... and more than a few years ago*—she worked her hands in front of her. *Why the hell is the whole right side of my face throbbing?*

That's when she remembered the unseen blow that knocked her out. *Bastards.* Now, the maneuver. *This is gonna hurt.* She raised her still-bound wrists high above her head and swung them down in front of her as fast as she was able, while throwing her elbows out. The theory was that the sudden force downward and outward against the relatively flimsy zip-ties should snap them and she'd be free. That was the theory, and it had worked at the academy. Now, however, it only broke both her wrists. Or, at least, that's what it felt like. Without thinking, she did it again in the next instant. And again, pain shot through her wrists and arms. But this time, the black plastic zip-ties snapped as the shock reverberated up through her shoulders. She yelped, but it worked! Her wrists hurt like hell, but weren't broken. Then, in her dazed condition, she realized she could have just used her kitchen scissors. *Stupid! Some FBI agent I am.*

Another nauseous wave of dizziness threatened to drop Letty to the floor again. She picked up the toppled chair and gingerly dropped into it again, this time of her own volition with less of a jar to her still-tender back. Sat there for a few minutes as the spell passed. *Yup, a concussion. Shit!* Once she recovered, she picked her steps with care, leaning on the counter next to the fridge. Didn't even need to find a mirror. She touched her cheek. Her fingers came away clean. *At least I'm not bleeding.* Grabbed a bag of frozen peas from the freezer and pressed it with care to her bruised face to mitigate the inevitable swelling.

On her way back to the safety of her chair, she snatched her Princess phone off the wall. Carried it back to her chair. She silently expressed gratitude for its long, spiraled cord. Too damn dizzy to dial, even with one eye closed to shutter half of her double vision. Jammed SAC Malone's speed dial. Something else to be thankful for. He answered on the first ring. Still in the office. "Sir, two masked men attacked me in my home. I think I'm okay, but need some help. Probable concussion. Not bleeding. Externally, anyway...." Then she laid the phone with its open line on her lap.

Suddenly drowsy, she dropped her head onto her forearms folded on the table in front of her. Malone's faint voice in the distance faded to a distorted echo. Figured she'd adequately briefed him. Rested her eyes. Just for a minute.

---

Letty's boss said, "Understood. Agent Mather? Letty? Letty! Shit!" Malone dispatched three agents to her house—lights and sirens—with a team of crime scene techs right behind them. They reported in. Then Malone called Sam Travis at home and warned him to be careful. Described Letty's call.

"Is she alright?"

"Says she is, but slightly damaged."

"*Slightly damaged?* How?"

"Help is on the way."

---

Letty realized she must have dozed off. Or passed out. She picked up the phone in her lap and dialed Sam. "Hey, partner."

"Letty, Malone called me. Said someone attacked you at home. You okay?"

"Sam, be careful. It's possible you're next. About the case."

"Yeah, don't worry 'bout that. *Are you okay?*"

"No, Sam, this attack was *because* of the case. Got a bruised face from a substantial blow by persons unknown. Two, I think. A few bruises elsewhere, but nothing significant. Help is on the way. Be careful, Sam. You may be next."

"Yeah, you already said that. Shit, Letty. Are you headed to a hospital?" Sam's voice shook with something between worry and seething anger.

"Yeah, I'm sure Malone has agents and EMTs on the way. S'protocol to take me in, check for a concussion. After that, I *will* be released if I have anything to say about it."

"Good. Call me. Please take care. I'll see you tomorrow, okay? We'll find these bastards and—"

"I'm okay, although a little shaken up. Sam, they threatened me to stop or they've got a bullet with my name on it."

"Fuckers. We'll get 'em. I promise."

---

Sam thought back to when his mother used to hit him. Sometimes it got bad. When she was using. Wasn't her fault. Got hooked after her accident. Then, she started stealing pills from the clinic where she worked. After she got fired and lost her nursing license, she hung out with dirtbags who'd feed her habit. For favors. He learned later what that meant. Broke his heart. She'd come home smelling like smoke, and... something...

sour. His dad got so mad at her, but never hit her. *Only she did that to me.* Sam recognized how Letty must be feeling, getting the shit kicked out of her. *Awful perception of powerlessness.* At least *her* attackers were strangers. Not sure if that made it better or worse. Nor did he dare ask.

# 29

Sam appeared shaken and angry. His rage bubbled and smoldered even more beneath the surface. That had gotten worse recently. And now, Letty? But he'd promised Kate and Brian dinner out. He'd keep that promise, but he needed to calm down, pretend all was well, which happened way too often. *Fuckin' job, but what else would I do that I love more than this shit?* After talking with Malone and Letty on the phone, he hurried out the front door, halfway down the sloped driveway. On the way out, he grabbed the wireless trail camera confiscated from the hunters down the road. Strapped it to a tree branch about seven feet off the ground. Aimed it toward the upper driveway and his house's steps leading up to his porch and front door. At just the right angle to make an ID if necessary. Sam had long ago reinforced every door in his house with double-slide-bar locks and solid two-inch-thick steel casings. A cop's mind.

He called to Kate and Brian as he breezed back in through the front door. "Hey, let's go, you guys. I'm starving!" Would they see through his crappy artificial smile? Didn't need them asking questions about what was going on, or even worse, asking if he was okay?

"Coming."

"Okay, Dad."

Kate descended the stairs from the second-floor bedroom. "Everything okay, Sam?"

*Fuck!* He smiled. "Yup, everything's fine. Let's eat." They drove the short distance into town. A booth at Hua Lai awaited them. Kate and Sam split a scorpion bowl—a killer cocktail disguised as what he called a foo-foo drink. Sweet, but packed a wallop. Just what the doctor ordered. Brian sipped a Coke. They chattered away until the food came. Like every time they ate here, they had ordered too much. But the left-overs always satisfied at home the next day.

A thirty-something couple slid into the booth next to theirs. Even in the dim light, Sam noticed the attractive young lady's left eye was yellowish purple. Old bruise. The man, about Sam's size, glared at Sam. "What are you lookin' at?"

"Nothing, nothing at all." Now, though, as an off-duty cop, Sam maintained his cool. He had to. But he knew this asshole beat this woman. He noticed he'd grabbed her left arm and was squeezing it enough to make the woman wince in pain. He thought of Letty. Bubbling rage.

Kate noticed it, too, along with the expression in Sam's now-flashing eyes. She knew that face and said, "Easy, big fella."

Brian picked up on it, too. "What's wrong, Dad?"

Sam dropped his gaze to the table in front of him before raising his head again to look across at Brian. "Son, what would you do if you saw anyone hurting Kate?"

"I'd try to stop it," Brian said without hesitation.

The waitress served the man in the next booth a heavy iced mug of cold beer while the woman got some kind of fruity umbrella-topped concoction. Sam spotted the woman's hand shaking. Took both hands to lift the drink to her lips. He tried to go on with his meal. Suddenly, the man grabbed the woman's arm and her drink spilled. "Stupid fucking bitch, now you've done it." The man wasn't shouting, but they heard every word of his seething half-whisper.

Under his breath, Sam asked Brian and Kate to move two booths down, leaving their food on the table. Kate saw Sam meant to say something to the man and was removing them from the line of fire, as they say. They moved quietly. Sam stood up and stared right at the man. "Mister, that's enough. Knock it off with the physical stuff with the lady and the filthy mouth or there will be trouble."

"Yeah, asshole, whatcha gonna do about it?"

"I'm a police officer and if I see one more issue here, I'll fill this place up with badges and guns. They'll take you away."

"Fuck you. Now it's your turn." The asshole picked up a fork with his right hand and aimed it with a swift downstroke toward Sam's hand, now on their table. With his left hand moving in a blur to avoid the fork, Travis grabbed the mutt's heavy beer mug in his right. Threw its contents in the man's face, and then with a full swing, slammed the mug down on the man's hand, still holding that fork. They both heard a few bones crunch. *Tough shit.* The man howled in pain. Other people had stopped eating and were now watching. Every server froze in their tracks.

The man dropped his now-twisted weapon, that mangled fork, and clutched his broken hand with the other. Then he let go and tried to hit Sam with his left fist while still sitting and dripping with beer.

"Bad idea, dude." Sam landed a powerful right against the left side of the still-sitting man's temple. Out cold. Sam turned. Told the manager, an acquaintance named Zhang, "Call 911, Mr. Z. Report a domestic assault. Tell them there is an officer on scene in civilian clothes." With a quick nod and a curt bow, Mr. Z disappeared without a word to make the call. Sam asked the woman, "Are you alright?"

"Yes, I think so."

"What's your name?"

"I'm Brenda, and that beast is Carlo Marconi."

"Brenda, it's none of my business, but you need to get away from this guy. He's a danger to you. And you deserve better than that piece of shit."

"I know. I've tried, but he keeps following me."

"Brenda, the police will be here in a few minutes. Show them your bruises. They'll lock him up. Go to a motel tonight and then tomorrow morning I'd like you to go to a safe house on Spring Street. Stay there until you *feel* safe. They have counselors who will help you. They'll also help you file a restraining order against him."

The police arrived. Recognized Sam, who gave them a short, concise report. The officer asked Sam to stop by the station for a complete statement. Sam said, "I'll be there first thing in the morning. And thanks for the quick response."

Officer Tryon said, "it's true, isn't it, Sam?"

"What's that, Bob?"

"You're a shit magnet."

"That's the rumor." They both smirked. More truth to that than Sam cared to admit. They handcuffed the man. On the way out, he screamed 'police brutality' down-nodding toward his swollen and broken hand. They led him away, first to the ER, then to lock-up, Sam assumed. Been there.

He turned back toward the woman who had

moved to a table until an EMT was finished with her. "I'll call a taxi for you if you'd like, Brenda."

"Thanks, Officer…"

"Travis. Sam Travis." He smiled and was glad he'd restrained himself. He'd had the strongest urge to pound that bully to a mealy pulp.

She smiled. "We came in my car, so I'll use that. And thank you for helping me." She had given her report to Officer Tryon. Now she approached Kate and Brian to apologize for disrupting their family meal. Brenda said to Kate, "Your husband is a good man. Not many will stand up to Carlo like that. Thank you." She dug out her car keys and left before Kate could utter a word.

Mr. Z approached Sam, Kate and Brian, now sitting two booths away from where they started. "We will prepare the same meal for you, nice and fresh, no charge. You are a brave man and you helped that poor woman. Your food will arrive shortly. I am grateful for your intercession. No customer needs to see that. No woman should have to endure that. Thank you all." Nods all around.

"Now where were we?" asked Sam, as if nothing happened. But it had. Especially inside.

"You were great, Dad!" Brian beamed. Kate kissed him on the cheek as their fresh round of appetizers arrived. She said, "Let's eat!"

They relaxed and chattered away during the rest of their meal. Pissed Sam off that violence around these two wonderful people seemed almost normal. Sam left a generous tip. He cursed to himself, though, for letting his anger interfere with what should have been a less bombastic takedown. *But I didn't mind at all, did I? Anyway, coulda been a lot worse.*

At home, Brian hugged Kate and planted a sincere kiss on her cheek, and then went to his father. He held him close with every bit of his early teen strength. "I love you, Dad. I wanna be like you." Sam kneeled, almost eye to eye, with tears welling up. "No, you'll be better than me. Love you, son. Why don't you hit the rack? We're running a bit late tonight, okay?"

"Okay, Dad. 'Night, Kate. Love you both."

Noting the sincerity in his voice, Kate purred, "Good night, Bri. Love you too, kiddo."

Kate and Sam dropped onto the couch. Kate fixed them both a strong belt of vodka with seltzer and a slice of lime slotted on the rim of each glass. The way Sam liked it. "You are something, Officer Travis. I'm grateful to you, too. I consider myself safe around you. Protected and loved."

They clinked glasses and kissed as Sam said, "Cheers, with a whole lotta love." But Sam needed to unload. "Kate, I lost my temper on that asshole. Felt good. And that's bad." She kissed his forehead and held the hand that now laid limp on his lap. But she said nothing. He reminded himself to check the trail cam outside before hitting the rack himself. But he needed no reminder to bolt the doors and secure the windows. Some things don't need reminders. Especially now. *I'll lose my temper alright, on the ass-hats that attacked Letty.*

# 30

Bingham and Lofton drove the ninety minutes back to Portsmouth after sending Ethan's unmistakable message to that FBI bitch. They were careful about speed and even used their blinker when changing lanes. Couldn't afford to get stopped, not after attacking a frickin' federal agent in her own frickin' house. After returning the van to the shop, they both headed home. No sooner had they walked through Bingham's front door en route to the fridge than his phone rang. Lofton snagged a beer for the road before heading home himself.

Josh answered, "Yeah?"

"Hey, ya Yankee bastard. How the hell are ya?"

"Carl?"

"Uh-huh. Y'all called my kin, so I thought I'd see 'bout dis reunion thing."

"Thanks for calling back, Johnnie Reb. Actually, ah was tryin' to reach ya ta see if you'd like to make some good solid cash money." Talking to this old country boy made it easy to slip back into his own gen-u-wine Bama twang.

"No reunion? A false PRE-tense from a damn Yankee? Dat ain't no s'prise! Whatcha cookin, brother?"

Josh said, "Yankee? Not by birth, ole son. I'm in need of somethin' special that only a guy like you might could get."

"What kinda special shit you be a needin', Josh?"

"Romeo Delta Xray." RDX is the explosive element of military grade plastic explosives, but it was dangerous to come right out and say that over an open phone line.

"Whoa, baby! I reckon there ain't no askin' what fer, is there?"

"Nah, best you know nothin' about it for your own good sake, but won't ever come back on ya."

"I do recall back in the day you knew what I was a peddlin' and y'all never said shit. I heard all y'all damn-near got jammed up fer dat dead lame-ass looey orderin' you guys into dat shitstorm at Tan Son Nhut. Was dat you?"

"Yeah."

"Good fer y'all. Right thing to do. Well, let's say I

jest might git you some a dat play-dough. How much ya willin to pay this poor ol southern boy?"

"Big money, Carl, big money. Name your price within reason and we got the cold, hard, green."

"How much shit you be needin?"

"Can you come up with about thirty pounds?"

"Whoo-whee, doggy! That's a lot of playin'! Ah don't have dat much inventory, but ah think I kin git it for ya, fer da right price."

"Name it, Carl."

"Hmmm. Pickup only. No delivery. How do a hun'rd large in used bills sound?"

"Done. When?"

"Gimmie two weeks. I'll call ya. Just you alone, buddy, with the green. Copy?"

"Yep, sounds good, Carl. Have to factor in the drive time from New Hampshire to ole Miss. But just me and the green is good with me."

"Alrighty. Got a pen? Take State Route 84 ta exit 33, Balfour Road. Go fourteen miles 'n turn left on Red Lick Road. Follow dat till ya come to a security fence with a keypad. Jus' ring 'n I'll open da gate. Ah be a callin' in about two weeks and we'll git 'ser done."

"Sounds great, Carl. Talk to ya later."

Josh was thrilled. Called Andrew, who said, "Man, the boss will be pleased. About that agent lady, too."

# 31

At Browning Diamond and Coin in Portsmouth, the three conspirators hunkered down in Ethan's office. Sometimes Ethan slept there on his couch. He'd not gone home. It was late. Josh and Andrew decided to deliver the news in person. All of it. Ethan only said, "Good job, men. And here's my news for you. Andrew, remember that deal I mentioned to you about something happening soon?"

"Yeah."

"Well, we're gonna hit a Liquid Natural Gas tanker coming into Boston Harbor on Bunker Hill Day. That's June seventeenth—four weeks from today. If we get the C-4 in two weeks, Josh.... It's all coming together, boys. The Patriot Guardsmen are gonna make a statement to the world."

"The who?"

"That's us, Josh. I decided it's time to give ourselves a proper name. On the phone or whatever, we'll just say 'PG.'"

Andrew was feeling the two brews he'd slammed down. One at Josh's place, and another at home before Josh picked him up. Said, "PG, huh? Well, that sure don't stand for no *'Parental Guidance,'* eh, boss?"

Seeing his buddy's remark and timing sucked, Josh covered. "Sounds great, boss. When do we start?"

"Right away. Andrew's already started gathering early stuff. Now it's time to put together the rest of your list—what you'll need for all of those remotely controlled boats to be operational and mission-ready."

Andrew jumped into serious fabrication mode. "Think I'll use a flared bow with step-back gunwales to shed water from any waves. Gotta be waterproofed, too, with lithium batteries, self-righting, and signal boosters for UHF frequencies. Ultra-long antennas, good ballast to offset the C-4's weight aboard, and—"

Browning was the big thinker, not a detail guy. "Okay, enough. That's your shit to do, Andrew. Make sure you do it right. One more thing. There will be two boats in tandem, one after another, to strike near the bow, and both mid-ship sides of the tanker. First charge will take out the outer layer of the hull. A second at the same impact points will penetrate the inner hull that doubles as the liquid's aluminum tank membrane. That will release the liquid into the atmosphere outside the ship, creating vapor, and that's when we'll ignite it."

Andrew said, "This is really gonna be something, boss."

"Make sure you're not being followed at all times. Report anything out of the ordinary. I'd be surprised if they didn't question me again after you guys spanked that lady agent. But I've got witnesses that I was at a town meeting with the Selectmen about a new ballpark for the local Little League teams. You guys never left NH. Got it?" The men both nodded. They still reeled from the audacity of Ethan's plan. He added, "Ok let's get to completing our prep. And Andrew, let's do make it seven boats. Six for the mission and one for pre-mission testing, like you suggested earlier."

# 32

Sam crawled out of bed early to answer the phone. He asked Letty, "How ya feelin'?"

"Bruised, sore, and not pretty. But mostly pissed off. At work."

"Really? I—"

"Yeah, I checked myself out. Listen, I have news from your requests for more data and our plans for a return visit to Browning's shop. Got the okay on surveillance, and pretty much everything else you asked for."

"Are you up for this, Let?"

"You're goddamn right I am. I want these bastards. They busted into my *home* and *assaulted* me." Sam found it unsettling how her voice was low and even, but he could feel the venom, even over the phone.

Letty may not yet be a seasoned field agent, but she was becoming one scary operator.

Travis thought to himself, *How many times have people come up the driveway and to my door looking for me?* Sometimes, the stair alarm would go off and Sam would go to the rear door. He'd walk around the house to the backside of the front entry and say, "Help you?" with his sidearm visible. *This* had changed the attitude of some first-time visitors. *But what if I were only five-three and a buck-twenty soaking wet?*

While choking down a quick fistful of breakfast burrito, Sam briefed his lieutenant and Captain Jamison with the kitchen wall phone's cord following him around like an annoying tail. Then he aimed his Bronco toward the Springfield FBI office. Arrived forty-five minutes later to run their security gauntlet again. Headed to the second floor, third door on the right. That's where Agent Letty Mather conducted her business at the edge of the "bullpen." Knocked and walked in to her office. Shock sculpted his expression upon seeing the damage to that beautiful face, all swollen, now migrating to every color in the rainbow.

"Did you get the plate of that truck?"

Letty looked up and said, "Fuck you, EPO Travis." There was that flat and even voice again. *Damn.* Smiling through her pain, she said, "Let's get down to it, Sam. I'm in the middle of a pity party and I'm anxious to nail these bastards. Frankly, I don't give a shit whether they are state or federal collars. You feel me?"

"Alright, then, show me what you got."

"These are the registration and descriptions of vehicles belonging to all three of our suspects. Also, a fourth vehicle, the van registered to Ethan Browning of Browning Diamond and Coin. The one we saw in front of his office."

"Yup, the one with our GPS device on it."

"Yes. We can download its hard drive here in our Info Systems tech lab as soon as we get our hands on it. That's presuming they haven't run a bug scan and discovered it."

"Are they that sophisticated?"

Letty said, "Hope not. Here's some interesting data on Browning's home from this property description. He has a detached four-car garage. Why would you need a four-car garage when, including the van, you only have two vehicles?"

"Could be he has a couple of muscle cars. He grew up in that era."

Letty's eyes widened as she studied an aerial photo. "Maybe. Hey, look at this image. What do you see, Sam?"

"Is this a *satellite* photo? Over *US soil*?"

"Yup. In cooperation with the US intelligence community, the Bureau has access to what are called 'engineering passes' of satellites designed to surveil

Europe or Asia. As they orbit, they pass over the US. Some of their spare capacity is dedicated to things like hydrology, oceanography, mapping, and emergency preparedness."

"You piggy-back on military satellites for your own surveillance purposes. Clever. Yeah, what's that?" He pointed to the property next to Browning's house."

"Looks like a neighbor with another big-ass detached garage back along the wood line. I checked the Brentwood Registry of deeds on his neighbor out of curiosity. Owned by an elderly couple—the Livingstons do the snowbird thing. But there was a sidebar on it that this couple has a permit from the town to rent or lease that building."

Sam scratched his chin. "Nothing on the other side of Browning?"

"As you can see from this aerial shot, no other neighbors around. Thirty-acre parcels."

That wiggled Sam's antennae. Serious privacy. "Are the Livingstons there now?"

Letty responded like she didn't know why that was important. "What are you thinking, Sam?"

"Dunno. My gut asked me that question. It needs to be answered."

"Why do you think?"

"Because Browning has the run of the whole hundred-twenty acres with only the Livingstons' there, and they're gone much of the time. Is the garage rented out now?"

"I'll check."

"What else you got?"

"Tax records all seem in order. The IRS did an audit five years ago and Browning was clean."

Sam grew a little more excited. "Okay, a couple more things. We need to pay Mr. Browning another visit. Ask him his whereabouts last night, if he has a car collection, or another hobby that requires space. Most importantly, we need to retrieve that bug from his van. See what that tells us."

"That's not very much reason to interview him again, Sam."

"No, but it'll still rattle him. We need to be aggressive here and keep him on his heels. Let him know we think whoever did this to you was him. Or possibly... what's their names?"

"Andrew Lofton and Josh Bingham, who happen to be the only two survivors that Browning pulled from that armored personnel carrier that blew up in Viet Nam. Definitely loyalists."

"Did your tech guys come up with anything at your house?"

Letty showed Sam a half-dozen interior and exterior black-and-white photos of her house. "Not much of anything. No prints and they're still running DNA, but I'm not too hopeful. If they wore masks and gloves...."

"What exactly did they say to you?"

"One guy spoke. His disguised voice sounded

broken and sort of whispered. He said, 'stop what you're doing or you'll never hear the bullet that hits you.' Something like that. I was a little woozy after they slammed me down."

"We're getting to them. For sure. What are they up to besides stolen coins, murder, and personal intimidation?"

"Oh, you want more than that?"

"Let's go rattle this dirtbag's cage again. You okay with that?"

"Yes, I am. Nobody violates my space without paying for it. Plus, somebody's gonna pay for my front door." She rewarded Sam with a devilish sneer.

"Let's roll then, partner."

# 33

They drove Letty's cruiser again. En route to Portsmouth, they both remained silent, deep in thought. Upon their arrival at Browning's store, the van was nowhere in sight. Sam said, "Pull around back. Let's check out the alley." There they spotted the van. "Keep your eyes peeled." Sam exited the car, closing the door with care behind him. Made like he just got out to stretch his legs. Did a full scan of the alley and the back of Browning's store. Nothing suspicious, and no windows or cameras. Sauntered to the rear of the van, which was backed up to within two feet of the building. Pulled out the "bug" which was half the size and weight of a brick. Tucked it inside his zipped-up jacket. Kept one hand outside his jacket, inside his pocket, to ensure the damn thing didn't fall out.

Sauntered alongside the van. Noticed something that wasn't there. He stopped, and did a double-take. No logo on the side of the van. But he saw the outline of... magnetic signs? But they'd been removed. *Interesting.* Returned to Letty's car. Through the driver's window, he pointed to the rear. She nodded and popped the trunk by pressing the button inside her glove box. He stashed the device.

Sam walked around to her open driver's window. Leaned on the frame and said, "Okay, let's pull around front and pay him a visit, rattle him some more. I'll take the lead again, if you don't mind. I seem to have a way of getting under his skin."

"No problem. Tough for me to talk, anyway. Let's go." She unconsciously rubbed her throat. Reminded her of her still-whopping headache. She needed something stronger than aspirin. Later.

They walked in. The bell tinkled. A voice from the back room said, "Be right out." Twenty seconds later, Ethan appeared from behind his curtain with his glass third eye still perched high on his forehead. "Ah, Agent Mather and EPO, what's your name again? I forgot."

"EPO Sam Travis, Mr. Browning. We have a couple more questions for you."

"Oh my, Agent Mather, what befell you? That's a nasty bruise."

"I ran into a door at my home last night."

"So sorry to hear that." He didn't *sound* sorry. "Let's go back into the office."

Sam started right in on him. "Tell me about your hobbies, Mr. Browning."

"Hobbies? You came back up here to ask about my hobbies?"

"Yeah, in a sense. We notice you have a four-car detached garage behind your house. Do you have a car collection?"

"No, I don't."

"Is there a reason for having a four-car garage when you only have two vehicles registered to you and your business?"

"No."

"I'm sorry to ask you, but having that kind of space begs for a reason."

"No, it doesn't, as I have already explained to you." He dropped into his chair behind the desk. Letty and Sam sat in the two guest chairs, *Deja Vu, all over again.*

"Okay, let's move on, then. Where were you last night?"

"I was at a Selectman's board meeting to discuss the construction of a new Little League baseball field."

"You or your men did not leave the state last night?"

"I can't speak for Josh or Andrew. I'm their employer, not their babysitter."

"Okay, then we'll ask them where they were."

"Your line of questioning is annoying and not to the point, EPO Travis. Maybe you should leave interrogations to a law enforcement officer whose training is more sophisticated than yours."

"Nah, Agent Mather loves the way I question potential suspects."

"Suspects? You suspect me of something? In what particular crime, Travis?"

"Officer Travis to you, Ssgt. Browning." The man's eyebrows took a short hike up onto his forehead. "Yeah, we're aware of your service record. Thank you for your service, I think."

"You *think?* Look at this, you arrogant...." Browning hoisted his prosthetic limb up onto the desk for them to see with a *clunk*. Took him grabbing his right pant leg cuff with both hands to get it up there. "You *think?* I lost a part of a leg serving my country in time of war, you idiot."

"Yeah, we saw what your service record says, and also what it doesn't say."

"What the hell is *that* supposed to mean?"

"Ever heard the term 'fragging,' Mr. Browning? I'm sure you have. Any first-hand knowledge of it, perhaps?"

"That's it. Either charge me with a crime or get the hell out of my office. And don't come back, or you'll be in court explaining why you are harassing a disabled and decorated veteran, not to mention a respected businessman in this community."

"Sure, thing, *Ethan*. We'll leave for now. We'll be in touch."

As they got into Letty's car, she croaked, "Man, you *do* know how to get under someone's skin." You lit him up light a firecracker. But what did we accomplish?"

"We made him uncomfortable. Criminals make mistakes when they're like that. Mission accomplished. We weren't going to get anything from him, anyway. Let's go to the Registry of Deeds and see if the Livingstons rented that garage out, to whom, for how long, and for what purpose. I smell something rotting. Oh, and did you see anything unusual about his van from the alley?"

"Like what?"

"No logos on its sides. Removable magnetic signs. Less obvious for stake-outs."

Letty wasn't really looking at Sam until he said that. She swiveled her sore neck to stare at him with some effort and winced before she said, "Son-of-a-bitch!"

The Portsmouth Registry of Deeds wasn't in Portsmouth, but in Brentwood, New Hampshire, a short drive south near Kingston. Letty flashed her badge and received immediate attention. Mrs. Keiger was eager to please a female FBI agent. She asked Sam if he was FBI, too. Sam offered his standard reply with a winning smile, "We're the green berets of law enforcement," and flashed his badge, not giving her the opportunity to read it. Letty did her thing. Mrs. Keiger produced a small file and handed it over. It showed the Livingstons had rented the garage only three times in recent years. Two of the occurrences appeared inconsequential, but the third and most current was to a Mr. Ethan Browning of 112 Main Street in Portsmouth, New Hampshire.

Letty asked, "Mrs. Keiger, this is a business address. Would you be able to provide us with his home address, please?"

"Of course. Please wait a moment and I'll look it up for you." One minute later, the administrator produced a piece of paper with Ethan Browning's home address at 274 Barnes Road in Portsmouth, which they already knew. But they did not know he had only rented that house for a three-month period, beginning two weeks earlier, renewable monthly upon request. Prior to that, he'd leased a small bungalow in town near his store.

"Thank you so much, Mrs. Keiger. You've been most helpful. Please keep this visit and its purpose confidential."

"Of course, Agent Mather. Is Mr. Browning in any sort of trouble?" asked Keiger.

"Not at the moment. Just routine background information that we're required to provide. Again, thank you for your assistance. Good day, Mrs. Keiger."

They left the registry and Sam had to ask. "As long as we're in town, how about a drive-by, Agent Mather?"

"Yes, since we're right down the road, why not?"

# 34

They cruised south on Barnes Road. A long curved driveway led to a two-story cape-style house on the west side of the road and about four-hundred feet uphill to their right. Even though oak trees lined the steep driveway, none obstructed their view of the house. The entire property was beautifully landscaped. The *No Trespassing* signs posted at twenty-foot intervals along the road looked brand new. Beyond the house, they spotted the north end of the four-car garage they'd observed on the satellite photos and described on the property's land record.

"I need to take advantage of nature's restroom, Agent Mather. How about you back up on the side of the road a bit to that stand of trees back there?

Strictly for my sense of modesty. You understand." He nodded over his right shoulder with a lop-sided grin.

"Why, of course, EPO Travis." She grinned, too.

"For about ten mikes?" That was military jargon for ten minutes. Once a Marine, always a Marine.

Letty smiled. "Roger that."

Off Sam went. He worked his way up the sloped property through the dense tree line between Browning's property and the Livingston's. Remained hyper-alert for booby traps, trail cameras, or any other surveillance equipment. Didn't come across any, but that didn't mean they weren't there. A well-camouflaged two-by-three-inch camera? Almost impossible to spot out here. He pressed on and approached what he assumed was the rear of the property. The entire south side of the big detached garage now lay before him. He also noticed a sizable pond behind the garage not visible from the road and wondered if Browning fished there.

Satisfied no one was inside or outside as there were no vehicles, he approached the garage. Spotted four security cameras around the building at its corners. He avoided their probable fields of view. The windows were blacked out from the inside by... plastic garbage bags? *Can't see a damn thing. Who does this? And why? What are you hiding, Ethan?* So he backtracked to Letty's car and jumped in. She had left the engine running in case the need for a hasty retreat was called for. "Guess you don't have to worry about the fuel bill, huh?"

"Funny boy, you're paying with your tax dollars. What did you find?"

"A large garage with windows blacked out. Plus, four security cameras on all four corners with overlapping fields of view. He's hiding something in there. I'm sure of it. Let's make a U-turn and head up to the Livingston place back there." He pointed back over his right shoulder again. They drove up the long blacktopped driveway next door to a large, white, three-story impeccably maintained Colonial with several large twelve-paned windows. They stopped short of seeing the two-car attached garage off to the right and set back from the house proper. An ornate front porch sheltered a fancy-ass front door. About two-hundred feet away, *another* large four-car garage. This place too displayed numerous posted *No Trespassing* signs as well, also brand new. One still had its price stuck to one corner.

Sam scratched his chin. "What's up with the four-car garages up here?"

"Dunno. Do you have to pee again?"

"Yup, leaky valve. Got binocs?"

"Yup, in the trunk. I'll pop it for you. Wouldn't want you to pee on a tree without your telescopic vision."

Sam retrieved the binoculars and hiked off. Once more, he came up through the tree line shared with

Browning's place to avoid any cameras. Circled around and looked for any signs of activity. Someone blacked out these windows in the same way. *Must have found a sale on garbage bags.* Four cameras visible, same as next door. No way to get closer without being spotted. Sam looked for tracks and found recent activity from light mud marks on the blacktopped driveway. A filthy area immediately around the garage's service door handle seemed like an anomaly on this otherwise impeccable property. *Huh.* Well, that and the garbage-bagged-windows, including every small window on all four overhead garage doors. He returned to Letty's cruiser and gave her the same news as the other garage. "What do you think, Let?"

"Obvious concealment of something. What, we don't know. My thought is to get eyes on both garages. Observe comings and goings. Find out what that reveals."

"Yeah, I agree. But what type of surveillance?"

"Well, you're fond of those trail cameras. I say we set cams up and aim them at the front and rear of both garages. Motion-activated FBI-issue cams with infrared capability and transmitters should suffice. They're effective day or night. We'll have our tech guys set us up with a small computer. When there's activity, it'll send us an email with video."

"You have those kinds of resources?"

"Yup. Bureau budget and reach. A warrant should be no problem. Plus, Malone likes me. A lot." She winked. "State-of-the-art and not available to the public. Let's get on it. What say we get out of here before someone spots us and rats us out?"

"Agree. How long for those cameras? And do we place them or do your feeb techs do it? Oh, and let's find out what's on the van's bug. Get a clue on what they were up to."

"Noah's lab rats don't go out in the field. Our tech agents do the set-ups. They're trained in concealment, evasion, and penetration into hostile territory. No one will know they were even there. They have their own infrared night vision, so they avoid any beams during their setup. I'm guessing about forty-eight hours."

"Nice." This impressed Sam.

"Let's get back to my office and check out the van's bug."

# 35

Ethan summoned Josh to his office. He arrived from the spacious back storage room of Brown Diamond and coin. They both headed into his small office. "Sit," said Ethan.

Josh complied and asked, "What's up, boss?"

"Your buddy?"

"He has the stuff."

"Alright, then. Time is running short. You need to get to Mississippi and meet with your guy to pick up the materiel. I want you to use my personal car. Here's cash for gas, food, and lodging. No cards, understood?"

"Yessir. When do you want me to leave?"

"Right now. Car is out back, full tank. Don't speed or get stopped by anyone. Straight there and straight back. Remember, you'll be carrying enough explosives to sink a cruise ship."

"Boss, if there's anything I know, it's explosives and I'll be real careful. No worries. Besides, without a high-temp ignition source, C-4 ain't that dangerous."

"Today's Tuesday. Figure a twenty-five-hour drive each way with one eight-hour rest stop. That's fifty-eight hours, plus allow two more hours for piss stops. So, I expect a phone call when you arrive down there, another when you've secured the stuff, a third when you leave, and also when you're halfway back. Here's a suitcase with a hundred grand plus another thousand for expenses. Don't get funny with me, Josh. I'll find you if you run and hide."

"No way, Ethan. It'll be just as you say. See you in sixty-ish hours."

"Good luck, son."

Josh called Carl to double-confirm his friend had the goods, and that they were ready for pick-up. He did, and Josh told him he was on his way down. He'd be knocking on his old Army buddy's door in about thirty hours. Followed routes 90, 81, 75, 59 and 84. Per the plan.

Meanwhile, Andrew had secured most of the materials he needed to modify the RC boats he found on-line, which would save a ton of time, now that they had a timeline. He bought seven. He'd first test one unit without the C-4 "plastic explosives," but with the equivalent weight.

While he waited for the boats and their controllers to be shipped to the Livingston garage, he prepped his custom electronics packages, including his navigation software. After the boats arrived, he'd disable their lights and drill holes in the decks for installing long-range antennas. He'd repackage the guts of each boat to accommodate signal extenders, and to ensure ample space low within each hull for the C-4. Also, strap-downs for everything. He figured thirty-six hours to mission readiness once he got his hands on the boats and the C-4.

He'd have to work at least three sixteen-hour days until the boats arrived, plus another day for rigging and final testing. After that, he'd instruct Ethan and Josh how to operate the controls. Less than two weeks out until party time now, or whenever Ethan gave the word. Ethan told them he'd learned from the Coast Guard's *Notice to Mariners* "their" LNG would indeed arrive two weeks from tomorrow. *That's a spare day to scope out our hides-slash-launch points. Perfect timing, so far.*

# 36

A dozen techies lived and worked in the lower level, a.k.a. the basement of the Springfield FBI field office. Home to both the lab rats and their version of a tech-SWAT team who would insert their surveillance gear in the field at what they now called 'the garages.' For this crew, a lack of windows in this basement was a plus. They kept the large space well-lit and crammed with electronic equipment that succeeded in glassing over Sam's eyes in wonder.

Letty introduced Sam to the supervisor, Noah Adams. Noah wasn't a typical youthful electronics geek with glasses, anemic complexion, and a slim build in a white lab coat. Rather, he was a forty-ish, well-built man with gray showing at the temples of his blonde hair. He wore jeans and a Celtics jersey. His greeting was warm and cordial. Reminded Sam that pre-conceived stereotypes could be deceiving, maybe even hazardous. He'd learned that long ago as an undercover operative.

Noah told Agent Mather and EPO Travis that the insertion of surveillance devices for the two properties out on Barnes Road in New Hampshire would take place the following night. Noah handed Letty a letter-paper-sized computer tablet about three inches thick. It was heavy, like it packed a lot of dense computing and communication power into a small portable package. Said it was a bleeding-edge prototype, whatever that meant. Noah then showed both her and Sam how to use it.

Sam was impressed, yet again, with the thoroughness of the work product. He complimented Noah and his team, especially considering the quick turnaround. Noah laughed out loud and said they had these in stock, as they were popular with the agents. "Beyond that, a little software tweak here and there to complete the package. No big deal."

Sam asked, "Can we look at our bug's recording, Noah? Of *Letty's* 'half-brick,' that is? We wanna find out what our suspects have been up to, where they've been. I planted this thing on their van."

"Sure, let's go on down to this table." He nodded up ahead to his right at a high-top table, obviously designed for use while standing. Sam handed over

Letty's device. Noah laughed, "Boy, this thing is an antique. Like last year's model."

Sam shook his head. *Antique? Last year? These folks move pretty fast.* Letty grinned, "Yeah, a prototype Magellan unit I got from the field agents upstairs. All they had on short notice. Or they didn't trust me with their fanciest toys. At least it's got the new GPS capabilities in a self-contained unit with a magnetic vehicle plate. Comes in handy on a tail, too, they tell me."

"No worries, these things had a good rep, even as limited as they are. Now less than half the size, a quarter of the weight, and better tracking using more birds concurrently—"

Sam interrupted, "Birds? You use *birds* for tracking?"

Noah chuckled. "Sorry. We call satellites birds. Let's check out what those boys were up to." He removed the recording device from its weatherproof plastic cover. Plugged it into one of his machines. The screen came to life displaying a map that contained red lines and time annotations.

"This is where and when they traveled, guys. It also notates the duration of each stop. I have to make a couple of adjustments to the program. Won't take but a minute." This further amazed Sam. He wasn't aware such capabilities existed. Then Noah said, "Bada-BING, people. Screen's up with everything you want to know, hopefully, or at least whatever this boat anchor offers. The red line shows travel around Portsmouth, assuming deliveries given these short-duration stops. Then, late in the afternoon the same day, the van travels from New Hampshire into Massachusetts. Based on its route, it appears the driver avoids toll roads and takes more time than necessary. Only a little clever," remarked Noah. "Once in Springfield, they travel to... our current location? Right across from our parking lot outside. Who's in this van? You're surveilling them and they're surveilling *us*? Never mind. Don't want to know, The van sits here for over an hour and then leaves. It then travels through a couple of small towns, stopping in East Longmeadow."

Letty fumed. "Those fuckers were following me. To my home. *It was them!*" Letty spoke loud enough to draw attention from most everyone in the cavernous room.

"Easy, Letty. Let it play out," said Sam.

After Noah settled down from watching Letty's nervous dancing around behind him, he continued. "The van stops at this location in East Longmeadow for exactly two hours, thirteen minutes." Noah pointed at the screen. "Then it leaves and goes back to Portsmouth using the same route as on the trip down. Goes stationary at its point of origin. That's it, Agent Mather."

Letty's visible shaking now caught Noah's undivided attention. He looked worried. Sam gritted his teeth, shook his head from side to side. His jaw muscles worked overtime. Observing Letty's reaction to this evidence, Noah didn't need to ask. He made a copy of the recording for SAC Malone and stuffed both it and the original into chain-of-custody evidence bags. Labeled both: 'Track recording and assault of FBI Agent Mather with date, times, and locations." He signed it and handed the two copies to Letty with sympathetic eyes.

Lightening the mood, Sam said, "That was fast."

"Oh, yeah, I programmed it to reproduce while we were viewing the data."

Sam saw Letty was still in shock, maybe shame, that she, a trained FBI agent, had let this happen, and this recording only scraped the scab off her still-bleeding emotional wound. He rested a hand on her shoulder. She muttered, "Sam, am I this stupid?"

"Could happen to any of us. Don't blame yourself. Now let's ditch the pity party and get on our game faces. Nail these bastards." One nod. Then again with more conviction. They offered thanks and goodbyes to Noah. Rushed to the elevator, rode it to the ground floor en route to kicking some thugs' asses. But then, they necessarily detoured up to the fifth floor in response to Letty's pager. Got right in to see Special Agent in Charge Jack Malone.

. . .

"Sit, please. Noah phoned me right after you left. What's your next move, Letty? Malone ignored Sam. This wasn't about him.

Letty got right to the point. "Noah says the bugs go in tonight and tomorrow. We wait a few days to see what happens. I suggest we get an AUSA on board because I'm convinced we'll need warrants, both search and arrest. And we'll also need field personnel to back up our play."

Malone stared at his analyst, now a seasoned field agent. *Baptism by fire.* He said, "You'll have to delay bringing the assault, threat to a federal agent, conspiracy, as well as breaking and entering charges. First, we find out what the actual crime is, or is about to happen. Agree?"

Letty responded through clenched teeth. "Yes, of course." Sam was relieved she'd returned to her professional self.

Malone swiveled his concerned focus on his agent to an apologetic gaze toward Sam. "EPO Travis, I wasn't ignoring you, please understand that. I appreciate the assistance you've provided the FBI to this point, and we'd appreciate you staying on this case with us. Agent Mather has kept me apprised of how helpful and professional you've been. Incidentally, Captain Jamison from your department called and brought me up to speed about you and your work history. I listened to the recording of the interview with Mr. Browning. Impressive. Sound tactics and control. Whatever either of you need, we will provide. Understood?"

Both replied in unison, "Yessir."

"Okay, take a day or two off and let this surveillance play out. If something breaks, let me know. That's it for now. Thank you both. Oh, by the way, Agent Mather, nice shiner. It's a beaut! Still like the idea of field work? Between this case and that trail predators case, I'd say you're now a seasoned field agent." Malone maintained half a grin. Sam liked this guy, even though he was a feeb. Letty lowered her eyes, before raising them to peer at her boss slantwise, but said nothing.

That expression was distant, cold. Sam wasn't sure if he liked what he saw. He nodded to Malone and they both left. Sam's thoughts swirled. *What's going on in her mind right now? Damn!*

# 37

Josh Bingham rolled down State Route 84 en route to Whistler, Mississippi, on time, but tired. Slept for six hours, ate breakfast, and got back on the road at six AM. He planned to arrive by two or three PM. After exiting on Balfour Road, he aimed Ethan's car east on Red Lick Road. Fourteen miles later, he looked for the gated fence Carl Devor had described. A little after three PM, Josh spotted a monster vertical steel-bar gate with a keypad on a pedestal. He didn't expect a "fence" composed of a crude-looking but formidable six-foot stone wall with a nasty spiral of three-foot high concertina wire U-bolted to its top. Pushed the button next to the speaker. "Carl, it's Josh at the gate."

Ten seconds later, about to call again, the speaker came to life. "Damn, Yank! Ya made real good time." The heavy gate inched away from him as it opened ever so slowly. Josh wondered, *That thing must weigh a thousand pounds.* He spurred Ethan's eighty-three Ford Crown Vic down a dirt road for a half-mile of roiling dust before pulling up in front of a medium-sized single-story log cabin. As he drew to a stop, the dust cloud caught up and swirled around the car. Two huge Doberman Pincers rose from the porch and bounded down the cabin's steps. Headed right for Josh, front claws scrabbling on his driver-side window, their snarling teeth and drool inches from his face. No way he'd get out of that car until Carl put those monsters on a leash. Preferably chains. Or in fuckin' cages.

Carl looked older, heavier, and more gray, but sure enough, the big dude descending the cabin's steps was his bud from Nam. He yelled at the dogs to shut the hell up and return to the porch, which they did on command. Josh got out of Ethan's sedan. Dragged the suitcase full of cash behind him. "Hah, Josh. That cold north ain't changed you much, 'cept you got older, heavier, and more gray. Not like me! Good trip?"

"Howdy, you confederate-flag-flyin' rebel." They shook hands and banged into a brief opposite-shoulder man-hug.

"C'mon inside and set a spell. I see you brought me a suitcase." Josh noticed Carl's cabin offered a simple open floor plan. A gun rack displayed an assortment of rifles, even a Barrett fifty caliber with a Leopold scope. One serious weapon. A few pictures of ducks, deer, and a couple of mounts adorned his walls. The place was unkempt and carried a distinctive odor, like that of rotting food competing with dirty socks and sweat.

"Yep, got what you asked for. Small-denomination used bills, all one-hundred-thousand clams." They sat in a couple of cushioned wooden chairs facing each other at a diagonal in front of a brick hearth. Said it was the coolest part of the cabin. Carl didn't ask why Josh needed the C-4, nor did Josh offer any explanation. Carl poured some home-brew moonshine into a Ball jar with a couple ice cubes out of a tray for each of them. They toasted to "victory." Josh handed him the suitcase. Carl cracked it open and grinned, revealing a few gaps in his smile where front teeth once resided.

"Wanna count it?"

"Don't reckon I need to. You ain't no buddy fucker or you'd be dead by now." He got up, limped out to the kitchen, and returned with a medium large metal suitcase guarded by two sturdy locks. He handed Josh the keys. "Open it and check out what ya done bought."

Josh did so and examined two-high stacks in rows of three, and in columns of two "bricks" each wrapped in yellowish, waxy, paper imprinted with the words,

## EXPLOSIVE MATERIAL
## U. S. ARMY C-4
## HANDLE WITH EXTREME CARE

Thirty one-pound bars. "Looks right, Carl. Can't thank you enough."

"You just did, boy, with this suitcase. Ah imagine ah be readin' 'bout it in the newspaper sometime soon. Good luck. You know how to handle it. Good stuff."

"Yeah, I remember." They finished their drinks. Josh already felt buzzed. Strong shine, alright.

"Ya gotta git goin' or will ya stay for a spell?"

"I'd love to hang with you and catch up, Carl, but my schedule's pretty tight."

"I reckoned that'd be the case. Holler if you be needin' any old thang else, buddy."

"I will, Carl. Appreciate what you did to help us protect our great land from sinking further into the swamp."

"You be fixin' to raise the dickens and ahm behind ya all the way. Be on yer way with good luck, my bruddah."

Josh set the metal case in the trunk of the Crown Vic. He crawled into the cockpit, and with a last wave, aimed the sedan toward the gate at the bottom of the hill. Ten miles away, he spotted a roadside phone booth. Called Ethan to inform him he had the stuff and was on his way back. He reconfirmed he'd call again when he reached the halfway point of his trip back to Portsmouth. Settled in for the fifteen-hundred-mile trek ahead of him. Now, he prayed to a god he didn't believe in that he wouldn't get stopped. Ethan'd kill him.

# 38

Meanwhile, Andrew Lofton's UPS packages arrived a day earlier than expected. He began assembling and modifying the remote-control boats in the Livingston's garage. Browning had accelerated their mission-ready date since Andrew no longer needed to build the boats from scratch. He reflected how much he loved the heat on his cheek from melting solder, combined with the smokey-metallic stench of hot flux as he customized control circuitry and mounted the long-range antennas on each of the seven boats. He focused on readying the test boat first. No sense building the other six until he achieved a successful prototype.

FBI cameras now hidden around the two properties on Barnes Road recorded everything and wirelessly sent notifications to Letty's computer. She called Sam after having two sorely needed days off. "Hello, Sam."

"Hey! Enjoying your down-time? Any news?" He hungered for an update on the case, but didn't want to sound like he didn't care about her home life, either.

Sounded like she didn't want to talk about personal stuff, anyway. Two minds of a single thought. "Oh, you know, tackling stuff at home that I've neglected for too long, ever since the move over from Boston and up from DC. Cams are up and recording, by the way. They're using Livingston's garage. Lofton's been in there working sixteen-or eighteen-hour days for the last four days. Looks like today, too. A UPS truck dropped off seven large boxes yesterday."

"The hell is he doing?"

"My guess is he's making or building something. Remember, he's a master fabricator. Plus, working long days like this? Another clue that whatever they're scheming is imminent."

"When do we hit 'em with warrants?"

"Malone wants us to wait. He's got a crew on Browning. Bingham has been missing for two days. Browning's Crown Victoria is gone, too. We don't want to alert any state authorities at this point. Rather, we're going to let it play out for now. Malone's theory is Bingham is retrieving something they need for their mission, whatever that might be. We need to know. So, we wait for him to return and surveil them all until we have a better idea of what they're up to."

"I guess that's the right move, but I'm more nervous than ever that whatever is going to happen, it'll be soon. Any major event imminent to warrant their kind of attention?"

Letty said, "If they'll make a statement with explosives, based on Bingham's expertise, it follows they'd want a lot of attention. That makes nearby large cities or large gatherings most likely. Boston or New York? Boston is closest. Plus, the profile for this sort of fanatic? They're often big on symbolism. Reasonable working assumption, for now, anyway. I'll poke around for events or celebrations, incoming or departing cruise ships, anything going on at Logan—"

"These idiots aren't dumb enough to hit a major international airport like Logan, are they? That's a pretty damn hard target." Sam puckered one cheek. "Although most criminals screw enough pooches to make a breeder blush."

That metaphor made Letty blush. "Yes, most criminals are not very smart. Not sure about this Browning, though. He's above average intelligence. We must consider every possibility, Sam. Meanwhile, with surveillance in place and based on what your gut is telling us, Malone has placed the FBI SWAT SOU on standby in case we need a multiple office deployment. Now we hurry up and wait."

"Yeah, I remember that part of military life. Your Special Operations Unit? Big guns. Glad to hear your boss is taking this seriously. I'm impressed. Stay in touch, Letty. And we gotta still be careful out there. Those guys might backtrack for more personalized attention."

"This time I'll be ready." Sam observed that cold and distant expression again. *Scary lady when she's pissed. Have to remember that.*

# 39

Bingham congratulated himself. He was on schedule at the half-way point on his trip back to Portsmouth off Route 79 in Virginia. Called Browning with his status and position.

Browning sounded pleased. "Bring it on home, son."

---

Browning broke out a nautical chart of Boston Harbor. He remained convinced that the shore at the southern tip of Deer Island not only offered convenient access to the harbor by vehicle, but was a good launch point. He chose the second launch point, the north end of Long

Island near Boston Harbor's entrance. Both locations were accessible by road. He researched anchoring and entrance points to the harbor for liquid natural gas tankers—LNGs. They'd enter during daylight hours, which meant they'd anchor somewhere outside the harbor, near its entrance, until daybreak the next day. He'd learned they'd be accompanied by escorts from the Coast Guard, EPO-manned vessels from Long Wharf, and the State Police from the H-4 barracks in Boston. The following morning, the tanker would be cleared to proceed to their wharf after picking up their harbor pilot. Making port was a day-long procedure.

The third point of attack would require a boat. Ethan estimated the George's Island area to be a perfect spot. *But which of us can navigate through the harbor's islands and shoals at night? Maybe a daytime visit first. Find a charter that uses that new satellite-based navigation shit to plot a safe course out to our third launch point.* One charter company advertised they carried the latest Magellan NAV 1000 on one of their boats—a twenty-foot bay boat with a four-stroke outboard. Nice and quiet. *His* launch platform. First, he'd charter the boat with her captain, get the GPS unit programmed. Then he'd be set to dispose of the captain and commandeer his boat.

Browning made some calls and hooked up with such a captain who skippered a GPS-equipped boat in Boston. Told him he wanted to do some night fishing for striped bass. Looked at the calendar and checked the arrival date of the LNG on the harbor's website. Perfect. LNG tanker *Hercules* was to arrive the day before Bunker Hill Day, Friday, June sixteenth. Two weeks from last Monday. She'd moor for the night on the edge of the north branch of the harbor's main entrance channel before proceeding into the harbor the following morning, like other LNG tankers had in the recent past. Ethan asked himself, *What if they planned on an early morning arrival and proceeded non-stop into the harbor with the Boston Pilot aboard en route into Everett Landing? We'd be aiming at a moving target in broad daylight! Not good.*

He needed intel. Browning hatched an idea. He still kept his camo uniform stashed in his footlocker, and still had kept his cane he used to get around when he was healing and learning to use his prosthesis. He'd make a trip to the US Coast Guard station on Boston's Hanover Street in full-dress uniform with his medals on full display. After exchanging pleasantries with the duty officer, he'd ask what they had going on. He was certain upon seeing his uniform and prosthesis they'd be more than happy to engage with an old disabled war dog. As long as he kept it casual and not too interrogatory.

Ethan closed the store early and drove home in his company van to prepare. He noticed the boys had not reinstalled the magnetic signs. Just as well. He'd iron the uniform, polish his left boot, making sure every square inch of his leather gleamed. For tomorrow morning.

---

The FBI noted the suspect's departure the following morning. A surveillance team tailed him.

# 40

Thursday dawned bright with perfect weather for Ethan Browning's trip down to Boston. Drove his van from his house to the shop where he'd had a rental delivered. Left his van in the parking lot. Once in the city, he walked down to 476 Hanover Street and chatted up the guard at the Coast Guard Station's security gate. The guard issued him a visitor's badge without question, only asking for his ID. He gave the young petty officer in dungarees and a chambray shirt his driver's license. Ignored the side arm and stern gaze that turned into a look of admiration once the kid spotted the medals and his missing leg. Ethan also flashed his VA ID card for good measure.

Down on the docks, four *Coasties* labored cleaning

one of the twenty-five-foot SPC-LEs—Special Purpose Craft for Law Enforcement. This was a Rigid-hull Inflatable Boat they called a *RIB* that featured twin two-hundred-horsepower Mercury engines and an M-60 machine gun perched over its permanent mount on the boat's heavy aluminum foredeck. The RIB was a serious piece of shallow-water law enforcement hardware. Ethan hobbled down to that boat on the dock and greeted the men, leaning on his cane with a theatrical flare. They returned the smiles and showed appreciation for this old war dog. One asked, "Why the uniform, sir?"

Browning replied, "I ain't no sir, son. I work for a living, like y'all. I'd appreciate it if you'd address me as Staff Sergeant. The Herald is doing a fluff piece on disabled veterans, and they asked me to show up for that dog and pony show. Respect for my fallen brothers, ya know. Long as I dug this out a moth balls," he motioned to his *costume* with a downward sweep of both arms, "why not pay you boys a visit?"

They saw an old soldier in an army uniform. His name tag read Staff Sergeant Rickman. Ethan Browning wasn't above using the ID of a deceased brother-in-arms. He had grabbed Rickman's name tag and wallet off his corpse after an exit wound had erased his face during the attack at Tan Son Nhut outside of Saigon. The youthful Coasties invited Ethan on board the RIB, offering him some unnecessary help, but he *worked the room*, as they say. Gave him a tour of the small but efficient craft. On the foredeck, Browning pointed toward the M-60 machine gun. "A nasty piece a work, right there. Loved the ole pig. Saved my bacon more 'n once. My back still aches, thinkin' about haulin' that thirty-pound lead-thrower around the jungle. But the damn thing was prone to either jammin' or runnin' away on me." *Yeah, workin' the room.*

A wide-eyed Seaman Apprentice followed Browning and the LT around like an eager puppy. "Huh?"

The sharp Lt. JG (Junior Grade) Connors took pity on the kid. "Alfy, earlier versions of the sixty used to jam a lot. This brand new model doesn't. Plus, the sear used to wear down. That'd result in a runaway gun. Stop pulling the trigger and she'd just keep slinging six-hundred-fifty rounds-per-minute. Pretty scary, I'd imagine."

Browning added, "And she'd keep slinging that river of lead up to twelve-hundred yards out, son. LT, imagine you're holding that sucker and she goes off on ya. Kicks like an ornery and pissed-off mule."

Alfy squealed, "Wow! You *carried* that thing?"

"Sure did. Love that beast. What are you guys getting ready for? A busy SAR weekend out on the harbor?" SAR was shorthand for *Search and Rescue*.

Ethan had already discovered the LNG was now about nine days out. The youthful lieutenant said, "Yeah, SAR's a major part of our daily mission, Staff

Sergeant, but we're gearing up for an escort detail. Takes some prep. The OIC likes us to drill. By the way, what happened to the leg?" He nodded down toward Ethan's prosthetic. Of course, Ethan regaled them with his tale of the Tet offensive, recounting how he and every one of his buddies suffered injuries or lost their lives in the action that took his leg outside of Saigon. Told them he was lucky to survive.

He embellished his combat story with a theatrical lump in his throat and a moment of silence, which they respected. It was obvious he had impressed them. The SA asked about his medals. The LT jumped in. "Alfy, that there is an honest-to-Jesus purple heart. And that one," his index finger came within about three inches of Ethan's chest, "is a Bronze Star with a V for valor. A real decorated combat vet. Right, Staff Sergeant?"

"That's right, son."

The SA said, "Amazing, man."

*Yeah, amazing, alright,* thought Browning. "What kind of escort? Must be important for you to be drilling so far in advance."

The LT again. "Oh, we got an LNG due in here late next week, and we really have to rig up for it. Kind of a big deal for us whenever one of those bad boys makes port."

Browning said, "A tanker? Boy, I'd sure 'nough like to see one a them babies up close. They say they're almost as big as an aircraft carrier. That true? When do you think the best time to see it?"

The lieutenant mentioned they hadn't communicated their arrival time yet, but it appeared they'd encounter a slight delay because of weather. "We heard they battled a tough beam sea. Not a problem though, Staff Sergeant. They'll moor outside the inner harbor in the North Channel until daylight if they arrive late in the day.

"Is there a place I can call to check when it comes in? I'd like to see that monster."

"Uh, yeah, the Boston Harbormaster has a direct line to the tanker *Hercules*. We just gear up and go when we're told."

Ethan chuckled, "Yeah, I remember those days. Get prepped and then wait for the order."

"Hey, Staff Sergeant, here's a card with the harbormaster's number. Call them. Don't want you to miss seeing this baby. It's something, alright."

Ethan accepted the card and said, "Thanks. Nice talking to you boys. Be safe out there." They waved and thanked him for his service and sacrifice. He'd call the harbormaster, courtesy of Lieutenant JG Connors of the Boston Harbor Coast Guard. He'd tell him a bunch of his vet buddies wanted to see the tanker come in. *Yeah, this'll work.* He returned the rental early and received a hefty discount from the rental agency. After all, a disabled veteran in uniform was to be treated better than almost anyone. *Not at all* like when they first returned from Nam.

The agency dropped Browning off at his store. He couldn't wait to shed that damn sham of a uniform and those phony fuckin' medals. Yeah, they were the real deal, but made him sick to wear them. He knew they'd rather have pegged his ass for fragging that stupid kid that got his whole crew killed. But the optics wouldn't allow it. *How fucked up is that?*

---

They'd want a stationary target, even as large as a tanker. She'd be easy enough to hit once underway. But they'd need two precise hits in the same impact point to penetrate first the outer hull, and then the inner hull in the same exact spot. Impossible underway. The exclusion area set up by the authorities as broadcast in a "Notice to Mariners" to all vessels defined a specific area to stay away from. Their target area. And if the Coasties were on the money, that'd be a small area around the tanker outside the harbor in the North Channel.

Ethan'd meet the charter captain at his dock in Hingham, get out a ways, and whack him after he programmed their course to his launch point into the boat's GPS. Then he'd have his boat and the navigational information to guide him to where he'd deploy his two RC boats. The programmed nav info ensured he'd return to his van, where he'd abandon the boat and make his escape. They'd planned for Andrew to pilot *his* two boats from the southeastern shore of Deer Island, targeting the tanker's starboard side. He'd drive his rental car there. Josh was to deploy his pair of boats from Long Island's northeastern shore, also accessible by vehicle. From these locations, they'd target both sides and the bow area of the tanker from their launch sites. Josh's bow angle was a low-percentage shot. At a minimum, his would be a diversion.

They agreed to plan further and drill ad nauseam until it was second nature to the three conspirators. Launch points and sequences, bearings, speed, time, and distances to achieve simultaneous strikes on their target. They'd also drill their escape routes and after-action strategies. Just another mission. But *this* time they'd obey orders from a commander who knew the damn probabilities and operational details. Not only every detailed mission parameter, but the calculated risks involved, and an established objective that held real meaning. They'd still conduct a trial run before mission day. Military precision was the clear rule. Ethan still worried.

# 41

Andrew Lofton neared completion of the trial RC—the remotely controlled prototype boat. On the Livingston's garage phone, "Ethan, please be out here at ten in the morning for a test run."

"I wouldn't miss it, son," Andrew's boss said over the phone, and Andrew convinced himself he heard him smiling.

---

Saturday, June tenth, FBI surveillance assets recorded the call and relayed the info to SAC Malone. "What kind of test are they talking about?"

"No idea, sir. We only know when it will take place."

"We need more intel, damn it!"

---

Ethan met Andrew with their test boat under wraps. They hiked from Livingston's enormous garage next door to the ten-acre pond behind Browning's garage. Andrew said, "See out there? I used your row boat to set up a small obstacle course marked with fluorescent buoys. I'm going two miles down the road and maneuver the boat through the buoys. You watch and I'll be on my bag phone with a portable video feed to pilot the boat. We'll still be able to talk."

"Ok Andrew, call me when you're in position." Ten minutes later, he did.

"Ready for this, boss?"

"Let her rip!" Instead of going straight to the buoys, Andrew showed off the RC's speed and maneuverability with figure eights and sweeping curves. The small boat made little noise, only a high-pitched whine, as it sped toward the buoys and weaved its way through the course with precision. Browning was impressed. "Okay, Andrew. Nice work. C'mon back."

They covered the test boat and Andrew carried it back to the Livingston garage. The other six boats perched obediently in a line on the workbench. They appeared close to completion. "Are these ready to go?"

"Not quite. Still have some soldering and wiring to do, but I'm close. One more long day. Satisfactory, Ethan?"

"Yes. We need time to finalize our course and time to target calculations from our launch sites, and to get that programmed into the controllers. After Bingham returns with the C-4, you'll have one day to stow it into each boat. Then we visit your launch points. That'll give us a two-day window just in case we run into an issue. I'm gonna jot down copies of our schedule so everyone knows what's going to happen and when. No screw-ups!"

"Yessir. Not the way we want history to remember us, for sure, boss."

# 42

Agent Mather met EPO Travis and Captain Larry Jamison at the Springfield FBI field office at nine AM the next day. Letty smiled. "Captain Jamison, so nice to see you again."

Larry looked dapper in his civilian suit and tie. He shook Letty's hand with both of his. "Great to be here with you, Letty. Run into a wall? Every time we get together, you're all banged up! Hangin' around with this guy does that to people."

Sam said to Letty while tossing a good-natured glare at his boss, "He's still a funny guy, ain't he?"

"Sam never mentioned you coming this morning, Captain."

"Well, I hid in the back of his cruiser. It was my

idea and I trust you don't mind my presence here today."

"Nonsense, you saved my butt on the trail predators case out on the AT, Larry, if it's ok to call you that. I am delighted to welcome you. Please join us. I assume Sam caught you up to date?"

"Yes. Sounds like this is about to get messy. And soon."

"Ready to get to work, boys?"

Sam said, "Yup, let's hear what we've got."

"I've arranged a ten AM meeting with my boss SAC Malone to go over everything. AUSA Timothy Riggins will be there as well."

"Well, it must be getting close to showtime if your Assistant US Attorney is here," said Sam.

"Let's go downstairs. We first need to talk with Noah Adams in the lab."

Letty introduced Larry to Noah, who said, "Pleased to meet you, sir. Welcome." They stood in front of a monitor. Noah lit it up with his remote. "Check out the date and time stamps on these surveillance videos taken over the last four days of both garages on Barnes Road outside Portsmouth. The most interesting one is the RC trial.

"What the—?" Sam blurted.

"Sam, it's a three- or four-foot radio-controlled boat modified for long-range control, probably through a portable video feed. Very bleeding-edge. Look at that antenna. I'll bet he's put in a signal booster, too. I'm guessing those new lithium-ion batteries, as well, if I were a betting man. He ran that boat for a good long while."

Letty looked confused. "Noah, what possible use would that have? Gotta be more than a hobbyist."

"Increases its controllable range. See where Lofton leaves with the boat's controller and Browning stays behind? The cameras weren't configured to cover the pond, but Lofton controlled a trial run from a couple miles away. That's per one of our ground units. And that's not even line-of-sight, meaning for the radio frequencies they're likely using even longer range is possible over water where trees and hills aren't in the way. Obviously using cellular data for a video feed. That's brilliant, guys. One of our techs went in last night and arranged cam coverage for that pond behind Browning's garage in case they use it again. I'd speculate they're going to put this boat in the water with some type of explosive device and send it on a suicide mission. I'm also speculating they'll use more than one boat based on the number and size of the boxes delivered a week ago by a UPS truck. What target? We don't have that info."

Sam piped up. "How many boxes were delivered? Safe to assume one box equals one boat?"

"Based on the size of this boat, assuming they're the same size, I'd guess seven boxes equals seven boats. Or maybe six boats and a box of controls or accessories."

Sam asked, "Can we get audio?"

"Can't get near enough to plant a bug inside. We do have the technology to splat a listening device against the wall of the garage or house, and Browning's store won't be a problem. But if they see it, the splat, we're blown."

"What do you think, Letty?"

Letty shrugged. "Let's go upstairs to Malone's office and discuss it with him and the AUSA. We don't want to screw this up on a fourth amendment snafu."

Sam shook the tech's hand. "Thanks, Noah. We'll get back to you on our decision." The two EPOs and Letty marched to the elevator. They buried themselves in silent thought during the ride to the fifth floor. On five, they exited and walked into SAC Malone's outer office. His assistant, Jen said, "You are to go right in. They're waiting for you."

Letty said, "The mood?"

"Not good."

# 43

The trio marched into SAC Malone's office. The new guy wore a fashionable dark blue suit and a white shirt with a blue and silver tie. He approached and introduced himself as AUSA Timothy Riggins. "EPO Sam Travis, I presume, and Agent Mather, of course. You would be....?"

"Captain Lawrence Jamison, Mass EPO."

SAC Malone also walked over to Captain Jamison, offered his hand and said, "I'm Special Agent in Charge Jack Malone. Pleased to meet you in person, Captain. Agent Mather has told me about you and I thank you for your, ah, intercession on the Appalachian Trail case. I've read the after-action report." They exchanged curt nods and knowing smiles. Then, Malone included Sam in his gaze and said, "Both you EPOs have distinguished yourselves." His eyes twinkled, but there was something else, too.

Larry offered a small smile. "Thank you, sir. Agent Mather is one of our favorite FBI agents."

Letty blushed. Malone returned Larry's smile. "Let's sit and go over what we know, what we don't, and what we suspect. Also, what we need to do with Tim navigating us through the legal maze to get these guys off the street."

AUSA Riggins projected his official tone of voice. "I have reviewed the reports submitted by Agent Mather. EPO Travis has a copy. I've also read EPO Travis's reports. There are some issues here, serious ones, that need to be addressed. Officer Travis, did you place a tracking device on a van belonging to Browning Diamond and Coin?"

"Yessir."

"What was the intended purpose of doing that?"

"To monitor the travel of Mr. Browning's vehicle by his associates, and I suppose Mr. Browning himself."

"And where was this done? The physical location?"

"Outside his place of business in Portsmouth, New Hampshire."

"Please tell me if you have police authority in the State of New Hampshire."

"Uh, no, sir, I do not."

"So, you placed an electronic monitoring device in a state where you had no authority implied or granted for police investigations. In New Hampshire." Not a question.

"Other than to interview Mr. Browning along with Agent Mather. We investigated the murders of two Massachusetts residents, as well as the theft of a considerable quantity of valuable Revolutionary War era coins."

"So, you were coat-tailing her multi-state police authority. Is that correct?"

"Where are you going with this, Mr. Riggins?"

Larry spoke up. "He's going to the Fourth Amendment of the US Constitution, Sam."

"Correct, Captain Jamison. EPO Travis, you lacked authorization to conduct surveillance or to place surveillance equipment. I know you must be aware of the 'fruits of the poisonous tree doctrine,' are you not?"

"Yessir."

"Well, I'm here to inform you that the charges against Messrs. Lofton and Bingham will go nowhere. That includes breaking and entering, assault and battery on a federal agent, as well as conspiracy. That is the fruit of the poisonous tree you planted, Officer. I'll never win that in a courtroom in a hundred years. Even in Massachusetts, General Law Chapter 272 section 99 explicitly forbids such activity. The

Commonwealth v. Hyde case has withstood several challenges without success for repeal or modification. Without getting into those challenges, from a legal perspective, you screwed up, Officer Travis."

AUSA Higgins continued. "*Federal* law leans towards a more progressive stance, with federal judges grounding their Fourth Amendment decisions on 18 U.S.C. section 2510-2520. You could be held liable under the US federal law, since you acted as a private citizen in that state in the eyes of the law. There is a supremacy exemption for federal officials or deputies. The federal government is more lenient with its interpretation under Hyde, but federal officials have said states may promulgate stricter laws than the federal government. Therefore, had Agent Mather placed that device on the motor vehicle, we'd have been fine. But official records, her report, and yours, cannot be altered or discarded. We can't put that genie back in the bottle.

"New Hampshire levies an identical statute as Massachusetts—also a 'two-party' permission state. You've committed a Class B felony under New Hampshire state law, Officer Travis. I am saddened to inform you that even though no charges will be filed against you, we cannot use any of the intelligence obtained from that device. That's despite it being a Bureau device. This affects Agent Mather's case in that the discovery of the perpetrators' whereabouts, including everything leading up to the assault and B & E, goes nowhere. My office will file no charges in this case, lacking further probative evidence."

Sam and Letty sat stunned speechless. Neither ever considered that. A mistake, an oversight, but a fact. They knew Riggins was right. Sam's impulsive move, though well-intentioned, was illegal as hell. *Shit.*

"But there is good news, too. Your case against Browning and his crew is still viable since search and seizure laws are much less restrictive at the federal level. Placing federal devices *by federal officers* on the Livingston and Browning properties is legal and evidence received as a result is prosecutable under federal law." SAC Malone sat in his desk chair, listening and watching their reactions. Higgins continued. "So my suggestions are that you continue to pursue leads, continue to surveil the two properties or a third if you choose to monitor Mr. Browning's place of business. But that, too, must be done with a warrant and only by the FBI.

"There is one exception. That is to appoint you a Special Federal Police Officer or a Deputy to the US Marshal Service. You may carry a firearm, perform warrantless arrests, but not carry out investigations without an experienced US Marshal, FBI, or other federal law enforcement officers or agents present. There have been cases where US Attorneys appoint a non-federal officer as a deputy on a case-by-case basis as a member of a joint task force involving multi-state jurisdictions. I will consult with my boss, the US Attorney, to see if this case will qualify you for such an appointment if you wish."

"What are the chances of that happening?" Travis asked this with a glimmer of hope in continuing to work this case across state lines.

"Quite good, given your recent history in working with the FBI on the Appalachian Trail serial killer case and their subsequent convictions based on your and Captain Jamison's testimony. You received the Meritorious Service Medal, the highest the FBI issues. My instinct, therefore, is to make that recommendation, setting aside this honest mistake. I will pursue that, coordinating through SAC Malone and Agent Mather. You will be advised as to that determination within the week. I understand time is of the essence, and we certainly want a similar outcome to the AT case. Are you good with that, EPO Travis?"

"Yessir. I appreciate the opportunity to solve the murders and to prevent a terrorist attack on our soil in whatever state."

"Very well. I will leave you to SAC Malone's guidance. He will advise me of this case's development. I will step in when warrants need to be drawn up and for any prosecutorial issues. I will take my leave now and wish you the best of luck." He winked at the officers on his way out and muttered under his breath, "Now go get these bastards."

The door closed. Utter silence consumed the room. But no proverbial pin dropped.

Malone startled the others with two emphatic but related questions. "So where are we? And what's the plan?"

# 44

Josh Bingham was a bit ahead of schedule. The metal suitcase sat by his nightstand. His Glock model 21, a forty-five-caliber man-stopper, rested within easy reach. As soon as he woke up, he called Ethan. "Boss, my eyes got real heavy last night, so I stopped for a few hours of shut-eye. I'm in Massachusetts and will be in Portsmouth in about an hour. "Where do you want me to bring the suitcase?"

"Good job and early by two hours, son. Meet me at the Livingston garage. I'll brief you on our current status."

"Okay, see you there, sir." After he hung up, he indulged in a deep and noisy sigh. "No rest for the wicked."

Ethan and Josh met at the garage mid-morning on Monday, June twelfth. Browning punched in the alarm code to disarm it. They entered the building together where Andrew was hard at work with his soldering gun. Country music blared. Ethan and Josh surveyed the seven RC boats, all blacked out with flat spray paint except for the test boat, sporting a gangly four-foot antenna, maybe even longer. Empty cardboard boxes surrounded Andrew. The entire area was in disarray. A huge workbench that took up the entire back length of the garage was covered not only by the boats, but an impressive array of Andrew's tools.

"Hey, guys." Their master fabricator's verged on giddiness.

Ethan said, "Turn off that shit-kickin' music and let's talk about our schedule. First, let's check the goods." Josh nodded. He slung the metal case up onto the workbench after Andrew cleared a space, unlocked and swung open the lid of his large suitcase stuffed full of C-4 bricks in their individual packets. They all stared at the explosives momentarily. Andrew whistled and smiled at his two fellow Patriot Guardsmen. Then he said, "I could use a hand cutting this stuff up to fit into the boats under their tie-downs."

Ethan waved him off. "In a minute. Let's review. Speak up if something doesn't sound right. The official Notice to Mariners is out. The *Hercules* will anchor late this coming Friday, the sixteenth in Boston's North Channel, right where we thought she'd be. Today is Monday and today we finish prepping, including testing all electronics and any last-minute instructions by Josh for our dress rehearsal tomorrow on my pond next door. On Wednesday, we rent vehicles, two vans and one pickup truck. We'll retrieve our rentals from Hertz using false IDs and stolen credit cards at Logan Airport. We'll leave my van in the short-term parking lot there and visit your two launch points on the harbor.

"Josh, per our plan, you'll be on the northernmost tip of Long Island. Andrew, you'll be on the southernmost tip of Deer Island. We drive to recon both locations. We then hustle back here, load up the rentals with all mission supplies, two vehicles in my garage and one in here. Josh, you're with me at my garage; Andrew, you clean and sanitize this garage after we're all loaded up. On Friday morning, we double-check every boat, controller, and the all batteries. Bring spares. We get to our positions by sunset. That's 2020 hours, forty minutes before zero hour at 2100 hours. I'll be leaving the dock in Weymouth well before sunset aboard a night fishing charter for striped bass. I'll take out the skipper and stow his body in the boat's cuddy cabin. Then I'll use his GPS to get to my launch point a mile east of the anchored tanker."

Andrew wrinkled his forehead and scratched his chin. "That's cuttin' it kinda close, ain't it, boss? On site only forty minutes before go-time?"

"Yes, timing is critical. But we sure don't want to sit too long with our "toys" at our launch points too much before sunset. Raises risk of exposure. After our walkthrough of the launch points on Wednesday, we'll know with precision where to go and how long it'll take to get there. We'll adjust our timing as necessary, but right now, this is the plan, okay?" They both nodded. "After the attack, we lay low for the night at the Boston Hyatt. I've made reservations for two rooms under a false name and credit card.

On Saturday morning, with heavy commuter traffic as a screen, we return the rentals and make our way back to a safe house. I'll tell you where that is at that time. I'm sure there'll be cops here at my house, so we won't be anywhere near here. I've also rented another car after we sanitize the mission rentals and leave. Worked on this guy's campaign and he owes me. So I'll lean on him and it won't be a problem. Because you know they're gonna come looking for us. But they won't find us or anything here.

"I've printed up this briefing summary on assignments and timeline for each of you as well as for myself. Here are your copies." He'd laid out the timeline in bullet points of the entire plan. As he handed these cards out, however, he delivered a stern warning accompanied by eye contact with each of his soldiers. "Protect these cards like your lives depend on them, because they do." They both nodded.

"Anyone have questions about any of this? Concerns? What-ifs?"

Josh said, "What if the weather is too rough?"

"We'll have a good idea of Friday's weather by Wednesday. If we need to delay, we'll do what we have to do. Rendezvous at the Hyatt after. If they get a search warrant for my place they'll never suspect the Livingston's. By then, they won't find anything here, either. Anything else?

Andrew asked, "what if we meet up with law enforcement before launching?"

"There's no law against running an RC boat is there?"

"Remember, I eliminated lighting on the boats so that's potentially problematic. And if they inspect the boats to see what's inside, we're cooked."

"Good point, Andrew. Alter the boat so they *can't* see inside them. Seal the hulls. But I agree, we must avoid contact with law enforcement. Remember, if you're taken into custody, you must have already destroyed these cards. Invoke your right to remain silent. I've got a law firm on standby. Your card also lists that phone number. *But you say nothing.* Don't make any deals or I'll get to you even if you're in prison. You do not say a single word. That's why I'm paying the law firm a good chunk of dough to protect each of us. Got it?"

They both replied, "Yessir."

"Andrew, what concern do you have about the

blast and wake from the first explosion affecting the second boat?"

"I think the shock wave will disperse enough for these boats to survive that if they're thirty seconds behind the first boat. They're self-righting, so even if a wave rolls 'em over, their waterproofing and ballast will keep them going."

"You think? Or know?"

"Boss, I've never used this shit on the water in an RC boat before. I'm giving you my best guess."

As the explosives guy, Josh piped up. "Almost five pounds of C-4 will create a hell of a first wave, but after ignition, I'm thinking it will subside quickly. The tricky part is getting the second boat into the hole where the first boat strikes. If we miss, we'll just put two holes in the outer hull without penetrating the inner hull, the tank membrane, and no BOOM."

"Andrew, get going on sealing the hulls. Use Josh for help if you need him. I have encrypted portable radios for each of us. Boys, I know you both love to lug those fancy new Nokia mobile phones around, but *do not use them or our pagers*. Not taking a chance on technology pinning this on any of us. After our boats have done their jobs, we meet at the Hyatt. Some roads will get blocked soon after our fireworks display, so speed will be of the essence. Today, we'll stash my antiques, art, drawers of valuable coins, everything of great value I've obtained over the years in a safe location. We'll transport everything in the big box truck parked outside."

Josh's eyes widened. "Boss, that's a lot of stuff."

"Yeah, but the proceeds will fund us until our next mission."

Andrew asked, "Where's that, boss?"

"You'll find out later. Let's get this stuff loaded and be careful handling it. There are cardboard cartons with tape and labels for the smaller items. Unless there are any further delays, the tanker is scheduled to dock on the seventeenth, this Saturday, a half-day late because of weather. The Coast Guard guys told me they hit some rough seas and had to tack, causing the delay. Arrives in Boston Harbor sometime on Friday. That's why they're anchoring at the entrance to the North Channel to await daylight before proceeding to the terminal in Everett. That's our window of opportunity, while they're still hanging on the hook in the North Channel anchorage."

# 45

They sat in SAC Jack Malone's small but opulent office in thoughtful silence. Travis spoke. "Damn, it never occurred to me. I apologize to everyone for my error."

Letty said, "I was there, and that never occurred to me, either. I'm accustomed to agents with nationwide authority and that got by me as well. So the blame doesn't fall on just you, Sam."

Malone said, "it's time we move on and let that lesson be one we never revisit. What are your thoughts, Captain?"

Larry responded, "We need to reassess what we know and what we suspect. But most important, how do we get enough probable cause to get into both garages?"

Letty rubbed her neck. "Our video surveillance revealed that Andrew Lofton, an expert fabricator and jack of all trades, is spending a great deal of time in the Livingston garage. Especially after a UPS delivery of seven large boxes to that garage on the eighth. What's he building or making? A bomb or bombs? Any reported thefts nationwide at armories or producers of explosives?"

"Good questions, Agent Mather," Malone pointed his right index finger at her in acknowledgment. "I'll assign a team to make inquiries."

Travis asked Letty's boss, "Sir, how do we find out exactly what Browning, Lofton or Bingham purchased and had delivered? That might establish what they intend to do."

Malone pondered that. Captain Jamison said, "What do we need to interview the UPS driver about his delivery: size, weight, quantity, or outside markings of the contents? Also, can we trace their credit cards for purchases and amounts?"

"Good angles, Captain. I worry about timing, though. My fear is that some clock is ticking and we need to move faster than the time it takes to trace credit cards."

As he finished voicing his fear, Jamison looked at Malone. "Sir, any contacts with the security department at UPS? What say we interview the driver without raising flags?"

Travis said, "What if his answers give us probable

cause? Then he'd be a witness in a criminal case. If found not guilty then, will UPS be on the hook as a co-respondent in a civil liability case?"

Letty said, "Good thought. But that's a lead we must follow and SAC Malone's approach to *requesting* an interview instead of waiting for a warrant to *demand* one saves us time."

Malone said, "Not that difficult to bring the driver in for a simple Q and A. Downplay it with security, so nothing falls back on them. They'd be reluctant to allow it if they get a whiff of liability in a civil matter. I'll put it in writing if necessary—no liability."

Everyone agreed. Malone picked up the phone and asked his assistant to get head of security at UPS Corp. on the line. Less than a minute passed. "Sir, Mr. Philip Wagner, head of UPS security, is on the line for you."

"Thank you, Jen." *Click.* "Mr. Wagner, thank you for taking the time. I need your help regarding an important case we're working on."

"Always willing to help the FBI if I'm able, sir. How can I be of assistance?"

"We'd like to interview a driver of yours who delivered some packages in the Barnes Road area of Portsmouth, New Hampshire."

They heard some paper shuffling and a few keys clacking on Malone's speakerphone. Then, "There are several drivers that cover that area. Can you be more specific, Agent Malone?"

"Yes, the delivery took place on the morning of

June eighth to..." He looked to Letty for the address. She grabbed a notepad from her rear pocket, flipped through a couple pages, and said, "276 Barnes Road, rural Portsmouth, New Hampshire." Malone then confirmed that with Wagner, who said, "Give me a moment to contact the warehouse supervisor and make an inquiry. May I ask the reason you're requesting this interview? Does my company have any liability in this matter?"

Malone broadcast his most confident voice, "The purpose of the inquiry must be confidential at this time, but I see no liability on your part here. We are looking into the size, weight and an outside description of the boxes' contents delivered to that address."

"If this case of yours becomes a criminal case, will my driver be a witness in a trial?"

"I can't rule that out until we know more. But I will assure you that UPS has no liability for delivering a legitimate order to a customer."

"Considering this, I will have to escalate this to a district manager and one of our attorneys to insure UPS is protected."

"I understand your dilemma here, Mr. Wagner, but this issue is far too urgent. I can bring him or her in for questioning without permission, but we prefer to do it with your cooperation and without fanfare. With or without your help, we must interview your employee, and quickly. I'm sure you'd want to avoid four FBI cars pulling up to your corporate headquarters facility, especially if someone leaked that, ah, *visit*, to the press."

Travis whispered to Jamison and Mather, "Now, that's polite muscle, pure and simple."

Wagner paused. Then, "Okay, Agent Malone, well played. I'll find out who was on that delivery. Where and when do you want to interview that driver?"

"We have a satellite office in Portsmouth. Call this number when you know the driver's name and I'll send up two agents for the interview."

"I'll call within the hour."

"Thank you for your cooperation, sir. The FBI will make note of that." Malone hung up and said, "Okay, Travis and Mather, you head to Portsmouth straightaway and meet this guy. Pump him hard. Officer Travis, you will be serving as a Special Federal Police Officer as of this afternoon. I had already contacted the US Attorney, and he granted my request to appoint you as such."

"Thank you, sir." He meant it. He and Letty bolted for the door en route to the Portsmouth FBI station, both smiling at Malone's strong-arm tactics.

---

"Captain Jamison, please stay for a few moments. I have a couple of questions for you." Jamison nodded.

Alone in the room together, Malone and Jamison, two savvy veteran supervisors, contemplated their next moves. Malone said, "EPO Travis is an exceptional officer setting aside that jurisdictional incident. I also note the chemistry between Mather and him. I was reluctant to assign any other agent to partner with EPO Travis because there was little time to have a new agent briefed and ready. Besides, I think she enjoys the field work and gives her a break from her analytical duties."

Larry didn't even wait a beat. "I agree. I think we both have placed a great deal of trust in them for good reason. Now, what can I do to help?"

"This looks to be an emerging waterborne threat we're dealing with here, and likely in Boston. You're more familiar with that sort of operation than I. Use your contacts with the Coast Guard, Mass State Police and your own department about beefing up patrols in and around the harbor, just in case. Our agents don't have webbed feet, so to speak, and the agencies I mentioned seem best-suited to support this case. Agree?"

"Yes. If we're dealing with a domestic terrorist threat, as we suspect, and it will be on the water, this will only enhance our ability to thwart these asshol—, these suspects."

"Thank you for coming in, Captain, and I am available to you twenty-four-seven. Here are my confidential contact numbers."

"Here are mine, Agent Malone. Pleasure to meet you and I welcome the opportunity to contribute." They shook hands as they exchanged cards.

Meeting adjourned.

# 46

Letty and Sam beat feet up Route 93 to Portsmouth. They arrived at the FBI station, passed through security, where the desk officer handed Travis a manilla envelope. "Thanks, what's in it?"

He was told, "Open it in the office on the second floor, room 215, your interview room." They entered 215 and almost bumped into the large conference table that dominated the small space. An American flag hung from a floor stand in the room's corner near a set of small high windows. Two large windows overlooked the parking lot. Framed and glassed portraits of the President of the United States and Director of the FBI appeared too large for the wall on which they hung, outboard of the windows, near the room's corners. Sam opened the envelope and extracted credentials that identified him as a Special Federal Police Officer and a badge that said so. "Huh. Never thought I'd ever, *ever* be a *feeb*."

Letty laughed. "Don't worry, Sam, it isn't permanent. Turning you loose on an unsuspecting nation? That is one frightening proposition."

He laughed at how she turned his insult into one of her own. Good humor. "What do we do now? Sit and wait until we get a phone call?"

"Yeah, pretty much. The SAC has this and will call us. If I know Malone, it won't be long."

Two hours later, the conference room phone rang. Jen, Malone's assistant, said, "Agent Mather, SAC Malone says that a Mr. Joseph Lewiston will arrive at your location in about thirty minutes."

"Thanks, Jen."

Twenty minutes later, the security officer called to let them know that one Joseph Lewiston awaited an escort. Letty met the UPS driver in the lobby where he was issued a visitor's badge. Introduced herself with a smile and a firm handshake. Kept it friendly, but official. Lewiston was a medium height and weight thirty-something, still wearing his UPS shirt. Despite Letty's amiable demeanor, he mumbled, "Uh, I'm not in any trouble, am I? Never talked to an FBI agent before."

"No, sir. We wish to ask you a few questions regarding a delivery." They rode the elevator and joined Travis in the conference room with the too-big table. Letty introduced Sam as *another federal officer*. Mr. Lewiston appeared intimidated and nervous as hell.

"Please have a seat." Letty kicked off the interview. "Mr. Lewiston, do you recall a delivery you made to 276 Barnes Road outside Portsmouth on June eighth?"

"Uh, that is my route." He paused. Then, his eyes widened. "Oh, yeah, the guy wanted the boxes delivered to the garage, not the house. I remember because it was a two-day air delivery. Had to have it there by ten AM that day. That's mighty spendy shipping right there."

"Are you able to describe that man?"

"Sure. Kind of a weirdo. Real geeky type, but also sorta looked like a soldier gone a little soft. About six feet, stocky, sandy short-cropped hair, didn't say much. He said, 'Put them down by bay three.' So, I unloaded them there. He signed for them, and I left. Didn't have any problem with him or the delivery."

"Did you see any markings on the boxes that you delivered that might have described their contents?" asked Travis.

"Hmm, I think there was a picture of a boat on each carton with the manufacturer's name on it. I can't recall which one, though."

Letty asked, "Can you describe the boat picture? And how large were the boxes?

"Had to be radio-controlled boats. Like hobbyists operate, ya know? Seen quite a few of them lately. But this was higher-end stuff, judging by the size and weight."

Both Letty and Sam glanced at one another. "About how many would you guess?" asks Travis.

"There were seven. It was on the signature slip."

Sam perked up. "We need a copy or the original of that slip."

"The office has the original."

"Who do we contact for that, Mr. Lewiston?"

"Butch McCall is the supervisor. He'd have it."

This was a huge clue *and* evidence that confirmed their working assumption. Sam continued. "Anything else or unusual about the man who signed for the delivery, Mr. Lewiston?"

"Uh, no, pretty routine. Although he was edgy, in a hurry. When I offered to move the boxes inside for him, he snapped at me, like something was a big secret in there. He was real careful not to open the garage door while I was there. Sorta hustled me off. I found it strange that all the windows on the overhead garage doors were blacked out. The boxes weren't all that heavy, but I remember each box was about four feet long and about eighteen inches deep and wide."

Travis asked Letty, "Anything else?"

"Nope, we have what we need."

Letty said to Lewiston, "Thank you for your cooperation, sir, and for your promptness in getting here."

"What's this about, anyway?" asks Lewiston.

"Just a routine inquiry at this point. I will see you out and thank you again."

Sam asked one more question. "Sir, you said you see more of these RC boats on your deliveries. Have you ever delivered that number to one location?"

"Nope."

"Okay, then, thanks, Mr. Lewiston."

Letty escorted him from the building. By the time she got back upstairs, Sam was already on the phone. "Yessir, we'll pick that up within the hour. Thank you so much for your cooperation."

"You're already on that bill of lading?"

"Let's go get it. I think with that, we just might have enough circumstantial evidence for a warrant." Sam looked proud of himself at the first use of his *federal officer* title. Admitted to himself it felt good. They drove to the local UPS warehouse to meet McCall, the guy with the original copy of the bill of lading signed for by Lofton.

Letty looked more worried than ever. "You sense we're looking for a bomb on a short fuse with a fast burn?"

"Yeah, these guys aren't only edgy, they're on a short timeline. Means we're running out of time here."

Letty pressed harder on the gas pedal. Her cruiser accelerated.

# 47

The investigation accelerated to where they risked losing control of it. SAC Malone coordinated with the IRS on Browning's finances, both private and business, on search and arrest warrants with AUSA Riggins, and he increased the number of agents assigned to the case. Captain Jamison focused on boat patrols in Boston Harbor with several agencies, including local and state police, the Coast Guard, and his own marine patrols. Agent Mather and EPO (now SFPO) Travis tracked down RC boat details, capabilities, and modifications. Every local, state, and federal agency was now on full alert for a potential domestic terrorist attack on our around the harbor. Location, date, time, and target or targets remained open questions. But Malone ensured continuous surveillance of the three suspects.

---

Andrew and Josh met Ethan in his garage. They had moved the boats and controllers to be close to the pond for their test run. Only three days remained before the LNG tanker *Hercules* was to anchor in the North Channel entrance to Boston Harbor to await daylight. She'd then make her way to Everett Landing, according to the latest Notice to Mariners. So, they began their final training on running the RCs. Andrew had completed the RC boats' course, time, speed, and distance programming for this test, as well as each boat's final configuration, with one exception. They carried lead ballast for this test, not C-4.

The weather had turned cloudy and threatened rain. Ethan surveyed the six boats resting on cradles fabricated by Andrew in the grass on the pond's shore. He envisioned he was surveying a school of ravenous sharks about to stalk their prey. He'd read somewhere that they also called them a *frenzy* or *a shiver* of sharks. Ethan liked that... a *shiver of sharks*.

---

It was Tuesday, the thirteenth. The previous day, Andrew had rowed out to the middle of the sizable lake behind the boss's garage to buoy a flag. That represented their target for this dress rehearsal. He had also placed three flags at various points on the lake's shoreline. He grinned at his own confidence over his control of these boats. With both pre-programming capabilities *and* manual override, including a concurrent video feed from each boat to each controller, the biggest variable was the person at the controls. Hence, the importance of this orientation, even though controlling the boats now was pretty much idiot-proof.

Each boat was bulky. At almost forty inches in overall length, a beam of just fourteen inches, yielded a sleek LBR, or Length-to-Beam Ratio, of less than 3:1. He had purchased boats with racy hulls that presented a minimal wetted surface for a reasonable balance between speed and stability, even with a cargo of almost five pounds of explosive strapped inside each hull for the mission. But those antennas were now damn long at sixty-three inches. Had to be. He'd ensured they were detachable with a twist-on fitting and flexible enough for transport, even in smaller vehicles. Those antennas lay on each boat's deck and attacked with tape for transport.

Ethan asked, "So, we're set except for the explosives, right?"

"Yeah, boss. Got too much time and energy in these babies to accidentally blow 'em up out here." Andrew chuckled with his omnipresent cigarette hanging out of the corner of his mouth. Some smoke found its way into his left eye. He squinted as he looked across his nose at his boss and commanding officer with a crooked smile and a loud but wet chuckle-slash-snort. The geeky smoker's laugh induced a fit of coughing. *Filthy habit. I gotta give it up. Some day.* "So, for today's test, I've programmed the controllers to guide the boats to the target, that yellow flag." He pointed toward the center of the pond that was more of a small lake than a large pond. The flag was a hundred yards northwest of their position.

Josh and Ethan stood almost shoulder-to-shoulder. Josh's brow furrowed at the daunting prospect of controlling two boats, each to such a small target that was so small. "So, what exactly do each of us need to do here, Andrew? Seems impossible, especially at night over long distances."

Andrew saw the doubt in both their eyes. "Not to worry. Most of the attack is automated. You won't need to do a damn thing. But in case something goes wrong, and we know happens in combat, I'll show you what to do. But that's only a backup. So, Ethan, Josh and I will each launch our two boats from our launch points on Friday night, as you've identified for us. You will launch your two boats from precise coordinates aboard a small craft one-and-a-half nautical miles due east of the tanker's anchorage. Josh, you'll launch from the northeast end of Long Island one-point-five miles southwest of the tanker. I'll launch from the southern tip of Deer Island one mile due west of the target. We'll hit it from three sides with two impacts each.

"The first strike will breach the outer hull. Thirty seconds later, each of our second boats will strike the ship in the same location to breach the inner hull, which is also the midship tanks' membranes. That will allow exposure of the liquid gas to hit the atmosphere, and the heat from the igniting C-4 in our second volley will do the trick. That explosion will drive secondary explosions in other tanks farther forward and aft of our broadside impact points."

Ethan's wrinkled forehead broadcast both admiration and concern. His eyes twinkled as he bounced a fisted hand on the part of his right leg that had not been blown off due to some politician's whim and ill-equipped leadership. "And that tanker's wretched carcass in the birthplace of America's original revolution will forever serve as a reminder of *our* Bunker Hill Day 1989. We attack in darkness before America awakens to a new day. This will be the useless government's darkness before *our* dawn. So what will we achieve with today's test, Andrew?"

"Right on, Ethan. Four things, sir. First, Josh and I will hike around the lake with a boat under each arm. That will demonstrate we'll be able to hoss this gear to our real launch points from our vehicles. Second, we practice with the controllers to initiate the pre-programmed navigation sequence. We'll launch at different times so our boats reach the target at the same instant. Instead of exploding for this test, the program will simply stop our boats at the target—the yellow flag out there." He nodded off to his left, toward the center of the large pond. "We'll then use the controllers to retrieve them after today's test. Today, the boats will travel at half of mission speed since this lake is smaller than the harbor. Third, we'll practice launching our second volley *precisely* thirty seconds after the first. And our last objective for today, we test my programming on this trial course. If all goes well, I'll drop the new code, the mission code, into each controller and replace the ballast with C-4 on each boat tonight, and we'll be good to go for Friday night's mission."

"Okay, Andrew. Show Josh and me what we need to practice." Browning appeared... giddy, which was uncustomary. Like this was a dream coming true.

Andrew spent the next ten minutes explaining how to operate each controller. They agreed it seemed straightforward. Then, each man would trundle to their respective launch points with a heavy boat under each arm along with two controllers and a walkie-talkie attached to their equipment belts with carabiners. The blacked-out boats and controllers were each labeled: A1 and A2 for Andrew's boats, J1 and J2 for Josh's, E1 and E2 for Ethan's. Andrew explained the importance of launching them in the correct order from their respective launch points at the correct time.

Before Andrew and Josh began their hike to distant points a third of the way around the lake in opposite directions and marked with red flags, Andrew offered to help Ethan with his boats, given he was a gimp. But Ethan pushed him away. "Gonna have to do this for myself Friday. I got this."

"Okay, boss. Guys, when we reach our flags, we'll walkie each other and I'll coordinate our launch times. Tomorrow night, though, we will simply launch each of our boats at a precise time unique to your launch points and distance from target. No communication will be necessary." Andrew looked at Josh. "Ready to hike to your launch point, big guy?"

"Yup, let's do this." Josh trudged off to his right carrying close to seventy-pounds of equipment. Andrew took off in the opposite direction. Took them all of fifteen minutes over irregular ground to arrive at the points marked by red flags on the shore. Ethan walked only thirty feet to his designated flag on the muddy water's edge behind his garage. He'd only be hauling his boats to the charter boat in a large backpack Andrew had cobbled together for Ethan's boats and controllers.

Time to see if they'd be making history in less than seventy-two hours, or if they'd merely make a mess today.

# 48

The three men arrived at their designated test launch points at three points around Ethan Browning's pond. Andrew got on his walkie. "E boat pilot, copy?" Ethan responded with a double-click of his PTT (push-to-talk) button. "J boat pilot copy?" Josh responded in the same fashion. Andrew said, "Okay, standby for launch of volley one. Ready?"

"E ready."

"J ready."

Since Andrew's launch point would be closest to the target on Friday night, he'd launch first. So, to simulate that, he'd do so today as well, but only by a few seconds. He launched his first boat. Then said into the walkie, "E and J, launch your number one boats... now." Twenty seconds later, Andrew launched A2. And thirty seconds after he'd directed Ethan and Josh to launch their #1 boats, he said into the walkie, "E and J, launch your #2 volley... now."

They watched as six boats in two volleys converged on the flag in the center of the lake at half of mission speed. They ran true. The first three boats arrived at the flag at the same moment and slowed to a stop, per Andrew's automation. They bumped into one another. Thirty seconds later, three more boats from the same three directions arrived at the target and drifted to a stop with a light bump of hulls. Andrew noted his arrived ahead of the other two by at least two seconds. Andrew clicked the *PTT* button on his walkie and said, "Okay guys, debrief in fifteen mikes behind the garage. Retrieve your boats." They used their respective controllers to pilot their boats back to Ethan's launch point instead of carrying them. Useful practice time on the controllers, too.

Once they reconvened behind Ethan's garage and retrieved their boats, Andrew said, "Okay, excellent test. I noticed my second boat beat both of yours to the target. Look, guys, you gotta have your boats *underway* at the exact appointed time on Friday night if we want them to reach the target at the same time."

It looked like Josh was about to belly-ache when Ethan said, "You're absolutely right, Andrew. We'll get it right Friday night. Excellent results." *Ethan sounds giddy again*, thought Andrew.

. . .

They met at Browning's shop the following morning and headed to Logan Airport in Boston to pick up their rental vehicles. They'd leave Ethan's van in short-term parking. From there, they caravanned to Long Island in Quincy, Mass. A brisk fifteen-knot wind scudded the low overcast sky toward the southwest. They reached the tip of the island and found a footpath that led to its boulder-strewn shoreline. Verified a clear sight line to the target area—they spotted through binoculars the green lighted bell buoy marking the north channel a mile-and-a-half distant. Few people milled around and were not likely to be out here after dark. The three Patriot Guardsmen grinned at each other over their selection of this launch site. This was where Josh'd wait for the appointed launch time of his pair of "toy" boats on Friday night—day after tomorrow.

They then drove the long way around Boston proper, into Winthrop, and out onto Deer Island. A lot more commercial and residential buildings out here, but the shoreline was muddy and would challenge a hiker to get to the water's edge through the mud flats. Great for clamming, but not for walking. Browning said, "Andrew, better bring your waders to get your boats out beyond the muck. What will the tide be at launch time?

"Slack turning to ebb—that's high and early outgoing, boss. It'll be better Friday night. Yeah, chest waders are still a must. Just in case."

Returning to their rentals, now confident these vehicles were capable of delivering them to their launch points, they headed toward the yacht club in Hull. Pulled into the parking lot. They spotted some fences. "Supply cutters for me Friday, just in case," Browning said to Bingham.

"Roger that, boss."

They proceeded to the docks and looked over the array of boats. Spotted their objective, a well-equipped fishing charter named *Codfather* on its transom. No one aboard.

Josh said, "Jeez, boss, that's a nice twenty-four-foot center-console with a cuddy cabin. A two-hundred-fifty horsepower Yamaha on its stern, radar, GPS, VHF marine radio, and well equipped with fishing tackle. Yeah, baby. Some day...."

Satisfied, they secured for the day and returned to Portsmouth. Parked their rentals in the alley behind the shop. Once inside, Browning said, "So, we're set for the mission Friday night. See you both tomorrow for loading up the box truck with my goods from the shop, say 0900 hours?" said Browning.

"Hell, yeah."

"Hoorah."

# 49

The radioman of the LNG tanker *Hercules* had reported their weather delay to the Boston Harbormaster via a marine frequency band on their single-sideband radio. He advised they'd anchor on the south side of the North Channel as planned. ETA 1900 hours (7:00 PM), Friday. Once within range, he updated the Harbormaster via the ship's shorter-range VHF marine radio. "Request Coast Guard and police escorts in place at least one hour before arrival to clear recreational vessels and commercial traffic. Will get underway at 0700 on Saturday en route to Everett berth. Also request harbor pilot on board at 0630 Saturday to guide us in. Thank you, sir."

Once the *Hercules* advised her intended anchoring

coordinates, the Harbormaster granted approval. Pete Segwith, a long-time captain of countless vessels from small craft to commuter boats to ships, including freighters and tankers, had served as Boston's harbormaster for eighteen years. Still, every time one of these mammoth tankers made port, he knew from experience he'd not sleep well, if at all, this weekend. The city paid him to worry.

---

Ethan Browning listened to his pre-programmed portable police scanner in his store's office. This custom rig received all short-range marine traffic conversations—public and private—between the LNG tanker *Hercules* and the Harbormaster. Lofton had ordered custom crystals (not legal) and installed them in this radio. Ethan also monitored conversations between the ship's bridge and the harbor pilot's base to arrange departing their anchorage on Saturday morning. This verified the Patriot Guardsmen *must* strike Friday night. But most important, he'd also be able to monitor the exclusion zone patrols on exclusive law enforcement frequencies. This included the US Coast Guard, EPO patrols, MSP's marine patrols, and BPD's marine patrol. They were charged with keeping civilian craft a mile or more from the tanker in every direction.

Ethan felt empowered. Confident.

## 50

Ethan placed a sign on his store's front door: *Closed For Remodeling To Serve You Better.* Browning had planned to meet Captain Jesse Pelligrini and his vessel, the *Codfather*, at the Hull Yacht Club at 1800 hours (6:00 PM) Friday for his "nocturnal fishing trip." But tonight, he'd tell the captain where he wished to go fishing.

The NOAA weather service advised fair weather and light north-northeast winds at five to ten knots through the weekend, resulting in a light chop on the harbor. Perfect. Surface chop created sufficient radar "noise" to further obscure their boats from detection. A full moon on Friday. Not ideal, but workable.

It was as if a lightning bolt struck Andrew. He realized they had made no *concrete* provision for the RC boats to detonate the C-4 when they struck the LNG. They were depending on the heat from impact to detonate the C-4. Not good enough in his mind. He wasn't the explosives expert, but knew a lot from working with guys who were like Josh and others. It surprised him that Mr. Bomb Tech Josh had not thought of this. *Some expert.*

After they had completed their recon sorties, they'd returned to Portsmouth. Andrew traveled directly to the garage and got right to work on the boats, but he needed to talk to his expert. Andrew called Josh at home. "Hey, Mr. Specialist, what are we doing to *guarantee* these things detonate?"

"Huh?" The question caught Josh off guard. Then he said, "I told you, the speed of the RC crashing into the steel hull creates enough impact to detonate the charge. Pretty simple, in fact. We just have to hit the LNG."

"How many pounds of force does it take to detonate a C-4 charge?"

"Well, back in the zone, we used blasting caps and RP-83 detonation cord. That delivers heat and pressure."

"Well, we have pressure from the impact but no heat. Doesn't it take like seventeen hundred degrees to detonate C-4? So now what? Where we gonna get blasting caps now, asshole?"

Silence. A grunt. Josh cleared his throat. "Shit. Fair point. Okay, don't panic. Simple enough. What say we configure a center-fire rifle cartridge on the tip of each boat's bow with, say, a ten-penny nail to serve as a firing pin? The impact acts like the firing pin of a gun striking its primer charge. That's gonna do the trick to *ensure* the C-4 detonates. Waterproof, of course. A plastic bag and rubber band'll do the trick. Even a condom taped up. And how about we throw a few cotton balls soaked in gas into that bag, too, just for insurance? Sorry, Andrew. I'm pretty sure the simple impact'll set off the charges, but you're right. This makes damn sure."

"Will this work?"

"Theoretically. Yes."

"*Theoretically?* That's what you got for me right now? He'll kill us both if this doesn't work. *That* we can count on."

"Okay, so we don't bother the boss with this technical shit. Those little black throwing knives of his scare the crap out a me. It'll work. Make this happen, brother?"

Andrew settled down. That's what pros do. "Alright, then I got some work to do before tomorrow. Bring me a box of rifle cartridges?"

"On it. Be there in fifteen."

. . .

Early the next morning, Friday, D-day, Andrew was satisfied with his make-shift detonators. The three Patriot Guardsmen stood in Livingston's garage surveying his handiwork. Andrew had lined the six boats up on the high workbench along the garage's back wall. Their flat foredecks featured four-inch gray-on-black labels: E1, E2, A1, A2, J1, & J2. It was as if those boats were staring at them, each with an accusative cyclops eye out front. Andrew explained to Ethan the final modifications were complete, including a failsafe detonator embedded in the bow of each boat. "They ain't pretty, Ethan, but we do *not* want to take any chances. Both Josh and I agreed this makes damn sure our party'll be a hit." Andrew caught Josh's eye, who offered him a grateful half-smile.

Browning looked at the wrapped and taped plastic protruding two inches from the bow of each boat. "Looks like shit, like a damn condom. That going to work?"

"Boss, you want pretty, or you wanna blow shit up? It'll work, alright. I got damn-near five pounds of C-4 strapped in near the bow of each hull right behind these detonators. Think firing pins. Added some ballast farther aft to keep their bows up in a chop. Tested this on the pond this afternoon. Good to go, boss."

"Fine. Good work, men."

Both breathed a sigh of relief. No knives. They loaded the boats and controllers into their rental vehicles, along with everything else they'd need for the mission. With little more than fourteen hours to go, Browning said, "Big night tonight. Before you boys head home to get a couple hours rest, finish sanitizing both garages. And I mean, there must be no fingerprints, no C-4 residue, no paperwork, nothing. I'd burn the damn building down, but Mr. Livingston might get suspicious."

A joke? Ethan made a *joke*? The boys looked at each other. Both shrugged. Josh said, "You got it, boss."

"We meet here at 1600 hours to caravan our three mission vehicles to our launch points." Saying nothing more, Browning headed into his house. His limp looked worse today.

---

Fifteen minutes later, Ethan pulled the box truck out of his garage, now loaded with antique furniture and paintings, coin collections, and diamonds from his business. Made one last phone call before leaving. Called three local friends and told them since the store was closed for renovations that he'd vacation in New York to visit an old friend. Also said he'd be staying down there for a few days.

He headed for the destination that was to serve as a hide until the dust settled. Drove seventy-eight miles to meet two hired men and backed the truck into a spacious garage to unload it. Took ninety minutes.

Browning paid the men in cash and secured their discretion with a generous tip. "Tell no one. No names." They thanked Browning and left. He then taped black plastic garbage bags over the windows of *that* garage.

Browning returned the truck to the rental company, picked up his Crown Victoria, and headed home. The ship-strike clock in his front hallway chimed six bells—3:00 PM. Exhausted, he mixed a drink and went over the entire mission again in his head. *Ready as we'll ever be, and an hour to rest before the boys'll be here. Time enough to get the leg up for a bit.*

## 51

Earlier in the day, District One Coast Guard and the Mass EPOs met for a briefing. This was business as usual for escorts to LNG tankers entering the harbor. But for this briefing, they discussed an additional element, *not* business as usual. The FBI had issued an alert for a possible terrorist attack in the area. Target or targets TBD, but most likely to be a water-based event in or around Boston Harbor. Several potential targets had an increased law enforcement presence leveraging Boston PD's marine unit, the Mass State Police Marine Unit, and EPOs all aboard their patrol vessels. Naturally, Old Ironsides, a symbolic target, received its share of resources. They also covered the Boston Fish Pier, Logan Airport and the LNG *Hercules* that was to anchor in the North

Channel that afternoon. Plus, the city paid overtime for additional roving patrols on both land and water.

SAC Malone paged Letty. She found a pay phone, as she hated using her new mobile. Some said the damn things caused brain tumors. Malone said, "I looked into the matter of Browning's 'closed file' by the IRS. The IRS audited him. Mr. Ethan Browning was not forthcoming with reporting his assets. Their principal focus was off-shore accounts. The auditors suspected he was fencing jewelry, valuable coins, and bearer bonds to private dealers, but acquired no proof. His balance sheets contained discrepancies that warranted another audit, which was to take place this coming tax season. Somehow, an informant inside the IRS warned Browning. Under the threat of a lawsuit, his attorneys squashed it.

"But the IRS did not give up. They put a case summary together and placed it in a closed file for that case to be reopened the following year. But this time, they'd do so with more agents, more intelligence, and resources devoted to uncovering the truth about his financials. It doesn't help us with a warrant to open Browning's offshore account. But I spoke with AUSA Riggins today, and he's filing for search and arrest warrants with what we have so far. He's shopping for a judge who sees more on those surveillance tapes than remote control boating hobbyists. He'll get those warrants based in part on this guy's shady background. I'd like you and Travis to meet our folks at noon to execute the warrants for Browning's garage, and the Livingston garage as well. But not Browning's house. We do not yet have enough probable cause for that and there is no evidence that ties the house to this op. I'm still working on that."

"Yessir. We'll be there. I'd love for us to head off whatever's coming."

Malone lowered his voice. In a serious tone, he said, "The harbor is buzzing. These RC boats are problematic. They're fast, reliable and undetectable on radar. Plus, this LNG tanker coming into port this afternoon offers these operators another potential target. We are dedicating appropriate resources there as well. Find something we can use, Letty. I, too, am convinced the stakes are high here."

"Yessir, we'll shake the tree until something drops." Letty called Travis, and they made their plans for the raid on the Barnes Road garages.

Sam answered the phone. He knew who it was. Said, "This is going to be a long day."

"Already is. Your gut queasy, big guy?"

"It's rumbling and burbling. Either gas from that meatball sub I grabbed for breakfast or an earthquake. Or.... See you at eleven in your office. We'll look over the warrants to make sure we know where we can search legally. Last thing we need is a Fourth Amendment issue if we find something."

"I love it. Yes, *when* we find something, *not if*. Some

gut you have, Special Federal Police Officer Travis." Sarcasm dripped from her lips.

"I have to check in with Larry. I'd like him to be there when we execute the warrants. You good with that, Letty?'

"Of course. We need to muster every bit of experience here."

## 52

On Friday, June sixteenth at 11:30 AM at the Portsmouth FBI field office, agents bristled, anticipating some action. They rarely saw much in Portsmouth, at least not like this. They checked and re-checked their search warrants for Browning's garage, Livingston's garage next door, as well as arrest warrants for Browning, Lofton and Bingham. SAC Malone had found a judge who granted a search warrant for Browning's house, too. A dozen men and women awaited the formal briefing. The Portsmouth SAC, Greg Bronzino, issued specific assignments to each agent. He assigned two to take photos before removing any items by other agents. Two women agents awaited apprehension of any female occupants. Two more agents were expected to focus on evidence labeling and security. A local towing company stood by in case they'd seize one or more motor vehicles. Plus, Bronzino ensured enough agents were on hand to take into custody up to three men—two agents per arrestee, those with plenty of take-down experience.

The dozen agents performed one final check of their gear, including firearms, handcuffs, and other restraints. Bronzino further assigned which vehicles were to transport the arrestees and to what destination they would be remanded. FBI Portsmouth had no lock-up or jail, only secure rooms. Four New Hampshire State Police troopers with a sergeant-in-charge accompanied Agent Mather, Special Federal Officer Travis, and Captain Lawrence Jamison.

Protocol included notifying the local police department. They advised Portsmouth PD that federal warrants were soon to be executed at 274 and 276 Barnes Rd. Asked for their help in handling traffic and onlookers. The Chief of the Portsmouth Police Department was cooperative and eager to assist. He assigned four officers and a lieutenant.

12:00 PM. Time to move. A dozen marked and unmarked cruisers pulled up to 274 and 276 Barnes Road. They split between the two addresses to search Browning's house and garage, with Livingston's garage all at the same time. They knocked. No answer.

Bronzino ordered the door breached by a fence pounder battering ram for speed of entry and for shock value rather than a Halligan Bar for a pried forced entry. The agents cleared the home—no occupants—and the search began in earnest for anything to provide intel on a potential attack. They removed electrical outlets and pulled pictures from walls to search their backing. Agents focused on collecting evidence. They opened up toilet tanks, looked for signs of false walls or floors, and emptied the refrigerator and freezer while examining each item. Others searched appliances, bureaus, beds, light fixtures, end tables, nightstands, filing cabinets, and under carpets. They all searched underneath anything standing that Browning might have taped to their backs or bottoms, but found nothing.

Same with both garages. Nothing. Someone in Browning's crew who knew what they were doing had sanitized Browning's garage. The smell of bleach caused the troopers and agents to reel. The techs found a few prints. Compared them to cards containing Browning's. A match. No surprise. No others. Another team had breached Livingston's garage. One agent silenced the alarm. Also nothing. Even the black plastic had been removed from the windows. Still, the techs checked the floors and work areas. One tech found trace evidence of military grade C-4.

Letty, Sam and Larry watched the search. Thought hard of what they were missing. Browning's file cabinets were empty. Letty said, "They knew we were coming and sanitized the whole place. The C-4 residue is all we have." Sam gazed, then stared. Spotted a length of rope hanging from a hole on the Livingston garage ceiling. Only obvious to him. He stood on a tall workbench stool and his six-foot frame still had to reach for a firm grip on the short pennant dangling from the twelve-foot ceiling.

As he pulled against resistance, a set of wooden steps unfolded and descended to the garage floor near the workbenches. The others watched him climb the rickety folding stairs that appeared wider than standard. Turned on a light by tugging on a pull-string to a bare bulb and fixture in this garage's attic. The shadows felt creepy. Old chairs, a table, some rugs rolled up, and various items they'd expect to find in an attic. The mess lay in disarray. But Sam's gut whispered to him. They'd left something behind. Letty followed him up and sneezed at the dust their passage had stirred up from the steps and the floor.

Sam thought, *These war dogs are military-trained men, but they aren't supermen or rocket scientists, and I'm betting they aren't masterminds, either. That'd be Browning. And he couldn't limp all the way up here.* Buried behind two large rolled carpets, a heavy china cabinet, and extra window screens he pulled away from the far wall, Travis spotted a large tool chest of drawers. *I wonder. Why a tool chest up here and not downstairs? And it's hidden.* "See anything out of place, Let?"

"What's piqued your interest? C'mon Sam, you're holding out on me."

## 53

Sam grumbled, "Get a photo guy and a tech up here. Now." Letty waved down at the techs standing near the base of the stairs. Moments later, two men in white coveralls ascended through the hole in the floor. Patches with *FBI* emblazoned in six-inch letters in typical yellow on their white body suits gave them the stereotypical appearance of lab rats. Sam said, "Photograph this and continue shooting as I uncover what I think is back there." Letty and the tech not taking pictures helped move the carpets and window screens while the other tech shot video and stills. Sam slid aside the china cabinet with a screeching wood-on-wood sound. "See that steel and chrome tool chest? Why is that here and not downstairs? And why hide it? Must have taken at least two strong men to get that monster up here, even empty, and it barely fits through the opening in the floor. Up those rickety folding stairs? Let's check it out."

The squat black box rode on casters, was trimmed in chrome, and had to be at least four feet wide, although not very deep. Featured tool-sized drawers except for the bottom one that was twelve or thirteen inches high. Sam opened that drawer. Inside, he found a forty-two-inch-long boat. He looked up at Letty. Said, "Now we know exactly what they plan to use, but where?"

Letty piled on, "And why leave this one behind?"

"Looks like a prototype. Get a tech up here who knows something about these things and open it up. Let's figure out what we're up against. Fast. I think my gut is telling me we're about out of time."

The techs moved the boat downstairs, still taking video. They tore away the flat-black plywood and fiberglass deck with chisels and hammers while another examined the flexible antenna that was in the drawer under the boat. It was longer than the boat by half-again as much. Another tech scrutinized what was inside the hull. He called out to the group of agents gathered around this new find, "Signal booster, GPS, and this looks like some type of autopilot hooked up to the GPS. Clever. Very clever. And extremely edgy stuff. This, in the rear, is ballast to offset the weight of something else meant to go into this empty space up front. Based on trace, I'm betting that's space for C-4. And, by the volume in here, plus the weight of the ballast, there's room for about... three to five *pounds*."

Sam's eyes widened and his jaw dropped before he said, "Holy shit!"

Word spread throughout the search team. SAC Bronzino arrived and looked at the now-disassembled boat, then at Sam and Letty. He asked, "How the hell did you find this? I thought we searched everywhere." Agent Mather shrugged and aimed a thumb at Sam. She told her on-scene boss for the day with half a smirk, "His gut gurgled at him."

"Okay, then, let's get word out to the marine patrols with pictures of this damn thing so they know what to look for. Nice job EPO, uh, Special Fed uh, never mind, doesn't matter. Sam, right?"

"Yessir. And this craft looks to be quite seaworthy. Suggests to me its counterparts are meant for big water, not a small pond or river. I'd bet coastal waters or more likely, Boston Harbor."

"Right. Possible prints on this, so let's start with that first. Then take this right to your tech guy in Springfield, Agent Mather. What's his name?"

"Noah Adams, sir."

"Right. Have him tear this machine down to confirm our suspicions, and *fast*. We need to know its capabilities, weaknesses, whether jamming its electronics is possible, the works. And anything else he can find. So, let's get it out of here and to Springfield.

Lights and sirens, people." A bustle of activity ensued. The feds released the New Hampshire State Police and the locals. The FBI sealed and wrapped Browning's house and the two garages with yellow tape labeled,

*POLICE LINE–DO NOT CROSS*
*UNDER PENALTY OF LAW*
*FBI*
*217-555-9675*

They had filled out the return on the warrant—that they'd seized the entire tool case and its contents. Even though there was a seven-day window to complete this piece of bureaucratic red tape, SAC Bronzino ordered all agents to complete it no later than the next day. That is, if they were satisfied that nothing else of interest remained on the property. But Sam wasn't ready to concede that just yet. He walked outside. His head still spun with his brain in overdrive. Letty said, "Excellent job, Sam. What tripped you?"

"Someone pulled the china closet away from the wall. Obviously, to set something behind it. The rolled-up carpets on either side of the cabinet hid that gap from the sides. Looked staged the way the window screens on top further hid the gap."

Larry joined them as some of the FBI cruisers peeled off down the sloped drive from Livingston's place. Lights and sirens to escort evidence en route to

Springfield FBI. Only the three of them remained standing in the now-quiet and deserted driveway in front of Browning's house.

"Ready?" asked Letty.

Sam scratched his chin. His gut gurgled again. "No, there's something else."

Larry chortled. "Okay Houdini. What's going on inside that block of cement your neck carries around for you?"

"Walk with me." Sam headed toward the back of Browning's house. Two garbage cans nestled inside a covered wooden box. Looked more like an air conditioner or gas meter enclosure. "Anyone search this? Doesn't look like it." Travis opened the box's hinged lid to expose two forty-gallon plastic garbage containers with bags lining them inside. "Huh, time to get dirty." They spread the contents of the first one on the patio block apron behind the enclosure. Nothing of interest.

The contents of the second container proved more interesting, especially toward the bottom. They uncrumpled newspapers and envelopes that once contained bills. That's when Larry spotted the remnants of an invoice torn to pieces. On his knees, after assembling the pieces like a jig-saw puzzle on the patio blocks, he read a receipt made out to Fred Kramer for a thousand dollars. "Hey, rent paid in cash on June first for a house at 457 Gull Drive, Penobscot, ME." Larry backed away and pointed to the assembled scraps of paper. He said to Letty, "*You* found this, not me, *Federal Agent* Mather. I'm a civilian up here. We're not making *that* mistake again." Sam jotted down that address. Letty whipped out a pair of plastic gloves and snapped them on. She examined the receipt, gathered up the pieces, and tucked them into an evidence bag that appeared from an inside jacket pocket.

Letty then puckered one cheek, wondering what else had they missed. She said, "A lot of stuff is missing inside Browning's house. Files gone, furniture and pictures missing, and the dust patterns on a couple of end tables near the couch and coffee table make it obvious that someone recently removed items. I think Browning rented a safe house under a false name and this is where it is."

Sam said, "I like it! But if true, would Browning be dumb enough to leave such a clue?"

Larry agreed and added, "Maybe. If he was in a hurry, and rattled. You kept him under pressure. Hey, there's no shortage of law enforcement coverage in Boston and the harbor now. We'll have to rely on the marine units to stop whatever those RCs are aimed at. Let's find this address and stake it out. I'll bet my pension they're going to Maine after their attack."

Sam rubbed his hands together, like he was ravenous and about to sit down to a steak dinner. "Okay, do we need to do anything before we head out? Notify SACs Malone and Bronzino?"

Letty broadcast her 'let there be no doubt' expression. "Can't leave them out, even though this is only a hunch, albeit a strong one."

Sam said, "And I'd like to have some backup, too."

"Yup, I'll take care of that. Do we take two cars or three?"

Larry said, "Two is less obvious."

"OK, what time is it now and what kind of ETA to Penobscot?"

Sam was already consulting a small book and said, "I looked it up in my pocket Atlas, here. Gull Drive is on Pleasant Lake. About eighty miles from here."

Larry rubbed his hollow gut. "No telling how long we'll need to wait. What say we pick up some fist food and coffee from a Quick Stop on the way?"

Sam shook his head in exasperation. His boss was always hungry, yet remained skinny as a rail, but knew he was right. Gotta keep the energy level up. He thought, *I could use a bite myself.*

Letty returned from her car. "Made the call to Bronzino. He'd sent his troops home and had to do a recall, but he's on it and has the address. Told him no lights or sirens when approaching within twenty miles of the place. We'll use our mobile phones for comms. Said he'd get Malone in the loop, too, but Jack's going to have his hands full if anything pops in Boston."

Sam looked like a dog with a bone. He grinned. "Let's roll. It's 1930 hours now."

Letty smirked. "Why can't you military types just use human time? It's seven thirty PM. Jeez." Both Larry and Sam looked at each other and grinned at their friend.

They jumped into the two unmarked cruisers—Larry's and Letty's, with Sam in the passenger's seat next to his favorite feeb. He remembered Larry liked driving alone, anyway. The two cars screamed out to Route 95 en route to 302.

## 54

Ethan Browning had made his way to the Hull Yacht Club to meet Captain Jesse Pelligrini at 1800 hours. The good weather had held. A southwest wind of five to ten knots was perfect for the op. Ethan's boats, E1 and E2, and their two controllers fit in a ridiculously large backpack. The boats' bows protruded from the top of the custom rig, but Browning had covered and bungeed them. When the captain saw the huge bundle, he joked, "We're only goin' on a four-hour charter, not four days, boss." Ethan laughed it off without comment. They shook hands, and Captain Jesse welcomed Browning aboard.

Pelligrini was a short, stout man in his sixties with white crow's feet outboard of each eye. The sun had bronzed the rest of his face. Ethan indulged in the expected pleasantries (how's the fishing been, what are we using for bait....). Stowed his backpack near the transom and took a seat next to the Captain who had shoved off. The pleasant summer evening required only lightweight windbreakers. Captain Pelligrini showed Ethan the life jackets and delivered the required safety briefing.

They headed through Nantasket Roads to the spot Captain Jesse had selected. Said he'd been a captain for thirty years and was damn good at it. Ethan kept his eyes peeled for other vessels and commercial traffic. Everyone else headed in as they settled in their chosen spot. As the evening wore on, they caught and released five short-striped bass. Ethan paid attention to how Pelligrini moved to the gunwale with his back to him and leaned over the water to net their catches.

It was nearing 1930. The time had arrived. After catching one more fish, darkness approached, like a curtain of doom. Ethan now needed to get to his launch point. Fifteen minutes later, he battled a large fish. As he brought it close to the boat, he saw his opportunity. Pelligrini leaned over the gunwale with the net to scoop up the fish. Ethan set down his pole now that the captain had taken control of his line. With the short aluminum bat in hand, the one used to subdue larger fish once close aboard, he struck his captain with a powerful downward stroke to the base of his skull. Lifted his legs and tossed him over. His rod, reel, line, and a large striper followed him. Ethan had ditched the plan to stow him below. The cuddy cabin was just too small. Pelligrini floated, but he was as dead as the striper in the fish-box they had not released.

No time for guilt over killing an innocent civilian. He liked Pelligrini. Casualty of war. With that out of the way, he peered at the Magellan GPS and plotted his course to his pre-selected launch site. Took a while. The original plan to get the captain to do it had failed, so he had to figure it out in the waning light. Fortunately, there was a gooseneck map light plugged into the cigarette lighter on the dash which he used to study the manual he located beneath the helm station. Twenty minutes later, he was on station, and he'd laid the RC boats on deck aft of the cockpit. A little over an hour to go.

---

Andrew Lofton arrived at the small parking lot near the southeastern end of Deer Island in the rented van at 2000 hours. Later than he wanted, but an accident closing off two lanes of traffic on the Southeast Expressway had snarled traffic. He was still ahead of Ethan's schedule, but he did *not* want to miss making history. Tonight's fireworks would set the stage for *their* Bunker Hill Day, only a few hours away, now. Too bad the tanker hadn't come in a day later. Oh, well.

A few people hiked near the end of the island, but

no threats, and they walked away from his location. From the parking lot, the monster tanker loomed about a mile due east of him, right where Ethan's intel had projected, and was already lit up like Gingerbread Lane on Christmas Eve. So far, so good. He worked his way down to the scouted area and removed the RCs from his pack. Checked the battery charge on both boats and both controllers. He remained confident in his last-minute Mickey Mouse detonation device. Just had to be careful not to bump that firing pin. Also checked and double-checked everything else he could think of. Ensured his walkie was on the programmed and encrypted channel he'd use to talk to Ethan and Josh, but only as a last resort.

He'd programmed the RCs with the simplest and most effective course possible. Once launched, his first boat, A1—part of what they called their first volley—was to accelerate to fifteen knots on a course of zero-nine-zero degrees. Precisely thirty seconds later, with hull A2 already floating at his side, he'd launch A2. If all went according to plan, three-and-a-half minutes later, boat A1 would strike *Hercules'* starboard side amidships, breaching her outer hull. Thirty seconds after that, boat A2 was to breach her inner hull, the midship tank's membrane, and all hell would break loose. He didn't want to be anywhere nearby when that happened.

So, the plan was to launch both boats and let the programming do its work. He'd then have a short three-and-a-half minutes to beat feet back to the van, secure himself inside, and make haste away from the shore. None of them had any idea the size of the lethal blast radius. Three RC boats in the first volley were all to impact the Hercules at 2100 hours. And the second volley of three boats from three different points of the compass were to hit a half-minute later. That was the plan. Nothing to do now but wait and listen to the gentle waves splashing on the boulders. He held both boats on short tethers clipped to his belt with carabiners until the appointed time arrived. The chill of the water seeped through his heavy waders even though he remained dry.

*Patriot Guardsmen? Stupid name, but the boss liked it, and the man knew how to make a statement!*

## 55

Meanwhile, Josh Bingham arrived a little early because of the muddy conditions at the shore they'd checked out during their recon on Wednesday. He thought he'd be glad he wore waders to get the RCs into deep enough water. But the tide was about to change. That meant he was at high tide and had plenty of depth. Might not even need the waders. He, too, wondered what tomorrow would bring. Would it change anything? Would they get caught and spend the rest of their lives in prison? Ethan and Andrew called him *the doubter*. But Josh owed his life to Staff Sergeant Ethan Browning, although Josh wasn't quite as radical as the other two. He remained loyal enough to get him to this point. *So, I guess I'm all the way in. If I turned and ran, Ethan would find me. But what if he was in jail? Could he do it anyway?* He felt conflicted, but would do as ordered.

Josh's nervousness subsided as he busied himself getting the RCs into the water. He tethered both J1 and J2 hulls to his equipment belt to prevent them drifting off while he waited.

---

Browning arrived at his launch point in the now-deceased Captain Pelligrini's center console craft, the *Codfather*. Everything was in place. They had planned everything. He also had his back-up plan in place. Browning had stashed enough funds offshore to live in comfort for the rest of his natural life, or until the Patriot Guardsmen's next mission if his boys survived. He did a radio check with his two accomplices on their mission's encrypted channel and they confirmed they were in position, too. But they were careful to speak in vague terms disguised as civilian chatter on an obscure frequency. They weren't going to use the radios at all, but Ethan *knew* Josh needed reassurance. *Mr. Doubter.*

Ethan'd had some difficulty getting the boats over the side of the *Codfather* while still maintaining control of them. His stump was killing him. He made a short bow line loop from each RC boat's padeye and attached it to a mid-ship cleat on the bigger boat. Rigged for quick release, he only needed to untie the line to each boat and they'd slip away in seconds. Scheduled first impact: 2100 hours, now mere minutes away. He was ready. He felt giddy. *Some dreams do come true.*

# 56

Adam Delaney fished out on Boston Harbor working the outgoing tide for stripers. Picked his spot east of Deer Island's southern end. Word was this spot had been hot all week. He'd judge for himself if that big-ass tanker ship half a mile to his east didn't screw up his fishing tonight. Delaney had anchored his twenty-two-foot Wellcraft dual-console fishing boat in about sixteen feet of water. But he did not display the required white anchor light on his bow, believing that'd discourage the fish. Called it his *fishing-stealthy* method. Had two lines in the water off his transom. He planned t use live eels tonight, the bait of choice for catching bass.

Delaney loved fishing at night when he didn't have

to deal with the *Googans* during the daytime. Those idiots were dangerous, oblivious, and lacked talent when operating boats, tying knots or choosing the correct fishing gear. Night fishing meant peace and quiet with a few beers and cold pizza while wetting a line or two. Though an Irishman, his favorite food was *not* corned beef and cabbage. It was pizza. A *pizzaholic,* his wife said. Cold, hot, warm, morning, noon, or night, pizza was his favorite.

He settled in. Wondered about that tanker, no doubt waiting for daylight before venturing in to their mooring in Everett. Everybody knew that's where those monsters tied up. Always a big deal whenever one came into port. Even from this distance, that ship was so gargantuan, her lighting made it look like an entire neighborhood of Christmas fanatics had gone overboard decorating. Once more, Delaney second-guessed whether this was a good spot tonight. If he'd had his VHF radio turned on, he'd have heard the warnings to steer clear of this area. Unnecessary noise while *fishing stealthy*.

---

The Coast Guard deployed three twenty-five-foot rigid-hull-inflatable patrol craft powered by twin two-hundred-horsepower Mercury engines each. Lieutenant JG Robert Connors was the officer-in-charge for this LNG detail. This young but experienced skipper commanded great respect among his peers and subordinates alike. When he shouted an order, you *moved*. Two savvy Bos'n's Mates, Johnson and Covington, piloted the other two RIBs. Both cox'ns (boat skippers) could brag of unparalleled training and experience, but they never did.

Crews of four were standard on each RIB, like tonight. Twelve pairs of eyes trained on the safety of the *Hercules* this night. LT stationed his boat astern of the tanker to guard against threats from seaward. He stationed BM1 Johnson's RIB off to the tanker's port side, and BM2 Covington's boat off the tanker's port bow. They carried twelve-gauge shotguns aboard each RIB. But their heavy hitters consisted of a deck-mounted M-60 machine gun on the bow of each RIB. They also kept at the ready MK 127 Star Parachute Illumination flares in aluminum gear boxes near their transoms. Those flares climbed to six- or seven-hundred feet ASL (above sea level), depending on launch angle, and lit up the sky for up to thirty-six seconds. They transformed night into day during their flight for a hundred-yard radius. Four Environmental Police boats cruised a half mile beyond the Coast Guard perimeter. They were to prevent any vessels from entering their perimeter, their *exclusion zone*.

The EPOs carried AR-15 assault rifles that clipped thirty-round magazines. They also carried parachute flares, twelve-gauge riot shotguns, and sidearms. Their rules of engagement with the Coasties were clear. "If anyone gets by you, get the hell out of the way. We're not letting anyone near the LNG and we'll open fire with our six-hundred-fifty round-per-minute M-60s. Also with crews of four, each EPO boat carried M-4 military rifles with thirty-round magazines. This detail was on duty from the tanker's arrival until relief arrived at 0600. Once the harbor pilot boarded at first light, the threat level would drop. But they'd remain diligent for the entire sortie into Everett, where normal dockside security comprised their relief.

Extra security was in place thanks to EPO Captain Larry Jamison coordinating the cross-agency protective barriers against a potential attack on more than one possible target. On high alert because of this current threat level, the State Police Marine Unit also had Logan Airport buttoned up tight. Boston PD covered the USS Constitution, also known as *Old Ironsides*.

---

As planned, Ethan Browning launched hull E1 at 2056 hours plus twenty-four seconds. His programmed course to the target was two-seven-zero, due west, from one-and-a-half nautical miles off the tanker's port beam. *What a big, beautiful target!* Precisely thirty seconds later, he launched hull E2. Both ran hot, straight, and normal. He watched the video screen, which turned out to be all but useless as he crammed the *Codfather's* throttle forward to carry him clear of the blast zone. *Gonna be big.*

---

Andrew Lofton still wondered about tomorrow. What headlines? How many injured and dead? Let the message go out. Congress and the President were killing the country he grew up in and defended. Maybe they'll even remember this as Bunker Hill Day 1989, the birth of the *new* revolution. People will care. Especially when this busy port's traffic would have to skirt around a new hazard to navigation—a sunken tanker ship at the mouth of the harbor, even though most of it would still be visible.

Night had descended, and the *Hercules* would burn all night. Starting now. The tide had risen, and the slack tide was soon to be outgoing, not that it mattered much to these tiny shallow-draft boats. 2056 hours. The time had arrived to send a message from within the flames of hell. A1 launched. Thirty seconds later, he sent A2 on its way, and he turned to run. As planned.

Josh Bingham launched hull J1 at the same precise time Andrew Lofton launched his. On a course of zero-five-four degrees, Josh watched his little remote-controlled boat in the moonlight making for the broad port bow of the *Hercules*. Thirty seconds later, he launched hull J2, turned his back to the shore and to the tanker's deck lights still glowing in the night sky northeast of him. He headed for the hills, as they say. *That brilliant mooring illumination will soon pale compared to thirty pounds of C-4 igniting a billion cubic feet of flammable gas!*

---

Adam Delaney never tired of the nighttime Boston skyline. Except for Logan's jets taking off nearby, it was pretty quiet. He had just hauled in a handsome striped bass. Rinsed his hands in the saltwater off his port side before accidentally touching his shirt. Didn't want Mary bitching about the smell on his clothes that were designated "for fishing only." It was gonna happen regardless. She'd get over it.

A few minutes before nine PM, Adam thought he heard a high-pitched whining sound coming from behind him. *What the heck is that?* He picked up his binoculars he always kept hanging inboard of the starboard-side helm station, and scanned for the source of the unusual noise. It grew louder. And coming right towards him. No lights, but it was moving pretty fast.

When one of Logan's jet's landing lights lit the sky and the water's light chop even brighter than the full moon, he spotted it. Looked like a toy boat with a powerful electric motor. It appeared blacked out, which is why he almost missed spotting it. He tracked the fast boat with his binocs. *Weird. Was this something to do with the gaggle of police boats in the harbor?*

It passed close off his starboard side. Guessed it ran by at twenty knots headed for... the tanker up ahead? *Oh, this can't be good.* He jumped onto VHF channel sixteen after switching it on and called, "Mayday, Mayday, Mayday. Calling any police boat or harbormaster." Boston PD Marine Patrol responded in an instant. Delaney was so excited the officer had to ask him to slow down. But the panic in his voice alerted every other station also monitoring channel sixteen, including the Coast Guard and EPO boats. Everyone in the law enforcement world already knew the harbor was on full alert.

"There's a small five-foot boat, no lights, running at twenty-plus knots straight toward the Deer Island side of the tanker anchored in the North Channel." The officer who took the call verified that all stations had been alerted. They had been warned to be on the lookout for small boats. Everyone acknowledged within the next instant. Only twenty seconds had elapsed since that small boat screamed past Delaney when he heard the same whining sound coming from the same direction. Knew what to look for this time and spotted it straightaway. Grabbed his radio's microphone off the dash above the wheel again. Crushed the push-to-talk button and shouted, "This is Delaney again! Here comes another one of those little boats, also headed toward the tanker from the east!"

---

Word had already spread when a huge explosion lit up the starboard side of the enormous ship. BOOM! A fireball clawed its way up from the water into the moonlit sky. Looked like slow motion. The Coasties surmised a small remote-control boat, likely launched from Deer Island, was a direct hit. Delaney could feel the wave of heat on his cheek before the explosion knocked him off his feet and pushed his boat toward the Island on a tremendous pressure wave. His mushroom anchor had broken free of its hold on the bottom.

---

Lt. Connors jumped on the radio to his vessels and the EPOs. "All hands, be prepared to fire upon small boats attacking the LNG. Send up flares, ready your weapons, and shoot anything out there that's moving. Be advised of a small civilian craft off Deer Island." As a precaution, he told the EPO Lieutenant for his detail to retreat into the harbor and out of their line of fire.

The EPOs gladly complied that instant since they did not have the equipment for this sort of engagement. The Coasties did.

---

Flares lit up the sky, turning night into day. BM2 Covington's RIB, now half a mile off the tanker's bow, spotted a second small boat's phosphorescent wake about a hundred yards out from the tanker's starboard side. Another crew member aboard Covington's RIB, armed with an M-4 on full auto, dumped both magazines and hit the boat with his last few rounds a few seconds after 2100. *BOOM!* The force of the explosion pushed the air out of everyone's lungs aboard Covington's boat. Took them a few seconds to get back up off their asses. The BM3 who fired the kill shot on that second boat had fallen overboard and lost his weapon. Six hands hauled his ass right back aboard an instant later before all eyes scanned the waters around the tanker once more.

---

More gunfire then issued from BM1 Johnson's M-60 from the port side of the LNG midship. Two more Coasties on Johnson's RIB took up positions with their M-4s on either side of a third member of the crew already on the M-60. All fired upon yet another small boat aimed at the tanker's port side. More flares went up. Johnson maneuvered his boat in the path of the "toy" boat coming from the east. Their 7.62x51 rounds hitting the water issued softball sized craters in the water. Seventy yards out, fifty yards, twenty-five, and *BOOM!* The little boat exploded before reaching the tanker or Johnson's RIB, but close enough to the RIB that it soaked the three men and knocked them on their asses. The pressure wave rocked the RIB to near capsizing, but it recovered, as designed.

Johnson hollered, "Another one bearing down on us. Light that fucker up!" Four guns, including Johnson's sidearm, blazed out at the twenty-knot four-foot boat. Brass shell casings rained all over the aluminum deck of the RIB. So much water sprayed from so many bullets it became impossible to see their target. But the hail of gunfire yielded another *BOOM*, and yet another pressure wave more intense than the last. They had defeated two attack boats en route to the tanker from the east.

---

Lt. Connors' crew launched more flares. The third Coast Guard RIB under the command of BM2 Covington stationed near the tanker's bow spotted yet another attack boat a hundred yards out coming in from the southwest. From outside the exclusion zone. Four machine guns aboard Covington's RIB targeted it.

Two of the crew ejected and dropped empty mags onto the deck, along with the pile of brass accumulating underfoot, before popping in fresh magazines. Covington's M-60 spewed a stream of shells faster than the eye could see. Visible tracers gave the illusion they were spraying a continuous beam of glowing lead at their target. The fusillade raged on. No confusion or panic, just concentration. *BOOM!*

But a second small boat approached from the same direction. Covington assumed it had been launched from Long Island to his southwest. It sped in almost immediately behind the first. Someone aboard pointed and yelled, "Get that fucker!" Conners now screamed in close alongside the tanker's port side toward Covington's RIB to reinforce his attack. Now eight guns rained lead out at the deadly little attack boat.

Lt. Connors thought to himself, *How the hell does anything survive in that?* No sense trying to converse over the incessant bombardment. He kept launching flares and rounds flying. A second attack boat coming from the southwest struck the bulb of the ship dead center on the bow less than thirty seconds after 2100 hours. *BOOM!* The tanker had taken two hits. They had suppressed four. A lull ensued. Everyone remained diligent. Lt. Connors unnecessarily commanded his men on the fleet of three RIBs to stay sharp. 'We don't know if this thing is over yet."

More flares. Five long minutes drifted by. The Coasties remained on highest alert, with adrenaline still cascading from every pore of every man. Then, at 2107 hours, Lt. Connors declared in a loud voice *and* over VHF channel 22, the Coasties' guard channel, "All secure from battle posture, but remain standing at the ready." Damage assessment came next. He discovered from a cruise-by close to the *Hercules* that they had sustained a small three-foot breach midship on the tanker's starboard side steel plating. Debris floated nearby. Insulation and bits of wood. *Hercules* reported their inner hull remained intact, and that pumps stayed ahead of the intra-hull inflow with no problem. No danger to the crew or its volatile cargo and no injuries. The other impact to the ship's bulbous bow caused minor damage. Had it struck a dozen feet to the left or the right on the broad bow? Would have been a very different story.

The sudden quiet, except for everyone's ears ringing, proved deafening. Those not close to the sustained din of firearms exploding all around them might have thought, *Why are these lunatics shouting at each other?* But that was the only way they were able to hear each other. Rapid-fire radio messages exchanged information about casualties (none) and damage assessments (containable). Lt. Connors informed the chain of command moments after the attack ended, and again after completing their initial damage assessment, with ten-minute checkpoints for an hour thereafter. As fast as it started, the attack was over in less than a few minutes from the first report by a fisherman to the last explosion. They'd let the brass handle the media. Lt. Connors congratulated every one of his men for their bravery under fire and for their deadly accuracy in defeating four of the six attack boats. He refused to call them "toy boats" as they were as deadly as six high-explosive torpedoes. Worse.

# 57

Browning heard the gunfire, felt the heat and pressure from the blasts behind him as he roared away from the scene at thirty-five knots. He berthed Captain Pellegrini's boat back at the Hull Yacht Club as if nothing had happened, tied her off, and drove away in his rented van. Proceeded the long way around the harbor to Logan to turn in the rental and pick up his own van, as planned. But Logan was closed. He saw traffic lined up ahead. Massachusetts State Police barricaded every entrance and exit to the huge airport. Returning their rentals and picking up his van? Not happening. Not today, anyway.

With their portable radios, the three conspirators agreed to meet in an old industrial yard outside of

Revere. Parked their three rentals hood-to-trunk out of sight of the street. They leaned shoulder-to-shoulder on the hood of Bingham's rented pickup truck. Browning said, "Change of plan, boys. Our boats caused damage, but to what extent we won't discover until at least tomorrow. We'll abandon the rented pickup and leave the keys in it. Odds are it will disappear. Same with the sedan miles away, also where stolen vehicles are common. We keep this van.

"What next, boss?" Bingham appeared casual about this new direction.

"Plan B. We head north."

Lofton jittered his hands on the hood. Looked like he had to pee or something. "Where?"

"I have a safe house for us in Maine. Not far. About an hour. It's stocked up with food, booze and clothes. I rented it under a phony name and stored the stuff you put in that box truck a few days ago. No one knows where it is except me, and soon, you two."

Upon hearing that, Andrew and Josh relaxed as they sauntered back to their rentals. They left Andrew's sedan parked between two buildings nearby. Andrew rode with Ethan and they followed Josh twelve miles south, where he ditched his rented pickup. Ethan's rented van transported the three conspirators, who would now be considered terrorists, just like the nation's founding fathers two centuries earlier. Ethan watched his speed and headed up Route 93. Jumped off at the Route 302 exit and headed northwest to Pleasant Lake. Not much talk or banter, more like reflection. Andrew worried. Josh slept. The night was gray and dreary with temperatures in the fifties. A cool northeast wind kicked up swift enough to shimmy the van now and then. Looked like a storm ahead.

## 58

Letty held her cruiser's speed at a steady eighty-five miles-per-hour on Route 95 on their way into Maine. Larry dozed while Sam consulted Letty's road atlas and his own pocket atlas several times during the drive. They turned onto Route 302. Sam estimated they still had about twenty-five minutes to go. The two-lane road with double yellows in the center didn't stop Letty from passing cars. Though angry drivers honked during close calls, she chose not to activate her emergency lights or siren. They might pass Browning's car without knowing it.

When Larry woke up, he leveraged the mobile phone installed in Letty's FBI cruiser to coordinate with SAC Bronzino. He was advised that Bronzino and his agents were about sixty minutes behind them.

They came to the intersection of Hammock Road and Gull Drive. Larry said, "Everyone, keep your eyes peeled for number 457." Letty slowed the cruiser to a crawl. They passed a mailbox with 457 scrawled on it and continued down the two-lane gravel road. They discovered a pull-off area and concealed the car in the shallow ditch halfway up a driveway of a nearby house that appeared vacant.

"What's the plan, boss?" asked Sam.

From the back seat, Larry laid a soft hand on Letty's right shoulder. "Does this crate have a twelve-gauge shotgun in the trunk?"

"Yes, with two boxes of rifled slugs and two of double-ought buckshot."

"Excellent, I'll take that since my pea shooter here is only good for close range. I might have to reach out and touch someone." They hiked back to 457's driveway that sloped up and curved to the right. Out of sight from the road, the modest but well-maintained log cabin perched on the top of a small hill. Big pine trees shaded the front yard. A freshly mowed lawn led down to a dock on a small lake behind the house. Likely Pleasant Lake. No neighbors close by. Larry nodded toward Letty and said, "Agent Mather, I'll assume command here, since this kind of work is more our style than yours. But we leverage your federal authority. Work for you?"

"No problem, Larry. Let's get this done and arrest these bastards."

"Good. Sam, you conceal yourself outside. Once they're inside, approach them from behind through the front door. Letty, you and I will be inside, waiting. Let's see if we need an invitation."

"Got it, boss," said Sam. He jiggled the doorknob. Locked. But he suspected its mechanism would not present much of a hindrance. He gave it a good bump with his shoulder. Smiled over his shoulder at his partners. "It's open."

Letty smirked at Sam's liberal interpretation of *open*. "I guess invitation extended, right, Sam? I did not see that!" They cleared the cabin with practiced efficiency. Three small bedrooms, a kitchen with a bar and three stools. One large bathroom featured a small shower, a picnic table for inside-dining in the kitchen, and a storage area in a short hallway leading to the attached two-car garage. They did a quick scan of the garage. Their flashlights revealed an array of high-end antique furniture, stacks of cardboard boxes full of art, cases of old coins, a small two-by-four-foot safe, presumably for the diamonds and precious stones and perhaps cash. Browning had emptied his store.

Sam muttered, "He's set to open a new business somewhere else. This is his exit strategy from Portsmouth and from his party in Boston." They closed the door to the garage.

Larry said, "Letty, how about you hide between the kitchen bar and the stove? I'll be in this bedroom doorway. Sam, you'll flank 'em."

Sam asked, "What about the rear door? And windows?"

"Not likely they'd enter from there. We play the percentages. Unless either of you has a better idea until the cavalry arrives. Front, outside and inside is all we can do. Once they're inside, we jump them hard and fast. Contain them inside. We don't want to be chasing these guys at night in the woods or even into other cabins.

# 59

Sam knew Larry didn't need to say it. But he looked at Letty who was not yet a veteran field agent, much less experienced in the takedown of three combat-hardened criminals. "Letty, check your ammo supply, handcuffs, and plastic ties for quick access. We find the light switches and light up the room once they're inside. You don't want to take these bastards down with a flashlight. Besides, you're gonna need both hands for your weapon." Larry then added, "On second thought, I think Browning will come in first and he'll flick the light on. Stay hidden until all three are inside."

Letty said, "Good plan, guys."

Sam fidgeted. "Yeah, until the first shot is fired.

Remember, these guys are combat-hardened war dogs, so be extra careful."

Letty smiled, but the left corner of her mouth twitched. Just once. Sam sensed the inevitable pre-action jitters in her.

He returned her smile. "Semper Fi."

With a solemn expression, Larry added, "When it's time to fight, you better fight like you're the third monkey on the ramp to Noah's Ark and it's starting to sprinkle."

Sam grinned, getting pumped himself. "Did you make that up or were you there, old man? I'll try to fix up the lock so it doesn't look like a B&E."

---

After that, they took up their positions and settled in for a wait. Letty peered over at Larry's nose, visible behind the bedroom door. And he watched her checking and rechecking her weapon, adjusting her position, and looking either anxious or scared. Or both. Larry offered her a reassuring nod, but said nothing. The hardest part of an op was the wait. Operators want it to happen as soon as possible so they don't lose their edge. Twenty-five minutes passed. Still no Bronzino and his troops.

Time had run out. Headlights lit up the room through the front windows. It wasn't Bronzino and his feds. Just as well. Element of surprise. A van crunched to a stop at the top of the driveway. Letty whispered the obvious toward Larry's direction. "They're here." She checked her weapon again. Got off her butt and crouched, ready to pounce. Larry smiled. *Rookies.*

---

Sam waited outside. Watched the threesome exit a strange van to indulge in a little post-trip stretching. Reminded himself they had just engaged in an act of terrorism, but hadn't heard if they were successful or not. At a minimum, they had escaped Boston. Sam seethed with an anger of his own. No amount of anger should drive a Marine to such violence against innocent civilians and property. But he understood rage. He stood at the ready, weapon drawn, behind a gigantic oak tree about twenty feet out, not sure what he would do next.

# 60

Ethan told his boys, "Wait here while I check it out." He left the two men standing by the van. He lit up the door lock with his flashlight. *Hmmm, something isn't right. The screws pulled out and haphazardly shoved back in?* With caution, he swung open the door. Flipped up the light switch to his right inside the jimmied door. With the room illuminated, he peered around with suspicion. Reached into one of his custom-fit pockets to retrieve one of his lethal five-inch throwing knives. With the knife in his right hand, he drew his Glock 22 with his left. This forty-caliber fifteen-shot handgun was serious hardware.

From outside, through the still open front door, Bingham shouted, "Everything good, boss?"

He spoke without turning, his gaze intent on the house's interior. "Yeah, great." He didn't get this far by being stupid. Gripped his gun low and ready. Cocked his right arm, prepared to launch his knife at somebody's throat.

---

Larry watched Browning through the crack between the bedroom door and its jamb. *This isn't going well. Should have come up with a better plan.* Seconds ticked by. Nobody moved. Larry thought, *This is nuts.*

---

Sam crept closer. Picked every step on soft pine needles, avoiding any twigs. Got within ten feet of Browning's two soldiers. Sized 'em up. Big boys a tad past their prime, but not by much. Considered their combat experience. *Nope, not pushovers, these two.* They still faced the cabin, now lit up inside, the front door still swung wide. Browning stood frozen in silhouette in the doorway. They awaited their boss's all-clear signal. That hadn't come. The bigger one had hollered, "Everything good, boss?" And he'd heard the muffled reply from just inside the cabin. But Browning was sharp and obviously suspected something was wrong. *He must have spotted those jammed screws in the door frame.* Now, Sam worried about Letty and Larry. He'd handle these two mutts. At least he remained pretty confident. With his heavy three-five-seven magnum in both hands, he considered his tactical approach. *Can't just shoot them. Let it play out. For now.*

# 61

With an abrupt motion, Browning fired twice through the pine door where Larry hid. One slug missed him. The other tore into his left arm. Letty jumped up from behind the kitchen counter and fired twice. Punched one round into Browning's left shoulder joint . He dropped the gun from that now-dead hand as if that piece had suddenly grown white hot. In a lightning motion, however, his right arm flashed forward. His first deadly throwing knife sunk into Letty's flesh close under her collarbone, two inches inboard of her left shoulder joint. She yelped in pain.

Larry flung open the bedroom door. Leaped out with the shotgun. Browning caught that movement in his peripheral vision. Retrieved and launched a second knife that appeared out of nowhere. It cut through Larry's jacket and grazed his arm, Blood seeped through. The twelve-gauge roared. Browning spun and flew back against the front door. Larry's massive slug damn-near tore off Browning's right arm at the shoulder joint. No surprise with three-thousand foot-pounds of energy propelling that slug at fifteen-hundred feet-per-second. The man landed face down, not moving. Larry stumbled over and kicked Browning's Glock away. His shotgun suddenly felt almost too heavy to keep elevated. *Good thing this asshole is down.*

Sam heard the two shots. He yelled, "Federal Agent, freeze or you die!" Both Bingham and Lofton spun around to face him in the dark, but did not freeze. Lofton drew his weapon from a shoulder holster. Sam dropped him with a double tap before the dirtbag even cleared leather. By the time Sam had done so, however, Bingham had already aimed his gun at Sam. But Sam already had a round en route to Bingham. He'd aimed for center mass. Instead, he hit the man's gun arm. But not until after a single round from Bingham's Sig Sauer P320 9mm punched Sam's left arm. The fire spread upward from his forearm spread. Caused him to feel dizzy. But his life depended on focusing, right now. Saw Bingham still standing, but his pistol had grown heavy in his right hand with Sam's bullet in that shoulder. *Shit, shoulda double-tapped that bastard, too.* Sam fired again. Put another round into the guy's gun arm. *BAM.* He fell backward, like a tree toppling. *If I hadn't pulled the trigger first just now....*

With a sense of eery calm, Sam approached, still holding his aim. Picked up Bingham's firearm with his wounded wing. The Sig dangled from Sam's index finger from its trigger guard. Took some effort to slash through the pain, but he could see the big man presented no further threat. Bingham screamed, "You killed my friend, you fuck!" Sam tucked the man's gun into his own belt with his good hand after securing his own weapon in his hip holster. With pain now radiating down and up from his left forearm, he dripped his own blood down onto his cuffs as he secured Bingham's arms behind his back. The man's arm was bleeding worse than his own. *Gotta stop both of us from bleeding to death right now.* Sam ripped off Bingham's belt and secured it semi-tight above his wound. Then he did the same for his own arm with practiced efficiency, even though it hurt like hellfire. Took thirty or forty seconds. Or was it longer? He grew woozy from blood loss, but he suspected that was more from afteraction adrenaline. *Gotta keep moving.*

With Bingham secured and Lofton dead, Sam clumped up toward the cabin to check on Letty and Larry. He first spotted Browning laying across the doorway, bleeding, face down. Then, there were Letty's legs visible from behind the kitchen lunch bar. *Oh, no!* He ran to her. She sat on her butt with her back to the stove, but her eyes were open and blinking rapidly in disbelief and shock. She wore an almost comically surprised expression. A nasty little knife protruded from high on her chest. He feared the worst, but saw she wasn't bleeding heavily. Sam grabbed a towel hanging from the oven door above her shoulder, and wrapped it around the knife with care. She moaned in pain. "Sorry, Let. You'll be okay. Not much blood, so it missed the artery. And well above your heart. Keep pressure on this, okay? Letty?" After a few beats, she nodded. Bit her lip. Said nothing through her rapid puppy panting. Her blinking slowed.

---

Larry was bleeding, too. But he walked over to the unconscious or dead Browning again and unnecessarily kicked the man's Glock again, farther away from him while Sam tended to Letty. He then slumped down onto the kitchen floor next to Letty to make sure she was keeping pressure on her wound. Larry looked over at Sam and snorted to nobody and everybody, "We're a mess." Larry gazed into Letty's questioning eyes and said, "Do *not* pull that out."

Now stumbling, Travis snatched the green Princess phone off the kitchen wall and punched 911. "Federal Officer Sam Travis. Three officers wounded. Three felons down at 457 Gull Drive. Need at least two ambos. Hurry." He dropped the phone onto a nearby counter, leaving the line open. Travis kept his feet under him with some effort. Checked Browning for a pulse. Weak, but regular. Walked back to the kitchen. After rummaging through a few drawers, found one full of dish towels. Grabbed two. As he came back to Letty and Larry, he tossed one towel to Larry who knew what to do. Sam turned his attention to Letty. "How you doing, Let?"

"I'm okay except for this knife sticking in me." Their smirks echoed one another's.

"Gonna check on those two birds outside. Be right back." Outside, Travis saw his double-tap to Lofton had indeed ended his life. Bingham was unconscious, but his three-fifty-seven had caused some serious damage to the guy's shoulder. Sam thought he'd survive. The belt wasn't working well as a tourniquet, though, so he cut off the big man's sleeve with his knife and knotted it around his upper right arm. That worked better. Had to work around the cuffs as there was no way he'd take them off. This bruiser could be faking unconsciousness.

Now-nurse Travis returned to the house. He'd tend to Browning next. If the man survived Larry's shotgun slug, Sam was betting he'd get a prosthetic arm in prison to go with his leg, or not. Didn't care. His mangled upper arm saturated another towel even as yet another tourniquet struggled to do its job. Browning remained unconscious as his body mustered its defenses against what had to be an appalling shock to his entire system.

Travis now took further stock of his own wound. He could move his arm, so he concluded that no bones got hit. He realized he was so high on a massive adrenaline dump he felt almost no pain. Pale from her own blood loss and shock, Letty asked, "How are *you* doing, Sam?"

"I'm okay, and damn lucky." They heard the sirens as the emergency vehicles roared up the gravel driveway, drawing a cloud of dust behind them. Some of it sifted in through the still-open and damaged front door under the covered porch. Sam stood out there to greet the cavalry. Held another towel against his wound as he offered the EMTs a triage report on wound priorities.

One EMT with round eyes, hands on her hips, muttered, "Holy shit! Is this the OK Corral, or what?"

"Yeah, what."

Browning was the worst, then Bingham, then Larry, then Letty. No rush on Lofton. Considered himself to be the last on the list of injured. They dressed Sam's wound. He insisted he was fine. A through-and-through, they said. He told the local PD officer who showed up with the two ambulances, "These two," he pointed first at Bingham being attended to by a pair EMTs and at Browning, already on a gurney, "will require guards at all times until we get our own people on them. They are dangerous terrorists."

The local officer's eyes widened, did a double-take

at their wounded prisoners, and saluted. "Yessir, will do."

Against the EMT's advice, Sam stumbled back into the small house to call SAC Bronzino. He plopped onto the picnic table's bench in the kitchen with the phone cord under his armpit. "Yeah, it's Travis. We got 'em. We took some hits too. One KIA and five wounded.... Yes, I said five. ETA?" Bronzino, already en route with his team, said they'd be on scene in five. "I'll wait for you, then."

# 62

A small crowd of various uniforms scurried around the cabin and its environs as SAC Bronzino arrived with six federal agents in two black SUVs. The supervisory agent from Portsmouth broadcast his reaction to the carnage with an astounded expression and a meandering stroll through the scene. He spotted Sam sitting at... a picnic table in the cabin's dining room-slash-kitchen? Face down, Sam rested his forehead on his unwounded right forearm on the tabletop. Bronzino approached. "Agent Mather?"

Sam raised his head in slow motion. He appeared pale, gaunt. No doubt from blood loss by the appearance of his clothes and the bandage and sling on his left arm. *Good Lord!* Bronzino was told on the way into the cabin that an EMT had insisted Officer Travis take a pain med. To keep him focused on anything other than the pain. Because he had insisted on waiting for the FBI's arrival. Sam joked with a sloppy smirk, "No, Special Federal Officer Travis, here...."

But Agent Bronzino reminded the smart-ass woods cop with a let-there-be-no-doubt expression that joking right now was not called for. At all. Not when he obviously expected a debrief. "Ah, yessir. A knife wound to Agent Mather's upper chest, but sounds like she'll be fine. In an ambulance now en route to... somewhere. Captain Jamison sustained a gunshot wound to his left shoulder, and a minor knife wound in his right. Lofton's dead. I shot him. Bingham sustained wounds, but he'll live. I shot him, too after he shot me." Sam nodded downward toward his bandages and the sling that embraced his left arm before continuing. His tone of voice grew even more flat and... vague. "Captain Jamison shot Browning with Letty's twelve-gauge. In the right arm. Just about severed it, I think. I directed the local PD to be vigilant with those two fuckers." Another vague nod toward the front door. "Agent Mather shot Browning in his left arm before he shot her. Browning's arm? Looked like raw hamburger. Larry's a pretty good shot with that FBI pump. Push-ups are out of the question for Browning." Slurred speech punctuated Sam's eyes seeking focus, but failing to do so.

"Are *you* okay, Agent Travis?"

Sam struggled to swing his gaze up at the still-standing Bronzino. His head bobbled as he smiled. "**Agent** Travis? Yup, that's me. Uh, yeah, I'll be okay, I guess. Just need some flushing, stitches, a few shots of vodka and a couple weeks off."

"What the fuck happened?"

"We were inside. We whipped together a quick plan, not knowing when or even if those assholes were comin'. I retreated to the tree line to flank 'em in case they got here before you guys. And then they were just here. You and your posse... weren't." Sam smacked his dry lips together, trying to wet his parched mouth. "Browning sensed something was wrong as he came through the front door and started shooting. He was quick and he was good. We underestimated him. We shot back."

"Why didn't you wait for us? Six people and six dead or wounded? That's some kind of success rate."

Sam gave this supervisory agent a drug-addled smirk. "Hey, we did what we had... in 20/20 hindsight...." his voice drifted off. "They surprised us. Had to improvise."

"Well, thank you, Officer Travis. You three broke this case wide open. I'm sure there'll be some criticism, but given the circumstances, I think the review board will look favorably on this operation."

"Review board, huh?"

*This guy is definitely well medicated.* "Yes, we require after-action reports, including all shootings per our procedures. We'll review everything."

"How did the tanker make out?"

"Fine. Minimal damage. She took two hits from two remotely controlled boats loaded with explosives. Some damage, but it's contained thanks to the Coast Guard's quick thinking and firepower. They saved the ship, Sam. We have a missing charter captain who is presumed dead by Browning's hand. Search teams will start tomorrow at first light. These criminals were clever. Ingenious, in fact. We had some luck too. A fisherman reported over his marine radio that a black *toy boat* was heading toward the tanker prior to the first of two explosions. That phone call resulted in the Coast Guard's quick response."

"Any casualties?"

"None."

"Excellent." It came out *egg-shell'nt*.

Bronzino said, "A fine debrief, Officer Travis. Let's get you to the hospital. They're out of ambulances, so I'll take you to Penobscot Medical Center myself.

"Sir, I think they're taking Browning to Portland due to the seriousness of his injuries after they stabilize him. I haven't heard where everybody else is going yet. I'd like to go wherever Agent Mather and Captain Jamison are."

"Let me see if I can make that happen."

Travis wanted to talk to both of them before a formal debriefing took place to ensure their stories about what happened were the same. Review board shenanigans. They'd be truthful, of course, but Sam wanted the tone of their narrative to support Letty's, her first shooting and all.

"Do I have to turn in this feeb badge and ID? I'm sure I'd put it to good use."

SAC Bronzino said, "You're too dangerous to be let loose on American soil, Sam. You're better off contained in one state, not fifty. But yes, you'll turn them in at some point. I must say, you've accounted very well for yourself in our sandbox once more, Agent Travis. I'd be proud to have you on my team."

"Thanks, but no thanks, sir. I like what I do and where I live." Their faces made it clear they shared a mutual respect.

# EPILOGUE

While in the hospital in Penobscot, Maine, Agent Mather, Captain Jamison and EPO Travis met in the recreation room at 0100 hours. This was just a few hours after they were admitted, and sooner than their respective attending physicians advised. All were groggy, but dead serious. They reviewed their after-action report before filing it or before any other interviews to ensure that they were consistent and using acceptable terminology. Letty ensured them it'd pass muster. At least, that's what she'd been told.

Two months later, the FBI review board concluded all shootings fell within acceptable parameters per FBI protocol. In fact, they lauded the combination FBI/EPO operation for their improvisation in subduing and apprehending a combat-hardened domestic terrorist cell.

Ethan Browning survived, but lost his right arm. Domestic terrorism is defined in the U.S. legal code but it is not codified as a law that can be prosecuted. But they charged him with capital murder, three counts as an accessory to capital murder, attempted murder, illegal weapons possession, Destruction of both public and private property, and conspiracy. They also charged him with attempted murder of one federal officer and one state law enforcement officer, along with a litany of lesser charges.

They charged Joshua Bingham with the capital murders of Walter and Rose Bedford. Plus three counts as an accessory before and after the fact to the murders of Walter Bedford, Rose Bedford and Captain Jesse Pelligrini. They also charged Bingham with the same charges, attempted murder of a federal law enforcement officer, and more. Those principal federal charges carried the death penalty.

Special Agent L. Mather recovered from her wound and was awarded the FBI's highest award, The Medal of Valor.

Captain Lawrence Jamison recovered from his injuries and was awarded the FBI Star. He resumed his duties with the Massachusetts Environmental Police, who also awarded him the Meritorious Service Award.

Special Federal Police Officer and Massachusetts Environmental Police Officer Sam Travis also recovered from his injury with a minor loss of strength and flexibility of his left arm. The FBI awarded him the FBI Star and he received a Meritorious Service award from the Massachusetts Environmental Police. During his convalescence, and after passing an examination, Captain Larry Jamison promoted Sam to sergeant. He resumed his duties in that new role.

Lt. JG Robert Connors of the USCG received the Coast Guard's highest award, the Coast Guard Cross, for his actions defending the LNG tanker *Hercules* in Boston Harbor. They also promoted him to full Lieutenant. Every member of his heroic detail received the Coast Guard Achievement Medal.

Civilian Adam Delaney received the Coast Guard's Distinguished Public Service Medal for his actions during the attack on the LNG tanker *Hercules*. Nobody talked about how his fishing boat had been within the Coast Guard's exclusion zone during the entire attack. They considered it a happy accident.

FBI Agents were able to return several items to their rightful owners or heirs that had been stolen or illegally acquired by Ethan Browning. Various museums received other historical articles from the

FBI for exhibition. The FBI placed an organization called the *Patriot Guardsmen* on their terrorist watch list based on documentation seized from Ethan Browning. An extremist manifesto written by Browning left doubt whether there were other members, and if so, how many.

No one ever recovered the treasure of Revolutionary War coins stolen from Walter Bedford and the people of the United States by Ethan Browning and his thugs. The FBI speculated they found their way into the hands of a wealthy private collector as someone's dirty little secret instead of on exhibition in a museum for everyone to appreciate. By analyzing the two dozen silver and gold coins as part of that find, the Bureau issued a bulletin and shared that bulletin with Interpol. They identified this bounty as evidence they sought in connection with a double homicide and funding an interstate conspiracy that resulted in an act of domestic terrorism. They'd recover this treasure. Just not today.

Two weeks after the shoot-out in Maine, Sam Travis married Katherine Miller. It was a private ceremony under the gazebo in Wedgewood's Municipal Park. The wedding party included Sam's now-fourteen-year-old son, Brian, Captain Lawrence Jamison, and FBI Profiler who was now officially FBI's freshest field agent, very Special Agent Leticia Mather, as witnesses.

Half an hour after the ceremony, the five of them sat in the largest booth at Beverly's Diner. It was crowded and cozy, not only because they were stuffed into the not-large semicircular booth, but also because three of them still wore slings. Kate wanted to wait with the wedding until everyone's wounds had healed, but Sam said, "No. I want to marry you now, Kate." How could she refuse?

Sam said, "Hey, this is fun, right? I mean, getting all shot up, getting married, and getting together to chow down on greasy food? What's not to love?" He noticed vegetarian Letty Mather chowed down on a chicken-fried steak drowning in brown gravy. He'd have to talk with her about that! Something in her eyes looked different. *Yeah, your first wound and your first kill does that to you. Or is it something else?* Sam thought about his own feelings. He enjoyed putting one of those mongrels down. Maybe too much. He'd consider talking with Kate about that. Maybe even with a professional.

Kate swiveled her gaze around the booth with misty eyes, her arm snug around Brian's shoulders, her head laying on Sam's good shoulder. "I agree. This is fun. But let's forego the bullet and knife wounds and mortal combat next time, okay, guys?"

Letty hoisted her mug of herbal tea with her non-slung arm and said, "Deal, Kate... Mrs. Travis, that is. To the happy couple, and to their son, Brian, our newest honorary Junior FBI agent!" But her smile didn't quite reach her dark eyes, nor did it match her chirpy voice.

Sam surveyed each face in the booth—his favorite people in the whole world. *How can one man be so blessed? Then why am I not happier?*

## WITHOUT END

# CAST OF CHARACTERS
## (ALPHABETICALLY)

- **Noah Adams**: FBI field office tech supervisor, Springfield Mass.
- **Rose Bedford**: Walter's wife.
- **Walter Bedford**: Detectionist and retired contractor. Discovered a Revolutionary War bounty.
- **Joshua (Josh) Bingham**: Ethan Browning's full-time employee at Browning's Diamond and Coin, Portsmouth, New Hampshire. Originally from Huxford, Alabama. Member of the *Patriot Guardsmen.*
- **Greg Bronzino**: Special Agent in Charge (SAC) of the Portsmouth, New Hampshire FBI field office.

# CAST OF CHARACTERS

- **Ethan Browning**: Owner of Browning Diamond and Coin in Portsmouth, New Hampshire. Also de facto leader of the *Patriot Guardsmen*. Originally from Seminole, Texas.
- **Robert Connors**: Lt. Junior Grade Connors, the OIC (Officer in Charge) of the LNG tanker protection detail.
- **Adam Delaney**: Fisherman who spotted the RC craft attacking a Liquid Natural Gas tanker in Boston Harbor and reported it to the authorities.
- **Carl Devors**: Viet Nam buddy of Josh Bingham and procurer of C-4 plastic explosives.
- **Lawrence (Larry) Jamison**: Environmental Police Captain. Travis's friend and 2nd-line supervisor. Also EPO Academy Commandant.
- **Abraham and Jacob Jenkins**: Revolutionary coin thieves circa 1775.
- **Henry Knox**: Artillery colonel in the Continental Army circa 1775.
- **Andrew (Andy) Lofton**: Ethan Browning's full-time employee at Browning Diamond and Coin. Viet Nam veteran corporal and co-conspirator in the *Patriot Guardsmen*.
- **John (Jack) Malone**: Special Agent in

Charge (SAC) of the FBI field office, Springfield, Mass.
- **Letty Mather**: FBI Special Agent recently transferred from FBI Quantico, Virginia to Springfield, Mass. Sam Travis's interagency partner.
- **Katherine (Kate) Miller**: Investigative journalist and Sam Travis' fiancée.
- **Paul O'Neill**: EPO Lieutenant and immediate supervisor of Sam Travis.
- **Timothy Riggins**: Assistant US Attorney, District of Massachusetts.
- **Brian Travis**: Sam Travis's teenage son.
- **Sam Travis**: Massachusetts Environmental Police Officer.

# BOSTON HARBOR

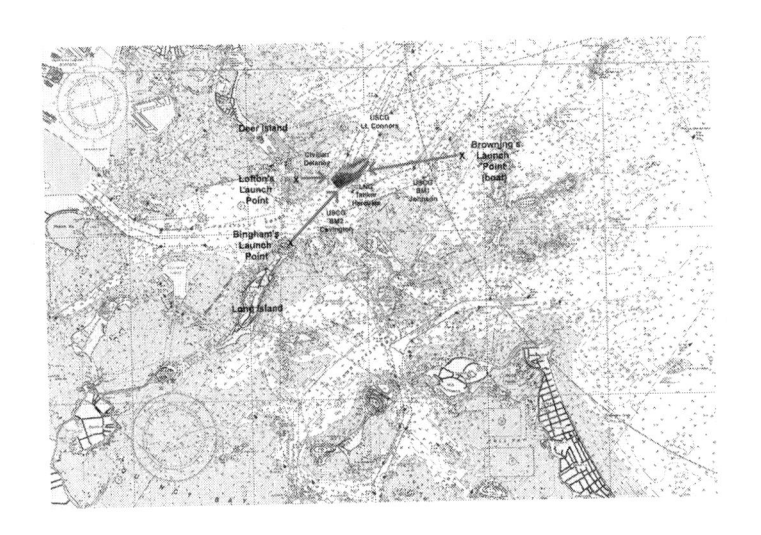

# GLOSSARY

- **Googans**: dangerous idiots in boats who are oblivious and lack talent when operating boats, tying knots and choosing the correct fishing gear.
- **Mass Pike**: Massachusetts Turnpike, also known as "the Pike"
- **NPRC:** National Archives Records Administration's National Personnel Records Center in St. Louis, Missouri, a government repository for archived military records.
- **OIC**: officer in charge, a military term.
- **PCGS (Professional Coin Grading Service) and NGC (Numismatic Guaranty Corporation):** the two most

important, independent, third-party coin grading services worldwide.
- **RIB:** Rigid Hull Inflatable Boat. Sometimes referred to as a RHIB. USCG vessels used for shallow water or boarding operations. In 1989, these were twenty-five-foot SPC-LEs—Special Purpose Craft for Law Enforcement. Feature twin two-hundred-horsepower Mercury engines and an M-60 machine gun perched over its permanent mount on the boat's heavy aluminum foredeck. RIBs are serious special-purpose law enforcement vessels.

# OTHER BOOKS BY GK JURRENS

**Historical Fiction (Great Depression Era Crime)**

- Black Blizzard: A Lyon County Adventure
- Murder in Purgatory: A Lyon County Mystery

**Aubrey Greigh Mysteries**

- Voodoo Vendetta - Culture That Kills
- Dancing With Death - Who Will Die? Or Disappear?
- Rogue's Gallery - Beyond Evidence (coming 1Q25)

## **Sam Travis Adventures:**

- **Lethal Game - Bears Under Siege**
- **Lethal Trail - No Body Is Safe**
- **Lethal Bounty - A Dirty Secret (this book)**

## **Contemporary Autobiographical Fiction (Drama)**

- **Dangerous Dreams: Dream Runners: Book 1**
- **Fractured Dreams: Dream Runners: Book 2**

## **Futuristic Fiction (Paranormal Mystery Thrillers)**

- **Underground, Mayhem: Book 1**
- **Mean Streets, Mayhem: Book 2**
- **Post Earth, Mayhem: Book 3**
- **A Glimpse of Mayhem: Companion Guide to the Mayhem Trilogy**

## **Non-fiction**

- **The Poetic Detective: Investigate Rhyme With Reason**
- **Why Write? Why Publish? Passion? Profit? Both?**

OTHER BOOKS BY GK JURRENS

- **Moving a Boat and Her Crew**
- **Restoring a Boat and Her Crew**

Turn the page to read an excerpt from Gene's new book: *Rogue's Gallery - Beyond Evidence*

# EARLY EXCERPT FROM ROGUE'S GALLERY
## AN AUBREY GREIGH MYSTERY

Available First Quarter 2025.
Subscribe at GKJurrens.com to be notified.

Chapter 1

It was late morning. Smoke from the camp's four damp-wood fires swirled through a dank mist and hung in the air with deliberation. Strings of lights that extended between a tight circle of two dozen small but colorful tents offered a festive sheen to the otherwise serene meadow. Music from a mandolin, a flute, and the soft thudding beat of a calf-skin drum tinkled and thrummed on the light breeze. A generator nestled in a small truck's bed just outside the camp's tight circle puttered away. Other sundry transports also lay in wait out there for the move to the next town, ready at a moment's notice. A smattering of costumed performers meandered among the sparse crowd. They'd offer an amusing diversion that preceded a semi-sad smile and an imploring expression behind an outstretched palm. *It isn't begging if they wear a costume and perform, is it?*

Hooded, her face was in shadows. She appeared unremarkable. Draped in ragged trousers down to her tattered flat slippers with frayed hems dragging in the still-dewy grass behind her, most considered her small. She was the visage of a local teenage boy with a well-practiced stroll. Ceija (SAY-ja) perused the carnival's fare, such as it was, as she worked the crowd—listening, observing, making mental notes with her photographic memory of *everything*. She made her way around the thin thread of strolling locals within their camp—their carnival.

Ceija Capriccio flexed her keen senses, assembling a mental dossier of at least a dozen potential clients. This was nothing like the rambling outskirts of Budapest, where teeming hordes would mill through their small show of oddities and entertainment day and night. Still, plenty of "clients" to choose from here in the countryside of Northeastern Italy. After all, their type of entertainment had become rare in these modern times. But clients still yearned to be relieved of their cash. They would oblige.

As Ceija passed her sister's tent, she thumbed her

nose and nodded toward the middle-aged man now in front of her with the proud gut and ridiculous hairpiece. Delia nodded back. They'd start small.

---

Two days earlier, their "kumpania" comprising six close-knit families had camped ten miles north of Udine (OO-dee-nay) in Northeastern Italy, less than three-hundred kilometers from the Croatian border. They called themselves Barátság Karaván, their *friendship caravan*. Much more than a close company of friends who journeyed together, they had followed the Sava River from Zagreb after making their way south from Budapest (BOO-da-pesht).

That had not been their home, just a place where some of them had been born or spent some time, and where Ceija and her sister Delia were orphaned. The sisters then spent more than a few years there, first in an orphanage, and then with these kind strangers. They were proud *Romani,* a people with no country *and* many countries. Most Romani had long-since settled down. Not Barátság Karaván.

It had taken most of the summer to get here. They had stopped and set up their little show whenever their larder needed replenishing. The women put up a few posters in the village. That and setting up their colorful tents in a high-traffic meadow with a few smoky fires never failed to draw a crowd. Their small carnival brought around several dozen locals today, each looking for a break from their boring and insignificant lives. At least that's how fourteen-year-old Delia Capriccio thought of them. *How small they must be to think what our little company offers is something special. Our humble little caravan!*

Ever amazed by this phenomenon, Delia remained a chronic cynic, unlike her dear, innocent sister Ceija. Delia loathed their nomadic lifestyle. *I grow so weary of having to hustle for every scrap, never knowing what having outsider friends must be like.* But then her mind once again shrugged at the inevitability of their fate. *Such is the life. At least I have a gift for languages. Learning Italiano? Easy. And we escaped those ridiculous charges of witchcraft by the Croats. All behind us now!*

Delia targeted the man with the hairpiece that her twin had identified as their next client, even though he did not yet know that. "Buongiorno, signore. You wish to learn what your future holds, yes? I shall read your palm for two Euros. My intuition is never wrong. Garantito." He walked past as if he didn't hear her. "Very well, signore. For you, only one Euro. And we'll not mention your secret to your wife shopping across the way there in the crimson babushka. You are seeing someone special on the side. Eh, my new friend?" Delia pointed at the frumpy woman Ceija had identified as the likely wife, or at least his companion, of their next client. As if she intended beckoning the woman's attention. They preferred calling them *clients* instead of *marks*. The rest was guesswork. She excelled at that.

The man froze in his tracks. He glared at her conspiratorial grin, then at the scrawled sign in front of her little tent:

*Signorina Delia*
*Divinator of Secrets & Fortunes*

Delia pressed forward. "You see, signore, my sight is clear, peering through the veil of the past, present, and sometimes, even the future. Not to worry, my new friend, your secrets are safe. You are my client, and I am now your trusted advisor. Come! Sit with Delia. You need to discover what mysteries the signora is keeping from you also, no?"

The middle-aged man, still handsome and hearty, at least in his own mind, paused. *Now* he *needed* to learn what this spit of a teenage gypsy really knew. He peered over his shoulder at his wife, still shopping across the encampment. Delia congratulated herself and her sister. *Ceija was right! Now we know.*

The ridiculous man approached Delia's tiny tent. She watched his expression transform from suspicion to appreciation as he took in her still-hooded but lovely face. His hesitation lessened with every step. Up to this point, she had camouflaged her youthful beauty with a caped robe under a bulky tribal shawl.

She knew her stunning beauty was her second greatest gift. The first? She and Ceija read people like a large print picture book. Sometimes... something else, too. And that frightened them both, a little.

They'd hooked the client. The man now sat across from her in the shadows of her open-door tent. He wrinkled his nose at the thin but dense tendrils of smoke from a stick of patchouli incense in the center of the table. Delia flung her robe and shawl over the back of her folding chair with a flourish to reveal her much more provocative patchwork halter-topped skirt. Her pale green eyes sparkled, threatening a hint of iridescence. Like twin almonds, they accented her razor-sharp cheekbones. Her smooth olive shoulders and back now lay bare, obscured only by her wavy raven hair. At fourteen, she had little cleavage to reveal. Still, only an idiot would miss the lascivious leer in this pig's eyes. *He likes his flesh young and petite,* she thought. She had read him with uncanny accuracy even before he had swaggered past her tent. Ceija had done well marking this one.

Now the big man leaned over the minuscule round table between them with greedy eyes, but said nothing. He wheezed as he breathed. The stench of garlic and sweat almost caused her alluring smile to crack, but she was a professional. "I am Delia, signore. Your Euro?" She extended her delicate hand, palm up and open, close enough to his folded ham fists on the tabletop to brush the coarse black hair on his knuckles, like the delicate touch of a butterfly's wing. "Let us begin. We have much to discuss."

## Chapter 2

Four years earlier, Absalon Lossár had rescued Ceija and Delia (no known last name) from an orphanage at the age of ten. In the town of Fot outside Budapest, the Marolyi Istvon Children's Center nestled on the grounds of a noble estate that had long-since seen better days.

As of late, Istvon had classified these two girls who had been abandoned at birth on the property—with a note indicating only their first names—as "un-adoptable." They were too wild, refused to be separated, and were no longer appealing cherub-like infants. Worse, they made no pretense at contrived civility for prospective adoptive families. They were wild prepubescent juvenile delinquents prone to acting out—non-stop.

But after a brief discussion with the beautiful twin girls, this handsome but unkempt young Romani said he and his extended family wished to adopt these two hellions. He offered a generous donation to the orphanage. The administrator was more than happy to shed her facility of this pair of demonic troublemakers. And the charismatic Úr. (Mr.) Lossár *was very persuasive.*

The girls were equally happy to be free of the old harpy and her human warehouse for cast-offs, even though they had no inkling what this bearded man with money and beautiful dark eyes and sliver tongue had in store for them. Delia whispered to her sister, "Whatever this old guy wants with us, it *must* be better than this place. Did you see how much he paid for us? Based on Elvét Szabó's wrinkled old face and the roundness of her squinty eyes, it was a prized sum!"

Ceija wasn't so sure. "Yes, he must be over *twenty years old!* Well, at least it will be different. Delia, we must watch out for each other."

They made a solemn pact to do so... forever.

---

Their new home? Barátság Karaván. The elder women of this traveling troupe immediately took a liking to these feisty young twins wearing the faces of angels and the demeanor of demons. One aging beauty, the most maternal of them all, Sasha Kristálygöm," (pronounced KREES-ty-gumb) took a special interest in them. Yes, they would become the daughters she never had. She'd teach them the ways.

---

# EARLY EXCERPT FROM ROGUE'S GALLERY

Already, the girls were pleased at this turn of events. The man who had bought them was stern... and devastatingly handsome... but hairy. Delia, especially, took a liking to this Úr. Absalon Lossár. He took them to his tent, sat them down on a large trunk, and spoke with stern eyes. "Girls, you are now part of kumpania—our company. We are a group of travelers, and we each earn our keep. You understand?" The girls nodded, even though they didn't. He continued. "I will school you in our ways. You will learn. That is the way of it. Sasha will teach you as well."

"Sir?" Delia spoke sheepishly. "What will we be learning?"

"It's not sir. My name is Absalon. You may call me Abs. I sensed something in you girls at the children's center. You have a talent that until now has gone unappreciated. Here, we will show you how to earn respect and make money with your talent. That is what I will teach you. Also, it is unacceptable to lack a surname. From now on, you shall be known as Delia and Ceija... *Capriccio*. Do you know what that means? A capriccio is a piece of music, free in form and of a lively character. The typical capriccio is one that is performed fast, intense, and by a very skilled musician. That is your spirit, and that is who you will become under my hand."

For several hours each day, Abs taught Delia and Ceija how to entertain. Specifically, how to read people, and to use what they discovered to their best advantage for the benefit of the troupe. And after they had done so, he taught them how to leave those same people—their customers, their audience, their clients—grateful for having been taken advantage of. The girls were naturals and found this premise fascinating. Over the next fifteen years, they learned rapidly from Abs and from others in the troupe until there was nothing left to learn, until *they* were the masters.

---

When Ceija and Delia were sixteen, six years after joining Barátság Karaván, their relationship with Abs changed. Instead of mentor to mentees, and big brother figure to little sisters, they changed to... something else. The girls were now young women of ravishing beauty and acquired charm, albeit rough compared to young ladies outside the troupe. Abs began paying special attention to Delia. She remained kind but uninterested. His frustration was clear. This became tedious to Delia. When she discovered her own sexuality, she found she only preferred the company of other young girls, not boys, and certainly not much older *men* like Abs. She unintentionally humiliated him more than once.

---

## EARLY EXCERPT FROM ROGUE'S GALLERY

At the age of thirty-five, after countless rebuffs over most of a decade of nurturing and teaching *his* Delia, and Ceija, Abs Lossár had grown embittered. He did not know of Delia's proclivities as she'd kept that a secret. He thought her an ungrateful little tart, and grew to resent her. Maybe even to hate her. Especially since the rest of the troupe fawned over his wards, treating him as if he no longer offered value. He could be with no woman other than *his* Delia. His jealously and spite drove him to a subtle madness he managed to hide. Mostly. That drove him from the Barátság Karaván.

---

The girls, now twenty-five and preposterously independent, also decided to leave the troupe. It was an agonizing decision, but most supported their decision. Most of their kumpania knew these young women had a larger destiny elsewhere in the world. With the blessing of most everyone except Abs Lossár who refused to even say goodbye before he himself left, they emigrated to America.

And so they found their way to America's largest city—Chicago. They deserved a brand-new start. And they would have it. No matter the cost.

### Chapter 3

# EARLY EXCERPT FROM ROGUE'S GALLERY

Eight years later, Aubrey Greigh awakened to the most enchanting sight in Chicago mere inches away. He nestled into the small of Detective Lieutenant Chance McQuillan's back. He buried his face in her auburn hair. She smelled like lilacs and felt like wispy silk. The fiery redhead reminded him so much of his dear Melissa. A Russian hitman had assassinated Mel and his six-year-old daughter almost five years ago, now. He'd love Mel and his little Clance until his final breath, but McQ had rescued him last year from his downward spiral when they thought they were going to die in each others' arms. If Mel were still alive, she'd love McQ, too. They were so similar—they even smelled the same. And yet the two women were so different they could have migrated from different planets. He reflected on that ridiculous notion. But only for a moment.

Without warning, McQ's eyes popped open. She shook her head, startling Greigh. She tapped her right temple. "McQ here... what? Okay, I'll be there in thirty." Double-tapped her temple to disconnect the incoming call from her comms implant. Then and only then did she lift her head off her pillow. Swiveled her gaze toward Greigh to her left. She only saw him in silhouette with the wall of windows seven floors above Harrison Street eight feet farther to their left. But she knew he stared at her with those dark doe eyes while she slept. Like every morning. She grinned, still incredulous that she now lived with this wonderful man who also happened to be a world-famous author of best-selling mysteries, and lived in this drop-dead-gorgeous suite—his contemporary condo—in the ancient Hotel Literati. This had been his home for the last ten years. Couldn't be more different from her closet-size studio apartment above Harrow's, the oldest cop bar in the city just two blocks from her precinct house. *What a difference five blocks makes!*

He reached out and brushed a thick lock of her auburn hair from her eyes. "Good morning, Red. Duty calls?"

She smiled and then smirked in a dreamy sort of way when shoving a harsh reality behind a startled awakening didn't really work for her. "Yup. Another body dropped. The captain wants me on it."

"The captain wants you to sit on top of a body? What on earth for? An innovative investigative technique to which you have not yet exposed me?"

She smiled, dragged her feet to the floor—she always slept with socks, Aubrey's sweat socks. They felt... nice. Warm. Comfortable. Intimate. Greigh often tried to restrain his sexy Sean Connery-like Scottish brogue, but sometimes failed, like now. "Shut up! You know what I mean. Are all writers like you?"

"I hope not. I imagine my brand of madness to be rather unique."

"Gotta shower and scoot." She hustled around the bed to peck him on the cheek, but he had a different idea. Pulled her down on top of him for an embrace and a longer kiss. She giggled, pulled away, and responded, "Greigh! I gotta run. Horrible breath, kind sir. Love you." And she was gone. Occurred to her she'd just uttered those last two words as a casual affectation for the first time. As she scurried to the bathroom, she pondered, *I guess we really are a couple now.* Another grin. *How did I get so lucky?*

But then she remembered Greigh still wrestled his own demons. She was better equipped to deal with hers. His still lived under a swirling cloud of doubt. A powerful Russian oligarch blamed both her and Greigh, as well as a few others, for the death of her twin brother, Ty Leonov, a year earlier. Mika Kuzmin vowed to avenge Ty's death. But Interpol and the United States government compelled Mika to return to Estonia, where she operated Obelisk Prime with an iron fist. OP... her international shipping empire and global criminal enterprise.

Neither McQ nor Greigh harbored any illusions. Kuzmin's reach was real. But McQ decided not to worry about that this morning. For a change. Off to the job she loved, while the man she loved still lay in *their bed,* no doubt dreaming up the plot for yet another murder mystery. Of late, he'd fallen into a state of lethargic doldrums between books. Or was he once more dwelling on the memory of his assassinated wife, Mel, and six-year-old daughter, Clance? Her heart ached for the precious man.

---

After McQ flew out of the front door of the huge suite like a prairie whirlwind, Greigh also grabbed a quick rinse. The air still hung heavy in their large Egyptian shower from McQ's time in there minutes earlier. *Lilacs!* The sun actually shone this morning. A few rays filtered through the wall of windows visible through the bathroom door beyond the bedroom that faced his covered balcony. Even that diffused light offered a pleasant glow to his morning ablutions. Still drying off, he said, "Butler, a stout cup of Bergamot in five, if you please." That was a strong English breakfast tea—Greigh's favorite. Americans called it Earl Grey. Nobody brewed Bergamot like Butler.

"Of course, Greigh. Anything to eat?" His apartment's automated control system dared not depend on Greigh for any regular habits, so every morning "he" would ask.

Greigh smiled. He hated being a foregone conclusion, and for some inexplicable reason, he liked to keep Butler guessing. "Nothing to eat this morning. Thank you, Butler." That was the system's default moniker, Butler. His daughter Clancy had liked that, so he never changed it. *Little Clance. Oh, how I miss you.* And his wife Mel had always tingled whenever she heard the voice of the old Scottish actor, Sean Connery. Not entirely unlike his own voice, some said. After all, like the actor, Greigh was born and educated in Edinburgh, even though his parents raised him in London.

He'd moved to Chicago almost eleven years earlier, met and fell in love with Melissa who had brought her haunting Columbian beauty to America with her. So Mel wanted Butler to sound like Connery. Greigh refused her nothing. Now, a small reminder of his past life. Like an old friend, or a painful memory, Butler had become his most trusted confidante. Plus, he proved to be an invaluable research assistant.

Life had become almost... comfortable, especially after the turmoil of the previous summer and fall. But then, he had no inkling the next few days would change everything, including maybe even his view of reality itself. That is, if he survived.

# DEDICATION

*To all law enforcement and military personnel who keep us blissfully ignorant civilians safe from bad actors, both foreign and domestic.*

# DISCLAIMERS

This is a work of fiction. Any similarity to actual persons, behaviors, places, or events should be considered coincidental and fictional.

No part of this publication may be stored in a retrieval system, transmitted, or reproduced in any way, including, but not limited to, digital copying and printing without prior agreement and written permission of the publisher, UpLife Press.

Research of this manuscript's period and its theme mandated judicious use of ethnic pejoratives and mild profanity, and are not meant to offend the reader. Quite the contrary, the use of these literary devices is intended to demonstrate the authentic commitment to a higher set of moral standards and to the strength of each character's faith, or lack thereof.

This entire novel is certified to be *"AI-free,"* that is, the authors—*certifiable humans*—wrote all 71,256 words, *not* artificially intelligent software. The authors reserve all rights. No distribution channel has any rights to sub-license, reproduce &/or otherwise use this work in any manner for purposes of training artificial intelligence technologies to generate text, video, or audio, including without limitation, technologies that are capable of generating works in the same style or genre as the work *without the authors' specific & express permission to do so.*

# ACKNOWLEDGMENTS

I'd like to acknowledge my awesome nationwide team of pre-publication readers, including:

- Dr. Jim Gardiner from South Dakota, a renowned neuropsychologist with training in music therapy,
- Larry Whiting from Alaska, who is a Revolutionary War aficionado and distant descendant of Henry Knox, President George Washington's Secretary of War shortly after the birth of our nation. Larry kept me honest on the finer points of that period's history.
- My Florida reader, Julia Stocksdale, who always tells it like it is as she leverages her expansive knowledge of the English language,
- Tom Kasprzak from Massachusetts, who is also my writing partner on our Sam Travis Outdoor Adventure series,

- My grammar specialist, Judy Rinehimer, hails from California's East Bay Area, and is the fastest beta reader on Planet Earth,
- Mark Mowry from Minnesota for his knowledge of all things medical lab-related,
- And Judy Howard in Brookings, Oregon, who continues to mentor writers of all genres, including yours truly.

My sincerest thanks to each of you, my friends.

- GK

# WHY THIS STORY NOW?

*International and domestic terrorism are both on the rise and have become a serious issue, not only for law enforcement, but for the average civilian. We are all at risk, and must remain vigilant. But we also live in the greatest nation on earth. Domestic terrorism is yet another storm to weather.*

*This story seemed appropriate in 2024, not only for its entertainment value, but as a reminder that sometimes deluded individuals may resort to violence in support of their cause.*

**Semper Paratus** *(Every Ready)!*

# ABOUT THE AUTHOR

*GK Jurrens writes with undiluted passion. He's published sixteen fiction and non-fiction titles to date including twelve action-oriented novels across five series. He also teaches writing and independent publishing seminars nationwide.*

With UpLife Press, GK has independently published:

- Outdoor Environmental Adventures
- Historical Crime Fiction
- Modern Murder Mysteries
- Contemporary Autobiographical Fiction
- Futuristic Paranormal Romantic Mysteries
- Science Fiction
- Poetry & Essays
- Writing & Publishing
- Nautical Travelogue
- Sailing Yacht Restoration

GK and his wife live and travel in a motorhome.

They wander their beloved North America as a source of endless inspiration. They've lived in forty-two states in the last decade for a few weeks to a few months each.

After studying Liberal Arts and Electronics Engineering Technology, GK earned a Bachelor of Science degree in Business and a Master of Science degree in Management of Technology from the University of Minnesota, USA.

Six years of government service (US Coast Guard Search & Rescue, Marine Law Enforcement) and a successful three-decade career in global high-technology (IBM) preceded more than a decade of voyaging on America's waterways, the Florida Keys, and the Eastern Caribbean from the British Virgin Islands to Granada, near the coasts of Venezuela and Trinidad.

Brief forays sailing around the Greek Cyclades Islands in the Aegean Sea as well as the San Juan Islands in the American Pacific Northwest offered Gene and his wife Kay more unique sailing challenges.

***With multiple works always in process, GK continues to write with a sense of urgency, and of course, passion. Always. He embeds contemporary social issues in each of his action-oriented stories.***

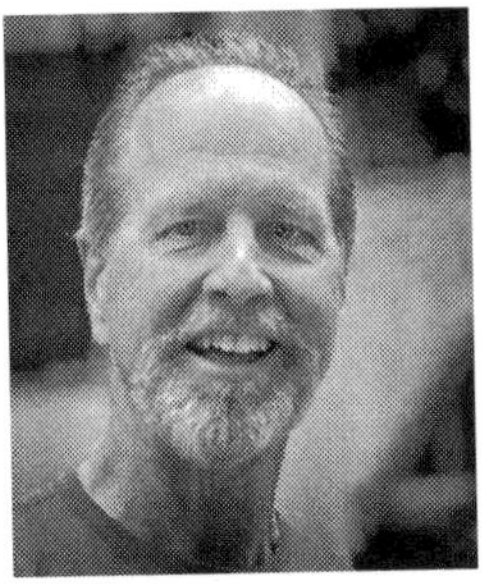

# ABOUT TOM KASPRZAK

"LT" spent thirty-two years as an environmental police officer for the Commonwealth of Massachusetts. Before graduating in 1977 from the Massachusetts State Police academy, Tom earned the coveted "top gun" award for superior marksmanship.

He began his EPO career as a field officer in various assignments involving both inland and marine law enforcement in places like Cape Cod, Boston Harbor and others. After transferring to the Berkshire Mountains in Western Massachusetts with skills honed from seven years of varied case involvement and courtroom testimony, he forged close relationships with local and state police.

Upon being promoted to lieutenant, he led a region of officers in search and rescue operations involving plane crashes, boating fatalities, narcotics, and the investigation and apprehension of various firearm violators.

Beginning in 1986, LT engaged in or supervised undercover operations focused on endangered wildlife. During that time, he worked with other local, state, and federal agencies on issues ranging from the environment to anti-terrorism.

Tom was selected to train in no fewer than three extended tours at the prestigious Federal Law Enforcement Training Center (FLETC) in Glynco, Georgia, where federal agents train.

Those intensive and immersive training tours honed his skills for inter-agency undercover operations, marine operations, and advanced operational readiness. He also trained for, and was an Incident Commander in several cases.

During his colorful career, Tom worked with the Massachusetts State Police air wing on helicopter operations, their dive team, apprehension team, marine law enforcement, and environmental police operations.

Tom spent his last seven years assigned to the State Police STOP (apprehension) team headquarters in Chicopee, Massachusetts, along with all the members of the region he supervised.

His undercover assignments brought dozens of individuals to justice who violated state and federal laws. He was also a Deputy National Marine Fisheries agent as well as a U.S Deputy Fish and Wildlife agent at the same time. Tom is also a US Air Force veteran with four-plus years assigned to Security Service and ultimately the majority of his enlistment was with the SR-71 Blackbird spy plane. His security clearance was one of extreme trust by the USAF.

His largest case—Operation Berkshire—closed one of the country's largest illegal commercial wildlife trafficking operations involving twenty-nine individuals, six states and two foreign countries.

The exploits of Tom and his fellow officers from his home state and others led to new exploits in crusading against illegal wildlife commercialization.

***National Geographic produced a special called "Wildlife Wars: Bears Under Siege" that featured Tom and his fellow undercover operatives after they closed Operation Berkshire.***

Tom taught new recruits at the State Police Academy courses in courtroom procedures, officer ethics and undercover operations. He also delivered endangered species lectures to schools, colleges, municipal police departments, as well as to other state and federal agencies including US Coast Guard District One in Boston with whom he was specifically trained in LNG (Liquid Natural Gas) tanker escort anti-terrorism protocols in Boston Harbor.

He made a name for himself during dozens of successful missing persons, body recovery cases, undercover operations, anti-terrorism and crime scene investigations. Tom and his life partner, Karen, now split their time between Western Massachusetts and Southwestern Florida.

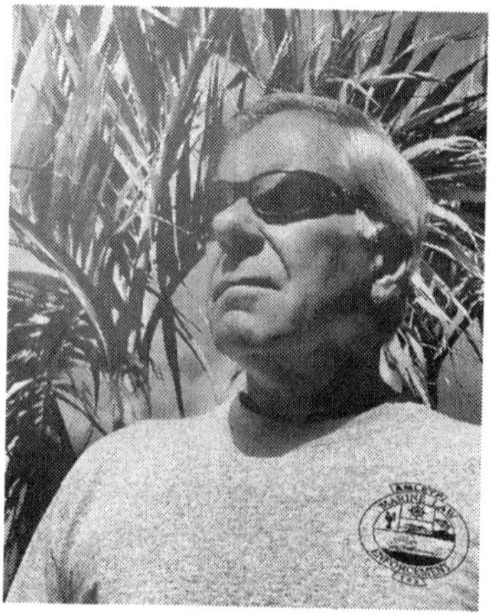

# BEFORE YOU GO

*Please post a brief review where you purchased this book.*

*Or email your thoughts to gjurrens@yahoo.com.*
Remember, other readers and I *need* to know what you think.
**I absolutely read every single review with gratitude. Thank you.**
Also, feel free to browse or subscribe at GKJurrens.com for announcements and giveaways.
See you there!
- GK

Made in the USA
Columbia, SC
04 February 2025